A FLOOD OF SORROW

BOOK 2 IN THE JOSEPH STONE THRILLER SERIES

J R SINCLAIR

VOICE FROM THE CLOUDS

Copyright 2023 © J R Sinclair

All rights reserved. This book or any portion thereof may not be reproduced or used in any manner whatsoever without the express written permission of the publisher except for the use of brief quotations in a book review.

This is a work of fiction. Any names or characters are fictitious. Any resemblance to actual persons, living or dead, or actual events is purely coincidental.

Published worldwide by Voice from the Clouds Ltd.

www.voicefromtheclouds.com

In memory of my sister Ione, the woman who was instrumental in lighting the fires of my love of reading.

CHAPTER ONE

THE RAIN HAMMERED down onto the roof of Alex's narrowboat, *The Kraken*, becoming more deafening by the second.

Tracey tore her attention away from the laptop screen she'd just been looking at with her boyfriend. They'd been attempting to finish the last episode of the crime show they had been binge-watching for the last two nights.

She cast a withering look towards the ceiling. 'Oh, I give up! I can barely hear myself think over all that racket.'

Alex paused the episode right in the middle of the big reveal about who the murderer was. 'I could sort out a Bluetooth speaker...' He frowned, spotting something move past the cabin window. No, not something but *everything* sliding past the port-hole at an increasing speed. That was a problem because right now *The Kraken* was meant to be safely moored to their regular spot on the embankment.

He jumped to his feet and rushed to the window. The bushes and trees lining the towpath were now under at least a foot of churning water.

Alex grabbed his waterproof cagoule jacket and shrugged it on over his shoulders.

'What is it?' Tracey asked as she surfaced from beneath the blanket that only a moment ago they'd been snuggled up under.

'That bloody flood they've been warning us about just ripped us from our mooring,' Alex called back as he headed to the door.

As he walked outside the air caught in his throat. He took in the transformation of the Isis, the name the locals gave this section of the Thames that snaked its way through Oxford.

Rain slammed down into the churning surface of the river like a hail of gunshots. The river was swollen and running fast, carrying a flotilla of broken branches and rubbish—and his home—right along with it.

Alex sucked air through his teeth, trying to assess the situation without panicking as dark storm clouds scudded overhead, erasing all the colour out of the world and pressing down on the city beneath them.

A few seconds later, Tracey appeared on deck wrapped in her yellow waterproof jacket. 'Bloody hell, this has turned ugly, real quick.'

'I know, I know, and I only have my own pig-headedness to blame. I heard the warnings. But unlike our neighbours, who sensibly moved their boats over to the Oxford Canal, I honestly thought we'd be fine on the river. I even took the piss out of them last week, pointing out the fact that a boat was probably the safest place to be if it did flood.'

Tracey shrugged. 'No biggie, just power up the engine, and we can find a new mooring to ride this thing out.'

He smiled at her. 'Yeah, you're right, there's no need to panic. What would I do without you?'

She grinned at him. 'Get your knickers in way too much of a twist.'

He laughed, leant over, and kissed the top of her head. 'Isn't that the truth.'

Alex reached down to the control panel and turned the key to the start position. Immediately the engine began to turn over, but three seconds became ten as the engine refused to catch. As their narrowboat gathered speed in the fast-flowing river, so did Alex's heartbeat.

'Come on,' he muttered to his boat.

'You did get the engine serviced like you said you were going to?' Tracey asked.

He grimaced. 'It's been on my to-do list, but I never had a chance to get round to it. You know how busy I've been at work.'

She shook her head at him, the whir of the starter beginning to slow as the battery drained.

He returned the key to the off position, threw out a silent prayer to the river gods, and tried again.

Three spins of the starter and then, with a glorious gurgling cough, the engine burbled into life with a puff of blue smoke.

'Ta-da!' Alex said, patting the top of the cabin.

'I had every confidence in you,' Tracey replied with a shrug.

He winked at her. 'Yeah, right.'

As the boat settled into a steady chugging, he threw it into reverse and gunned the throttle.

With a roar from the diesel engine, *The Kraken* started to slow, but she was still being carried forward by the strengthening current.

'Is it too late to try and turn her round?' Tracey asked as the wind howled around the narrowboat, driving the rain into a slanting angle.

'No dice, in this torrent. The moment I try that, the boat will probably pitch over. The best we can do is ride this thing out until the river slows,' Alex replied.

'Okay, but we're *so* looking at buying a flat after this. So much for the romantic life on the water you sold to me when we first met. Not one mention of chemical toilets and having to empty them practically every week, more often if you've had curry.'

He grinned at her. 'It must have slipped my mind.'

Tracey gave him a mock punch in the arm and shook her head.

The banter was a good distraction because Alex didn't want to let his girlfriend know just how worried he really was. Even in full reverse, *The Kraken* was moving as fast as a speedboat by the time Iffley Lock appeared in the distance.

It was then Alex realised why the current was getting even faster. Both lock gates ahead of them had been left wide open by the keeper, no doubt to let the storm water pass through to avoid flooding across Oxford. He'd sailed through Iffley Lock many times, but this wasn't going to be the usual slow-speed crawl he was used to. It would be more like riding an out-of-control runaway express train.

'Jesus, can't you slow this thing down any more than this?' Tracey asked, her eyes widening as they were pulled towards their imminent destruction on the lock walls.

'I've already got the throttle wide open in reverse as it is,' Alex finally admitted. 'This is as slow as it gets, so you better hang onto something and keep everything crossed we make it through in one piece.'

His girlfriend shot him a lip-chewing look as she grabbed hold of the railing.

With his heart thumping in his chest like a drum solo, Alex began to make rapid adjustments to the tiller. All he could do was aim for the rushing torrent of water being channelled through the middle of the lock and pray they made it through intact.

The open gates rushed towards them at a shocking speed

and suddenly they were inside the roaring waters hurtling through the lock. There was absolutely nothing Alex could do to keep *The Kraken* on a straight path, and suddenly she began to slip sideways.

With a huge bang, the prow hit the wall, almost throwing them both overboard. Adrenaline made his blood hum as a brief sound of splintering wood scraping over brick echoed off the walls of the manmade canyon. But then with a rush of spray, the narrowboat shot out of the other side of the lock into the vast expanse of calmer floodwater beyond.

Alex sucked in another breath as he took in the lake. There was no sign of the shores of the river anywhere. The Isis had burst its banks, spreading far and wide into the floodplain of fields surrounding Oxford. Trees pointed up out of the water like the gnarled fingers of old men.

After the deafening noise of the roaring water, the sudden silence that descended was almost as shocking. No longer contained, the river's flow had dropped to a crawl, and the narrowboat finally began to slow. It was then Alex realised there wasn't even the sound of their diesel engine running.

'No, no, no,' he muttered as he tried the key again.

But apart from a clicking noise coming from the compartment beneath his feet, nothing else happened. Without power, *The Kraken* quickly began to drift out into the newly formed lake.

Tracey pointed ahead towards a large oak tree directly in their path.

Alex shook his head. 'Don't worry. Even without the engine, I can still use the tiller to steer us round it.'

Tracey nodded. 'Okay, but please just get us and our home through this in one piece.'

'No pressure then,' he replied, forcing a smile. He deftly manoeuvred *The Kraken* around the obstruction, his heart rate finally beginning to decelerate as he considered their predicament.

What the hell am I going to do now? he thought.

Their boat was effectively adrift without power. The hull almost certainly had significant damage from the impact with the lock. In the longer term, Alex had no idea how the hell he was going to pay for the repairs.

'So what happens now?' Tracey asked, loosening her white-knuckled grip on the railing.

'I would say we should ring emergency services. But which one? Police, the fire brigade, or the bloody coast guard?'

Tracey snorted, but then her expression widened when she caught sight of something ahead. 'Actually, that might not be necessary.'

Alex looked to where she was pointing to see their narrow-boat was being carried towards a grassy island rising above the floodwater, which he was pretty sure was actually a raised section of the river embankment.

'You're saying we could ground the boat on that?' Alex asked, gesturing towards it.

'Exactly, then all we have to do is wait for the water to go down and get someone to give us a tow back up the river.'

'You mean we're not going to end up in the middle of a dry field like some sort of modern-day Noah's Ark?'

Tracey laughed. 'Now there's a thought, although someone must have forgotten to load all the animals.'

Alex chuckled as he steered the narrowboat towards the island.

After everything they'd just been through, it wouldn't have been too much to ask for things to go smoothly. But no, the river wasn't finished having its fun with them yet.

As they closed in on the embankment, an invisible current caught hold of *The Kraken* and started to turn the boat at an angle to the island. Despite leaning hard on the rudder, there was nothing Alex could do to slow the narrowboat as it hit hard, gouging out a great chunk of the mound. As a landslide of mud and turf slid into the water with a whoosh, they finally came to a shuddering rest.

Alex immediately jumped off the boat and drove metal stakes into the embankment, securing ropes from the narrow-boat as Tracey threw them across to him.

The adrenaline ebbing from his system, he looked at their new mooring as he secured the narrowboat. Then he laughed, a massive sense of relief surging through him.

'What?' Tracey asked.

'The lads at work aren't going to believe me when I tell them about our whitewater ride on a canal boat.'

But the smile that had started to form on Tracey's lips fell away as she looked down at the gap between the boat and the embankment. 'What's that, Alex?'

He peered down at the object bobbing on the surface of the water. It was heavily covered in mud but had patches of blue showing in between. He was used to seeing no end of flotsam sailing past on the Thames, everything from milk cartons to used condoms. But there was something about this that was different from the usual rubbish.

'Pass me the pole from the roof and I'll fish it out,' he said.

A few moments later, Tracey handed him the pole they usually used for keeping the narrowboat away from the walls of the lock. Alex used the end of it to guide the object within reach. He lifted the mud-covered thing clear of the water, and dropped it by their feet. A moment later he had cleared enough off to reveal an expensive-looking blue running shoe, a woman's going by the size of it.

Alex shook his head. 'The things people sling into the river.'

Tracey frowned. 'Actually, I think it might have been buried in that mud we just knocked into the river. But how could it have got there in the first place?'

Before Alex could reply, a series of bubbles came from the same spot in the water where he'd just recovered the running shoe. Almost in slow motion, something much bigger broke the surface.

It took several heartbeats for Alex's brain to catch up with what they were now both staring at. A human hand floated on the surface, its bloated, mottled fingers pointing to the sky like an echo of the flooded tree branches all around them. Then, like a mermaid rising from the depths, the rest of the body surfaced as well.

Alex found himself gawping at a woman's lifeless face, her mouth frozen open as though she'd been gasping for breath, her eyes gone leaving gaping sockets. Strips of flesh hung from her ribcage like ribbons of silvery seaweed rippling in the water.

His brain busy rebooting from the shock, it took him a moment to realise Tracey was screaming. He scrambled back up the embankment, nausea spinning through his stomach. The moment he stood, breathing hard, Tracey threw her arms around him, sobbing. As she buried her head into his chest, Alex yanked his mobile from his pocket. He punched in 999, looking anywhere but at the woman floating in her watery grave and staring up at them with those cold dead eyes.

CHAPTER TWO

THE CANAL WATER was rising fast as a squall pounded on Joseph's cagoule. He cast a pissed-off look at the leaden sky, and offered up a silent curse.

Dylan was standing next to him, grey hair stuck to his forehead and peeking out from beneath his beanie hat. He looked as wet as the proverbial drowned rat. The professor gripped a mooring spike, his hand slipping on the wet iron Joseph was frantically hammering into the ground.

'Flipping Nora, I thought they said this bloody flood had already peaked,' Dylan said. He glanced over his shoulder towards the normally sedate canal, which was rushing past them with swollen frothing water.

Joseph grimaced. 'No need to tell me. The sooner we get these extra mooring ropes tied down for both our boats, the happier I'll be.'

The detective and the professor weren't the only boat owners experiencing heart palpitations right now. As the storm filled the canal with floodwater at an increasingly alarming rate, similar scenes of frenzied activity were playing out all around them. Owners up and down the length of the canal were all desperately trying to secure their craft.

There were also a lot of extra craft that would normally have been moored over on the River Isis. With all the warnings of severe flooding the Met Office had been banging on about for the last week, many had sought out sanctuary on the Oxford Canal in the middle of the city. That had been a good call until the floodwater had begun finding its way into the canal system as well.

The moment Joseph had finished driving the stake in, Dylan wrapped the rope around it with a bowline knot to secure his boat, *Avalon*, to the shore.

White Fang and Max, Dylan's dogs, were sitting on the roof of his floating home, giving both humans barks of approval for a job well done. Up until now, they'd been running up and down the boat to inspect the water rushing by. Particular excitement had been caused by a supermarket plastic bag sailing past like a mini iceberg. They'd been wagging their tails the whole time, obviously seeing the flood as a *great craic* as Joseph might say—unlike their humans.

'Right, now for some extra mooring ropes for yours,' the professor said.

The DI nodded, but they had literally taken two steps towards his boat, *Tús Nua,* when a loud bang came from one of its mooring spikes as it tore free and slammed into the hull. Immediately, the narrowboat's prow began to swing out into the current.

Joseph didn't so much run as leap for the fast disappearing rope as it snaked its way towards the canal's edge. With a sterling effort that would have made a rugby forward proud, Joseph lunged and just managed to catch the end before it disappeared into the water. The DI bounced to his feet, leaning back as he hung on, scrabbling to hold his position as the swollen floodwaters caught hold of his floating home and threatened to snatch her away.

Dylan grabbed onto the rope too. The dogs barked with even greater enthusiasm at this latest performance, like the humans were their own personal circus act.

Joseph and Dylan dug their heels into the gravelled path, but despite their best efforts, they were still being pulled steadily towards the edge.

It was at that moment the detective heard someone splashing through the puddled path towards them. A second later, his daughter Ellie was by their side and hanging onto the line as well.

'You seemed to be having a bit of trouble here, Dad,' she said, raising her eyebrows at him.

'Some might say that, but we had it all under control, didn't we, Dylan?' Joseph replied as he gritted his teeth and tightened his grip on the slippery rope.

'Only in your mind, Joseph,' the professor said, shaking his head at his friend.

Slowly, breathing hard, they managed to start hauling the prow of *Tús Nua* back towards the embankment. A short while later, with a few rope-burn battle scars between them, they had the boat safely secured to four fresh mooring spikes.

Mother Nature obviously decided she'd thrown enough at them for one day, because the tempest suddenly drizzled to a stop. That was followed by a break in the clouds, bathing everything in instant bright sunlight.

'The big man upstairs will be throwing in a bloody rainbow next as a bonus,' Joseph muttered to himself.

'What's that, Dad?' Ellie asked as she pulled her hood down.

'Don't mind me, just having a go at the world in general.

Anyway, to what do I owe this unexpected visit from my lovely daughter?'

'I saw a Tweet from the Oxford Chronicle that the river was flooding and there was some overspill into the canal. So I thought I'd better pop down to see if you were both doing okay. Seems just as well I did.'

'Isn't that the truth?' Joseph said, wrapping his arm around her shoulders and giving them a squeeze.

'Enough to treat me to breakfast?' she replied with a grin.

Dylan looked between them. 'That sounds like a splendid idea, but I insist it's going to be on me rather than your father. If it wasn't for Joseph, my home would be a receding speck on the canal now. As it isn't, I'm in the mood for a cheeky full English breakfast over at Blues. My treat.'

'Hey, I'm never going to say no to that, even if it is English,' Joseph said.

'You'll get no argument from me,' Ellie added.

'In that case...' Dylan put two fingers in his mouth and whistled. In milliseconds, both Max and White Fang had leapt down off *Avalon* onto the towpath, and were all doggy smiles and dancing bodies. Ellie made the usual fuss of greeting the Border Terrier and Beagle, and was rewarded for her troubles with a smacker on the lips by White Fang.

Her dog greeting duties done, her gaze turned up to the professor. 'But isn't Blues a bit posh to allow dogs in?'

'Not if they're hearing dogs,' Dylan replied.

'Hang on, you're not deaf,' Joseph said with a puzzled expression.

Dylan screwed his eyes up as he glanced at the DI. 'Pardon?'

Joseph snorted. 'They broke the mould after you were born, didn't they?'

The professor grinned at them. 'I flipping hope so. After all, there's only enough room for one person like me in this world.' He hooked his thumbs under imaginary braces and pulled them out.

Then with a click of his tongue, followed by a tunefully whistled version of *Happy*, Joseph, Ellie, and the dogs fell in behind Dylan. Like some modern-day Pied Piper, he led them away along the towpath towards the bustling heart of Oxford.

Humans and dogs were now sitting in the splendour of Blues Restaurant. Joseph had always thought this particular establishment exuded more than a slight whiff of an exclusive gentlemen's club. Not that he'd ever actually been to one, but he imagined it would be very much like this. The restaurant certainly attracted a large number of well-heeled tutors and students from the colleges.

The interior was bathed in a soft light from the ceiling lantern that made it seem much brighter than the now-grey-again weather might suggest. Its wooden counter positively shone with all the layers of polish, worked into it over many years. Behind it was an impressive collection of fine wines and spirits. There were also large palms dotted everywhere across the dining area, and plenty of tasteful sketches adorning the walls. Black-waistcoated waiting staff glided between the tables making sure every guest was well attended to.

Thankfully, and most importantly for Joseph, Blues excelled when it came to producing a splendid, fill-your-boots, breakfast.

The DI pushed away the empty plate that had contained smoked bacon, sausages, black pudding, two fried eggs, baked beans, flat mushrooms, grilled tomato, and toasted sourdough bread. In a shockingly small amount of time, the whole lot seemed to have evaporated. That possibly had something to do with the two dogs under the table. Whenever the detective had made the mistake of looking down at them, he was met with puppy-eyed looks, and any resolve he'd had to not feed them immediately broke. Hardened criminals he had a cast iron will to deal with. Soft dogs, less so.

Joseph sat back, breathing in the scent of money in the esteemed eatery. How Dylan had managed to blag his way into Blues with White Fang and Max was a sight to behold and was certainly a master class in guile. The professor had claimed that, *yes*, he really did require two hearing dogs, *one for each ear*. That had left the manager so flummoxed that he had simply waved their whole party in, dogs and all, with a bemused expression.

'That breakfast certainly hit the spot,' the DI said, raising his cup of tea towards Dylan and Ellie sitting opposite him.

His friend nodded. 'Yes, although not a word to my doctor.'

Ellie immediately looked concerned. 'What, you're on some sort of diet now?'

Dylan patted the slight paunch bulging over his belt. 'No, but that sounds like the sort of thing you should say when you've had a breakfast this splendid, especially at my age. Anyway, how were your eggs, my dear?'

'Really good, although Mum's eggs Benedict will always take some beating.'

Joseph nodded. 'Kate has always been the champion of creating an award-winning breakfast. It was one of the many reasons I fell for her back in the day. Talking of her, how's your mum doing, Ellie? I haven't heard from her in ages.'

'She's keeping her head down as she's researching some new major news story.'

'Which is?' Dylan replied, taking a sip of his tea.

Ellie shrugged. 'No idea. Whatever it is, Mum is keeping it close to her chest.'

'Is she working late into the night as well, by any chance?' Joseph asked.

'How did you guess?'

'Because it's the same old Kate when she gets the bit between her teeth. When she's on the hunt for a big story, she always becomes like a woman possessed.'

'Look who's talking,' Dylan said. 'You're exactly the same when you're involved in any major investigation.'

Joseph held up his hands. 'I know, I know. Kate and I are like two peas in a pod when it comes to our jobs, both driven people. That's why we've always understood each other, and got on so well.'

Ellie gave him a calculating look. 'Talking of which, isn't it long past time that you should have started dating again, Dad?'

Joseph groaned. 'Not this again.'

His daughter's gaze developed a laser focus. 'Have you even tried out that dating app I installed on your phone?'

'Look, we all know that's not me. I've never been a man for casual dating, even for a quick roll in the hay, no matter how charming the lady. I'm basically an Irish romantic at heart, and I'm all in on finding a soulmate. The bottom line is that your mum is a tough act to follow...'

A familiar ache squeezed his heart. The problem was even if Kate had moved on, Joseph certainly hadn't managed to yet. Also, just to really rub salt in the wound, his ex-wife had somehow ended up marrying Derrick, his boss and a prick of the highest order. The universe had a cruel sense of humour sometimes.

As Joseph's silence lingered, he caught Dylan and Ellie exchanging knowing looks.

He raised his palms. 'Look, just let me be. I'm happy in my bachelor ways and you both need to accept that.'

Dylan's brow knotted. 'I know I'm not exactly a shining role model myself, but you make that sound like the self-imposed sentence of someone determined to be lonely. Besides, you're not exactly likely to meet anyone tucked away on your boat, are you?'

Ellie quickly jumped onto the rapidly accelerating bandwagon. 'Exactly. I could always set you up on a blind date or something, Dad.'

Joseph gave her an appalled look. 'Bloody hell, I can't date a student.'

'Hey, believe it or not, there are some mature students at Oxford. But I actually had one of my lecturers at the Blavatnik School of Government in mind. She's single, very intelligent, with a sharp sense of humour. Just your type. Leave it to me and I'll sort out something.'

Before Joseph could reply, his police-issued phone warbled on the table. When he read the screen, he saw DC Megan Anderson's name. Not wanting to look a very timely gift horse in the mouth, he immediately pressed the call accept button as a way to get out of this torturous conversation.

'Hey, Joseph, sorry to disturb you, but a body has just been found in the River Isis. Chris is calling everyone in. It's all hands on deck for this one.'

Normally Joseph would have moaned about it being his day off, but not on this occasion when his daughter was actively plotting to make his lack of a love life her personal mission to sort out.

'Can you swing by Blues to pick me up, Megan?' Joseph said.

'No problem. I can be there in ten.'

'Make it five and I'll bribe you with a Danish.'

'Pastry or the male variety?' the DC replied.

'As I'm not talking about a guy with a horned helmet, a tasty snack it will have to be.'

'Shame. I'll see you soon.'

Putting the phone down, Joseph was already waving towards one of the waiters to order a Danish to go as he slipped his coat on.

'Hey, where do you think you're going?' Ellie asked. 'I was in the middle of setting you up on a hot date.'

'Exactly. Why do you think I'm trying to get out of here like my arse is on fire?'

Dylan chuckled. Ellie just shook her head at her father.

'This conversation so isn't over,' she said, crossing her arms.

'That's why I'm going to be incredibly busy at work for as long as possible,' Joseph replied, winking at her.

The detective had no idea just how true that statement was about to become.

CHAPTER THREE

As the flood had subsided over the last few days, the river had gradually returned to the confines of its banks. That had finally allowed the forensic team to have full access to the location where the victim's body had been discovered. After finding themselves assigned to DCI Chris Faulkner's team, this was the first opportunity either Joseph or Megan had to make it over to the actual crime scene.

That was why Joseph was wearing the tallest wellies he'd been able to track down in the equipment store back at St Aldates Police Station. Now suitably equipped for this muddiest of expeditions, the DI was trudging next to Megan, making their way along the edge of the Isis on a puddle filled footpath towards the hive of police activity ahead of them.

Megan cursed when, for the third time, one of her wellies got stuck in the mud. With a few swears, she managed to pull her leg partly out, swaying like a drunk who'd just stumbled out of a pub. She reached out and grabbed onto Joseph's shoulder to balance herself.

'Bloody hell, is the mud extra sticky round here or something?' she muttered as she leaned on the DI to pull her wellie free with a glopping, popping sound.

'That's good old Oxford clay for you; the very finest,' Joseph replied. 'When it gets this wet, it can certainly give Glastonbury festival a run for its money.'

Megan gave him a sideways glance. 'That sounds like the voice of experience. Have you been then?'

'Hey, stop looking at me as though I'm over the hill. I'm only in my forties, I'll have you know. And like any true Irishman is born to do, I've partied a bit in my time. It's part of our cultural DNA to pursue hedonistic experiences.'

Megan raised her eyebrows at him.

When she didn't actually say anything, Joseph was fairly sure he could see the cogs spinning behind her eyes. No doubt the DC was mentally recategorising him from the *old man* box she'd placed him in, into the *there's still hope for him* one.

Together, the detectives continued their slow but steady calf-grinding slog towards the large forensic tent that had been erected at a jaunty angle over the section of embankment that led down to the River Isis. A launch was towing a battered red narrowboat back upstream in the direction of Iffley Lock, just visible in the distance. There was also a police RIB, rigid inflatable boat, supporting the diving team, who were currently examining the riverbed. Amy, the head forensic officer, was hopeful more clues might have slipped into the water where the body had been disturbed.

Joseph gestured towards the receding craft. 'At least the owners will be happy to finally get their home back.'

'I bet they will,' Megan replied. 'As though the stress of finding that dead woman wasn't already bad enough for them.'

The DI nodded. 'At least we won't have to bother them with any more questions now they've been ruled out as suspects. The pathologist already told Chris that the body has been in the ground for at least three years. That was long before either Alex or Tracey ever moved to Oxford.'

Megan's gaze settled back on the tent. 'If it hadn't been for their narrowboat taking a bloody great chunk out of the embankment, I doubt that woman's body would've ever been found.'

'We certainly got lucky that the corpse was discovered, even if it was because of a freak accident.'

His colleague grimaced. 'I doubt that young couple sees it quite like that.'

'I don't suppose they do,' Joseph replied as DI Ian McDowel, in a decidedly mud-splattered forensic suit, emerged from the tent.

Seeing them, he waved. 'You guys are a bit late to the party, aren't you?'

'Only because DSU Walker insisted we finish up the paperwork on that series of garage break-ins in Botley,' Joseph replied.

'Well, that's *Wanker* for you. I sometimes think his only role in life is to suck out as much joy as possible from the job for the rest of us.'

'There's a *joy* part—since when exactly?' Joseph asked.

Ian rolled his eyes at Megan. 'Don't be fooled by his grumpy copper act. Joseph's never happier than when he's up to his neck in other people's shit—or maybe I should say, *shite*—and solving a crime.'

Megan chuckled. 'I think you're definitely on the money there.'

Joseph shrugged. Ian certainly wasn't wrong. The start of the year had been one of the best of the DI's career since the *Midwinter Butcher* case had finally been solved. In doing so, he'd finally achieved some level of closure in the death of his son, Eoin.

The same seemed to be true for Joseph's ex-wife, Kate, and even his daughter Ellie, who both seemed to be carrying far less weight on their shoulders these days. Yes, it had been much better for their family, although, as always in moments like now, the grim reality of his job often had a knack of dragging him back down to Earth.

Ian began stripping off his forensic suit. 'Right, that's me done. Now you're both here, I need to report back to DSU *Fucker* with the latest findings.'

'Which are?'

Ian was about to answer when the tent flap rustled and Amy emerged from inside.

'I'll leave it to the expert to brief you,' he said, nodding towards her. He finished struggling out of the coverall, and began the long trudge back to the unmarked police Volvo parked up back on the main road with the other vehicles.

'So how's it going in there?' Megan asked.

'I'm afraid it's been slow-going sifting through all the mud,' Amy, the crime scene manager in charge of the other SOCOs, replied.

'I don't suppose the victim had some ID on her?' Joseph asked.

'Sadly not, but then we don't want life to be too easy and me being put out of a job, do we?' Amy replied, her German humour as dry as ever. 'My team is waiting to hear back on the dental records.'

'What about cause of death?' Megan asked.

Amy gave Megan a thoughtful look. 'You need to talk to our friendly pathologist about that. I believe Doctor Jacobs was due to begin his examination of the body first thing this morning.'

Joseph turned to Megan. 'What do you say? Are you ready to attend your first postmortem?'

Megan's eyes widened. 'I can't say I'm terribly keen.'

'I think it's incredibly instructive for a young officer to attend an examination,' Amy said. 'You'll learn a lot, Megan.'

Joseph scraped his hand through his hair. 'I agree and it's another one of those rites of passage that we all go through at some point and there's no better tutor than Rob. He'll teach you a lot about the clues to look for at a crime scene when someone's been murdered.'

'Like them not breathing, for example?' Megan replied.

Amy's gaze travelled to the DI. 'I see that you've taught her well in the ways of dark humour, Joseph.'

'It's been my duty, although in fairness, she's been a quick study,' the DI replied.

Megan cocked her head to one side, gazing at him. 'I've learned from the best. Anyway, despite the whole idea filling me with nausea, it sounds like I really should attend. But you may need to give me a bucketful of Silvermints to see me through it, Joseph.'

'You expect me to be there with you?' the DI replied.

Her eyes widened. 'Bloody hell, I thought you would be there for a bit of moral support, or at least to stop me redecorating the inside of the pathology lab with a fine splatter of vomit.'

Joseph grinned at her. 'Only pulling your chain, Megan. Of course, I'll be there, Silvermints and all.'

Megan sighed. 'Then it seems I'm in.'

Amy nodded. 'Good. I don't think you'll regret it. However, before you rush off to find out all the gory details from Rob, maybe have a look at the crime scene first?'

'You heard the woman, so we better get to it,' Joseph said, snapping Amy a salute. She rolled her eyes at him.

A short time later Joseph and Megan, suited and booted, entered the forensic tent along with Amy. The first thing the DI noticed, apart from an abundance of slimy mud, was the large hole that had been excavated into the side of the embankment. A number of SOCOs were painstakingly using trowels to excavate the site like archaeologists. There was also a measuring stick driven into the ground, and one of the officers was using a theodolite to survey the site. The other thing that immediately caught his attention was a group of yellow numbered markers showing where objects of interest had already been removed. Amy and her team had been very busy.

'So, where does it look like the body was buried before it was disturbed?' Joseph asked her.

Amy pointed to a scooped out depression to one side of the hole. 'Going by the impression, the victim's body was originally placed there, and the prow of the narrowboat acted like a huge shovel to scoop the body out of the embankment. We found a bin liner with her clothes still in them, next to where her body originally was. By our estimate, the victim was buried at least six feet down.'

'But that's the depth of a regular grave,' Megan said. 'It must have taken a lot of work.'

'Exactly,' Amy replied. 'Whoever it was that buried her here, they were obviously keen for her body never to be found.'

'I agree, but digging a grave that deep isn't exactly something you can do during the daytime, especially with all the boats that pass by this spot,' Joseph replied.

'In that case, could the murderer have done it at night?' Megan asked.

'Yes, that makes sense, but even then it's risky,' Joseph replied. 'All it takes is one dog owner to be out late and the murderer could have easily been spotted.'

Megan nodded. 'Also, why not choose somewhere like a wood with plenty of cover, far away from anywhere busy?'

'That's a good question. Maybe the murderer was local, so it was simply convenient, or perhaps this was near where the victim was originally killed so they just wanted to bury...' Joseph spotted one of the evidence bags that had been stacked with the others on the far side of the hole. In it was a blue running shoe with yellow laces.

'Oh shite,' the DI said, as he went over and picked it up for a closer inspection.

'We just unearthed that during the dig, but the other matching running shoe was actually recovered on the day that the body was discovered,' Amy said, before narrowing her gaze at him. 'Hang on, going by the expression currently on your face, it looks like you might recognise it?'

Joseph slowly nodded, as a case that had kept him up many a night came rushing back.

'This could be a cold case I originally worked on with Derrick, when he was still a DCI. If I'm right, that running shoe belonged to Hannah Emmerson, a student from Oxford University who went missing four years ago. Although there was no evidence to support the theory that she'd been murdered, well Derrick being Derrick... Well, you know what he's like.'

Amy gave the detective a thoughtful look. 'If the superintendent was true to form, I expect he'd be in a rush to close the case because of a lack of evidence?'

'In one. But I thought you said that this corpse was buried three years ago, not four when Hannah disappeared?' Joseph said.

'It's always hard to be exact. That's a rough estimate. Doctor Jacobs might be able to give you a better idea, but I think you'll find that number is in the ballpark.'

The DI scratched his chin as he turned the thought over in his head. 'But that suggests the victim was being held somewhere before her body was dumped here.'

Megan's eyes widened. 'You're saying she was abducted and held prisoner somewhere for up to a year?'

'Jesus, I suppose I am. And that would mean that Hannah might still have been alive when Derrick decided to close the case two months in.' He covered his hand with his mouth. 'Feck, we could have still had a chance to rescue her, if we hadn't just bloody given up.'

'If Derrick hadn't given up, you mean?' Amy corrected him.

'Yes, I suppose that's true. The one thing I do know for sure is that this isn't going to look good for our superintendent when it all comes to light.'

Megan exchanged a look with Amy as they both nodded.

'So what happened in Hannah's case?' Megan asked.

'She disappeared early one morning while she was out running through Christ Church Meadow by the River Isis. In Derrick's defence, he negotiated with the superintendent at the time to have lots of resources thrown at the case. We had sniffer dogs, the works. We even had a section of the Isis dredged in case she had slipped, or even been thrown in. But despite everything, we couldn't find a sign of her. It was like she disappeared off the face of the planet. Eventually, Derrick wrote her off as just another missing person case.'

'But not you?' Amy asked.

Joseph shook his head.

'Well, there's absolutely no way you would have known to look here, unless someone had tipped you off,' Amy said.

Joseph sighed. 'I suppose you're not wrong. But the problem with the original investigation was that we had zero information to go on. Hannah was the very definition of a loner, a student who liked to keep to herself. That was, apart from her passion for rowing. She was actually a member of the women's Oxford Boat Team, where she was a cox on the Blue team. Despite interviewing all the team members and staff, as well as fellow students at her college, we had absolutely nothing to lead us to a suspect. Still, giving up on the case has certainly never sat easy with me all these years.'

Amy nodded. 'Then it sounds like you're going to get a second crack at solving this.'

'Let's hope so,' Joseph said. He stared down at Hannah's final resting place, breathing deeply and trying to loosen the knot of tension that had already taken up residency in his chest.

CHAPTER FOUR

JOSEPH AND MEGAN headed into the pathology observation room. It looked directly into the immaculate lab where two doctors were wearing full PPE, including white long-sleeved gowns. Their face shields, and masks, had been put aside for a moment.

An old veteran when it came to attending an autopsy, the DI could barely hear the whir of the fans of the exhaust ventilation system the postmortem lab used. By the sound of it, they were cranked right down. That was a good sign, as it meant the smell of the body was going to be far milder than many he'd been exposed to over the years.

He could see the two police pathologists were currently sitting at a bench and drinking cups of tea. That was despite the presence of the dead body covered with a sheet less than a few metres away from them. Pathologists were often hardcore like that and corpses, smell and all, didn't seem to really bother them.

Joseph waved through the window at the older grey-haired man in his late fifties. A few moments later the pathologist stepped out of the lab to join them.

'DI Stone, it's been a while,' the man said.

'Yes, but maybe not long enough in our line of work, hey, Doctor Jacobs?'

'Very true,' the doctor replied, turning his attention to Megan. 'And you are?'

'DC Anderson. I'm glad to meet you.' She extended a hand and shook the doctor's.

'Your first autopsy by any chance?'

'How did you guess?'

'Maybe something to do with your current grey complexion.'

That elicited a faint smile from Megan that she really didn't put her heart into.

Doctor Rob Jacobs turned his attention to the DI. 'Before we head in there, I should let you know that we've already confirmed that the body is indeed that of Hannah Emmerson. We've checked her dental records, and I'm afraid it's a match.'

'No surprises there then,' Joseph replied with a grim face.

At that moment the door opened and the young woman who'd been having tea with Jacobs put her head around the door.

'I've just finished sewing the body up, Doctor Jacobs.'

'Excellent.' He gestured to the woman to join them. 'May I introduce you both to my prodigy, Doctor Clara Reece. I'm training her up to take over from me. That is, when I eventually get round to retiring.'

She raised her eyebrows at the detectives. 'I wouldn't listen to Doctor Jacobs. No one around here takes that seriously, or believes that he's going to retire anytime soon.'

'Glad to hear it, because this man's expert testimony has helped to put more than one murderer away,' Joseph replied, casting a gaze towards the sheet covering the body on the autopsy slab in the next room.

'Would you like us to talk you through what we've found so far?' Doctor Reece asked, noticing where his attention was currently focused.

'That would be grand,' Joseph replied.

Jacobs nodded and headed over to a closet, where he dug out the two masks he handed to the detectives.

'That will help with the smell which although mild is still rather pungent,' the doctor said, answering the questioning look Megan gave him.

That turned out to be a significant understatement. Despite the mask, the odour still struck Joseph squarely at the back of the nostrils as they entered the room. The doctor's definition of *mild* was significantly different to his own.

As he breathed the scent in, it was a strange combination of earthy compost mixed with an underlying scent of decaying fruit. It was almost pleasant compared to some of the dead body smells that the DI dealt with over the years. A fresh corpse hit you straight in the face at a good twenty metres and instantly made you want to gag. At least on this occasion, the passage of time had helped to diffuse the putrid stink. Hopefully, because of that, Megan would be able to hang onto her breakfast.

Just to play it on the safe side, the DI checked he had his Silvermints in his jacket pocket, his chosen method to combat the awful smell autopsies frequently exposed him to.

The DC was already taking several deep breaths as she eyed up all the stainless steel surgical instruments on a small table, including a saw. It didn't take too much of a leap of imagination to work out where the organic slimy green matter on them had come from.

'Are you ready, DC Anderson?' Doctor Reece asked as she caught the pale expression on her face.

'As I'll ever be,' Megan replied, with only a slight quaver in her voice.

Joseph patted her on the shoulder. 'You'll be fine.'

Megan nodded, the mask sucking in and out over her nose and mouth a couple times, before glancing at Doctor Reece.

Without so much as a *ta-da*, the doctor pulled the sheet off.

The DC, to her credit, barely blinked as the corpse was revealed. However, the same wasn't true for Joseph. He felt an instant swirl of nausea as he tried to reconcile the ruined body of the victim before them with the young woman who had disappeared four years ago.

When Hannah had vanished, she'd been a fit runner. However, in death, her body had been reduced to a hollowed-out shell, strips of flesh hanging loose to reveal the yellowing bone beneath. The most obvious transformation, apart from the lack of eyes, were the stitches right up the middle of the woman's collapsed sternum.

'As you can see, the victim is very well preserved considering how long she was buried,' Doctor Reece said.

It wasn't lost on Joseph that Clara, like her mentor, didn't actually use Hannah's name. The senior pathologist had once confided in the DI that it was a deliberate strategy, and one way the pathologists used to keep an emotional detachment so they could do their job.

Joseph, like most officers, had learned to do the same, but not anything to the degree their chief pathologist could. That's why Hannah's face would now be added to the parade of others that often haunted Joseph's own nightmares and made him wake in a cold sweat in the middle of the night.

'You've already finished the postmortem?' Megan asked, also peering at the stitches with a lot more stoicism than Joseph was currently managing.

'Yes, and trust me, that was probably a good thing for your very first visit to the lab,' Doctor Jacobs said. 'I'm afraid there wasn't a lot left of the victim's internal organs, and they'd all broken down into something of a soup.'

Without saying a word, Joseph lifted his mask and popped a Silvermint into his mouth, relying on the menthol to suppress the bile rising up the back of his throat. He offered one to Megan who, much to his surprise, waved it away as she went in for a closer look at the corpse.

A real sense of pride filled him that Megan had come so far in just three months. The first time he'd met her, she'd been puking her guts out behind a forensic tent that contained a decapitated goat, one of the Midwinter Butcher's animal victims.

The DC looked intently at the missing sections of flesh around the ankles of the corpse, before she returned her attention to Jacobs and Reece with a frown. 'Are those animal bites that I can see in the flesh?'

Doctor Reece beamed at her. 'Ten out of ten for your observational skills, DC Anderson. Those are actually rat teeth marks.'

'Hang on, how's that even possible when she was buried under six feet of earth?' Joseph asked.

'It's not, at least for a rat to burrow that deep. So that suggests the victim was held somewhere else first. That's where, presumably, the rodent damage happened, before the body was moved to its final resting place.'

Joseph nodded. 'Okay.'

'That makes sense, but what about cause of death?' Megan asked.

Doctor Jacobs was about to answer, but Joseph held up his hand to stop him, because he'd just noticed the marks around the victim's neck. Now it was his turn to lean in for a closer look.

'Looking at those lines, I'd say she was strangled, but not with hands. Maybe with a ligature? Also, based on how deep it has cut into her neck, I would say it was done by someone who was pretty strong.'

Doctor Jacobs nodded. 'Nailed it in one, DI Stone, but then I'd expect nothing less from you.'

Joseph shrugged. 'I'm glad not to disappoint. Is there anything else you can tell us?'

'We're still trying to determine a rough date of the victim's death. That's been complicated by the highly saturated clay of the embankment acting as something of a preservative.'

'A bit like the Lindow Man?' Megan asked.

Doctor Jacobs shot her an impressed look. 'Exactly.'

'Sorry?' Joseph asked, looking between them. 'The Lindow Man, who was that then?'

'He was that man from the Iron Age, well-preserved in a peat bog in Cheshire,' Megan replied. 'Through analysis of the guy's remains, they discovered he had been in his mid-twenties. He apparently died from a combination of a blow to the head, strangulation, and a cut to the throat.'

'His murderer really wasn't taking any chances then?'

'Something like that,' Megan replied with a small smile.

'You seem to know a lot about it DC Anderson,' Doctor Jacobs said.

'Archaeology is something of a passion of mine. I've even helped out on a few digs.'

Joseph stared at her. 'Aren't you a dark horse?'

'Hey, it's nice to still be able to surprise people sometimes.'

Doctor Jacobs gave her something approaching an awestruck look. 'I'd love to talk to you about that sometime, as it's something that I've always wanted to do.'

Megan beamed at him. 'No problem. I'll give you my number and we can get together for a drink sometime.'

Joseph exchanged a look with Doctor Reece who was also watching this exchange with an almost anthropological fascination. It was easy to see there was an immediate spark between Megan and Jacobs, despite the age difference. Maybe one day they would tell their grandchildren how their eyes had first met over a corpse.

'As interesting as that all is, we should concentrate on the job in hand,' the DI said, giving Megan a sharp look.

'Sorry, don't mind me,' she replied.

'No, it was actually a very good point, DC Anderson,' Doctor Jacobs said. 'Just like a peat bog, the clay slowed down the decomposition of the victim's body. That makes dating the death far more challenging than normal. We're going to be relying on taphonomy to see how the body has changed since death. To help with that, Doctor Reece has already sent mud samples from the site to be analysed for the acidity and the anaerobic conditions. That's why we won't know exactly when she was murdered until we get the lab report back, and even then it will be an estimate. I'm hoping to have those lab results ready for briefing the investigation team tomorrow.'

'Then we look forward to hearing your report,' Joseph replied. 'The only problem is that any trail that might lead us to the murderer has probably gone very cold by now.'

'Hey, never say never, Joseph,' Megan said.

Doctor Jacobs smiled at her. 'That's the spirit, Detective. And you could do with some of that self-belief too, DI Stone.'

'Aye, I probably could,' Joseph replied, as his attention returned to the woman lying dead on a cold steel slab.

At least there would be some form of closure for her parents. One thing that was certain, now that Joseph knew what had happened to Hannah, he wasn't going to stop until they found the bastard responsible, and locked them away so they could never harm another soul ever again.

CHAPTER FIVE

THE FOLLOWING DAY, the incident room was positively heaving with detectives and uniformed officers. Joseph noted with some surprise that even the big man himself—DSU Derrick Walker—was standing at the back. For someone who was almost permanently stuck behind his desk in his glass citadel of an office, it was something of a departure for the superintendent to grace them with his presence.

If nothing else, that told Joseph that the man had more than a passing interest in this case. Maybe Derrick was even experiencing some level of guilt about terminating the original investigation way too soon. After all, who was the DI to say miracles couldn't happen and the eejit wasn't experiencing some remorse?

In preparation for the briefing, Joseph had gone through all of the original case files for Hannah's disappearance. He'd also dug out the images that were now placed at one end of the evidence board. Among the photos already up, there were also ones taken at the original crime scene along the path where she had vanished that fateful morning. Alongside those, were photos of the narrow boat owners, struck through with a red marker, indicating they'd already been eliminated as potential suspects.

There was also a group shot of the original women's Oxford Boat crew of which Hannah had been a member. She sat crouched in the front row, a big cheesy grin on her face. That photo had been taken just a month before she had disappeared. Finally, there were photos of the blue running shoes with the yellow laces that had been recovered from the current crime scene, together with close-up photos of the marks around Hannah's neck, taken at the autopsy. But the biggest reaction from the team had been reserved for the pictures of the rat bite marks around her ankles. That told everyone that even in death, the murderer hadn't shown her body any respect.

As Joseph looked around the room, he couldn't help but feel a sense of gloom hanging over him, despite all the warm bodies Derrick had allocated to the case. In the original investigation, every avenue they'd looked into had quickly run into a dead end. Standing here today, despite finding her body, it was hard to see why it would be any different this time around.

Finishing his conversation with Amy and Doctor Jacobs, Chris picked up the remote for the TV set behind him.

'Okay, everyone, let's make a start,' he announced.

With a click, the Thames Valley Police, TVP, logo was replaced with a photo of Hannah in a dark blue tracksuit, holding up a gold medal to the camera and grinning.

'This is Hannah Emmerson, who disappeared over four years ago whilst running along the path that edges Christ Church Meadow, next to the River Isis.'

Joseph zoned out slightly as Chris went over details he already knew, keeping his attention discreetly on Derrick—the man who had once stabbed him in the back, all in the name of climbing over him to secure his promotion.

It was hard for Joseph not to take some satisfaction in seeing

Derrick looking distinctly uncomfortable as he listened to the briefing, and it was little wonder why. Once the press joined the dots that Derrick had been the SIO on the case, at the very least it would be a stain on his career, possibly worse if Hannah's parents decided to put in a complaint about police negligence.

In Joseph's opinion, Derrick had certainly given up far too early. Although, again in fairness to the man, there had been absolutely no further leads to pursue at the time. If Joseph had been the one in charge, yes, he might have hung in there doggedly for a bit longer. But then, ultimately, he too would have been forced to throw in the towel.

It was only when Amy and Doctor Jacobs stepped forward that Joseph tuned in again to what was being said.

'Dental records confirm that the victim was indeed Hannah Emmerson,' Doctor Jacobs said.

Amy pressed the remote button to display a photo of the two blue running shoes on the desk. 'Of course, we already knew that, thanks to DI Stone's sharp memory. He was able to identify her running shoe based on a photo he hadn't seen in over four years.' She clicked the remote again.

A new photo of Hannah appeared on the screen, this time with her wearing the same blue running shoes.

'Lab tests of the soil deposits have also confirmed that there is a possible discrepancy in the likely date of death and when Hannah was placed in the improvised grave by the Isis,' Doctor Jacobs said. 'However, we can't be certain due to the clay that her corpse was found in. The lower oxygen content of the soil and its saturated water content slowed the rate of decomposition. That means the clay effectively acted as a preservative and slowed the breakdown of the victim's flesh and bone material. However, due to the rodent damage, it appears that Hannah was almost certainly killed in another location, where her body was left long enough for the rats to gnaw on her corpse.'

Several of the officers in the room shook their heads, exchanging grim looks.

'The result of all of this is that we have no way yet of precisely saying when she died,' Doctor Jacobs continued. 'It could have been within hours of when she was first reported missing, or as much as twelve months later.'

Ian's hand shot up, and Chris nodded towards him. 'I don't suppose there is any DNA evidence left to help identify the killer?'

'Unfortunately not. Even with the preservative qualities of the mud, if the murderer left any DNA behind, it's long since been lost to time,' Amy said.

'So what about any leads from the original case?' another officer asked from the side of the room.

Immediately all eyes turned, not to Derrick, but to Joseph, as though he'd been the SIO on the case.

For feck's sake! the DI thought to himself.

'Yes, would you like to answer that, Joseph?' Chris said, as Derrick stayed determinedly thin-lipped and mute.

He cleared his throat and nodded. 'During the original investigation, we interviewed absolutely everyone, including all members of the Oxford Boat crews, both men and women, as well as senior staff, including the coach and his assistant, along with Hannah's family. None of them appeared to have any motive.'

'What about some sort of professional jealousy? Maybe someone who was after Hannah's seat on the boat crew?' Ian asked.

'That's what we wondered, too. It's no secret that it's highly competitive to get onto the Oxford crews, even for a cox position. But anyone who might have had even the vaguest of motives was able to produce credible alibis.'

'So this could be just a random murder, then?' Ian said,

pursuing his line of thought like a dog with a tasty bone. 'Maybe Hannah was simply in the wrong place at the wrong time and fell into the crosshairs of some psycho, who then abducted and killed her?'

Before Joseph could answer, Chris jumped in. 'All of that is speculation at this point, Ian. We need facts rather than guesses at this stage of the investigation. So to begin with, we need to go over every old lead that Joseph and his team were able to come up with at the time, and let's see if we can't come up with a few new ones of our own.'

His team? Yes, Joseph could already see the trajectory of this, even if it was just by inference. Once again, it wasn't lost on him, no one looked at Derrick. The superintendent obviously wasn't going to volunteer anything. It was almost as though the man fully intended to use Joseph as a lightning rod to hide behind. What a surprise.

But it was then, when the DI's greatest level of cynicism had kicked into high gear, the superintendent actually decided to speak.

'So, what are you thinking about prioritising with this investigation, Chris?' Derrick asked.

'To begin with, interviewing old witnesses again, and anyone who might have had even the mildest reason for wishing Hannah harm,' the DCI replied. 'Also, someone should go over the old case notes to see if anything was missed.'

'I'm happy to do that,' Joseph said.

But Chris didn't exactly look enthusiastic about the idea. 'Okay, but maybe Megan should do that with you. Two sets of eyes and all that.'

Megan nodded at Joseph and smiled.

The DI obviously didn't have any problem with the DC helping him, but he still felt a spike of irritation. Although Chris hadn't come out and said it, there was another implication here:

that the original investigation had been slack and they'd over-looked something obvious.

Joseph heard the door softly shut, and he glanced back to see Derrick had just vanished from the room. Of course he had, the little fecker. The superintendent had probably already had a quiet word with Chris, suggesting that if anyone was to blame for negligence, it was Joseph. Of course, he might just be para-noid, but he'd had enough run-ins with Derrick over the years to know the man would be more than happy for him to take the rap.

Then a deeply troubling thought hit Joseph. What if he really was the one who had missed something obvious? There had certainly been a bum-rush, thanks to Derrick, to get things tidied up in double-time. Maybe in all the haste to close the case, Joseph hadn't picked up on a detail that might have led to rescuing Hannah, especially if there'd been a window of time when she'd still been alive.

A sense of deep unease swept over him.

Thankfully, everyone else's gazes had now pivoted to Megan as she asked a question, almost like she was deliberately drawing the spotlight away from Joseph.

'So what about putting out a plea to the public to see if anyone has any information that's relevant?' she said. 'The news might prompt someone who didn't come forward during the original investigation, especially since we have a body now. That could motivate someone to say something, even if they think what they know is trivial. It could lead to a breakthrough.'

Chris shook his head. 'I'd like us to keep our powder dry, at least for now, in case we tip off the murderer that we're on their trail. My instinct is that the less warning we give them, the more likely we are to catch them. But never say never. If nothing else pans out, we can always turn to that as a last resort.'

Megan nodded, but then leant across to Joseph. 'I wonder if

that news embargo includes Derrick not tipping Kate off?' she whispered.

Joseph knew the DC had a point. Kate was, and would always be, a newshound at heart. It would be hard for her to resist leaning on her husband for information.

'I suspect even our DSU won't be inclined to let his wife know about this particular case,' Joseph replied.

Megan gave him a questioning look, but when he didn't elaborate any further, she just shrugged.

As Chris wrapped up the meeting, Joseph was lost in thought. It took Megan several attempts, waving her hand in front of his face, for him to realise she was trying to get his attention.

'What do you think, Joseph?' she asked as the other officers headed over to their desks in the incident room.

'I think we've just been served a shite sandwich without any ketchup. The truth is, I reckon we'll end up chasing our tails just like we did four years ago.'

'Hey, we won't know until we try,' Megan replied with the bright enthusiasm of a young officer who hadn't been ground down by the office politics of something like this.

Joseph did his best to smile, but it was hard not to see dead ends wherever he looked, just like they had before.

'Wow, you look like you just swallowed a fart,' Ian said as he wandered over with his Batman mug in his hand. 'What's the problem, my Irish friend?'

By way of an answer, Joseph just raised his eyebrows at him.

He grimaced. 'Yeah, stupid question. What you probably need right now is some caffeine rocket fuel to cheer you up.' He tapped the side of his mug. 'I'm doing a run to the kitchen. Fancy a cup of old Joe?'

'No, I'm good,' Joseph said.

'Then cheer up, you miserable bugger,' Ian said. 'Anyway, how about you, Megan? Fancy a mug?'

She managed an almost genuine smile. 'Thanks for the offer, but I'm okay.'

Ian nodded, and with a cheery whistle headed off.

'A proper cup of coffee from that barista who runs that van round the corner?' Joseph said to Megan the moment that Ian was out of earshot.

'God, yes. I don't want to hurt the poor guy's feelings, but his tea and coffee-making skills, as you might say, are a bit *shite*.'

'Yes, the phrase "dishwater with milk" comes to mind.'

Megan smirked as they both grabbed their coats and headed for the door.

As the detectives stepped out into the general office, Joseph couldn't help but glance across to Derrick's glass-walled office, where the superintendent currently had his head in his hands. It seemed Joseph wasn't the only one worried he might have slipped up.

Nevertheless, he was determined to do whatever it took to crack this case, regardless of the cost to his or Derrick's career.

CHAPTER SIX

SEVERAL HOURS LATER, dozens of phone conversations were underway in the incident room. Officers were reaching out to everyone who had been interviewed as part of the original investigation. Megan, whose desk was next to Joseph's, chewed on the end of her pen and scanned through the files on her computer screen. She, like Joseph, was going through every statement she could find. To say the least, it was tedious, mind-numbing work.

Ian, who was sitting opposite them, put the phone down with an exasperated sigh. 'Give me strength. That's the third person on the list who's left the flipping country.'

'That's Oxford students for you, with the world literally waiting to fall at the feet of many of them,' Megan said.

Joseph massaged his neck muscles as the sense of despondency deepened inside him. 'Yes, and that, of course, may also include our murderer.'

'Maybe, maybe not,' Ian said, in a far too cheerful tone, despite his own lack of success with his phone calls.

'Did you get out of the right side of the bed or something?' Joseph asked.

'Let's just say I'm still enjoying the afterglow of date night with the missus. That's why I have a certain spring in my step this morning.'

Megan pulled her chin in. 'Too much information.'

'He did ask,' Ian said, grinning at her.

Joseph quickly held up his mug. 'Did I hear you say you were doing a tea run?'

At first, Ian gave him a baffled look that quickly morphed into one of delight. 'I didn't, but now you mention it I am parched. I'll happily do a brew.' A moment later, the DI had gathered up their mugs and was checking to see if anyone else wanted a cuppa. Not surprisingly, everyone quickly shook their heads, and some even produced water bottles out of their bags to prove just how hydrated they were.

'Did you really just voluntarily ask Ian for a cup of tea, or was I hearing things?' Megan asked the moment Ian was out of the room.

'I just needed to distract him before he hit us with the sordid details of his love life.'

'Ah, and I expect Ian, being Ian, wouldn't hold back on the details,' Megan replied.

'In one. So if we have to suffer a cup of his awful tea, it's a small mercy for us, trust me.'

Megan grinned at him and nodded.

Joseph returned to the soul-sapping task of going through record after record on the HOLMES2 database. It was a few minutes later when something snagged his attention. There was a short report that had been added to the investigation notes. It was a phone message transcript that had been taken at the front desk from a woman called Joanne Keating, an Oxford student. Apparently, she'd rung the police station with some new information about Hannah a year after the case had been closed.

Joseph leaned towards the screen as he started reading the message the desk sergeant had taken.

'Hannah told me that she was worried about her mental health. Apparently, she kept forgetting that she'd moved things in her flat. Like, she said she'd been studying and put her textbooks on the shelf afterward, only to find them back on her desk the next morning. She even claimed to remember turning off the TV when she left one morning, only to find it on when she returned. The thing was, she had absolutely no recollection of doing those things, and was wondering if the pressure of all the training for the Oxford Boat crew on top of her studies was starting to get to her.'

Joseph sucked air over his teeth as he continued reading. The duty sergeant who'd taken the call had forwarded the message to...

The DI stared at Derrick Walker's name at the bottom of the screen.

Multiple questions immediately spun through his mind. Why was this the first he was hearing about it? Could it be that Derrick had followed up on the message but found nothing of real value in the woman's report? But if so, since Joseph had been part of the original investigation team, why hadn't Derrick said anything? Also, if Hannah's mental health was an issue, might that have relevance to their investigation now? There was also another obvious theory. What if Hannah had a stalker?

Joseph quickly hit the print key, and a moment later had a hard copy of the message in his hand.

'Found something interesting?' Megan asked, looking up at him.

'Not sure, but I'm going to kick the tyres on it to find out.'

'Keep me posted.'

'Don't worry, I will,' Joseph replied as he headed to the door.

On his way out, he almost collided with Ian coming through the door with a tray of mugs.

'Whoa, slow down there, speedy,' Ian said, managing to swerve just enough to not spill a drop of the grey-looking tea.

'Sorry, someone I need to see in a hurry.'

'Right...' Ian angled the tray towards him. 'Grab your mug then.'

'Nah, just leave it on my desk and I'll have it when I get back,' Joseph replied, having absolutely no intention of drinking the insipid brew in this or any other lifetime.

———

In the superintendent's office, Derrick's gaze flicked up from the printout of the phone call transcript. He gave Joseph a wary look, his jaw muscles clenching.

'So I was wondering if you could tell me about this message,' Joseph said. 'When you spoke to Joanne Keating, was she able to cast any more light on these things that happened in Hannah's flat?'

The DSU blinked, but remained mute, his eyes narrowed.

After a good five seconds had crawled past, Joseph finally decided to jump in again.

'I'm assuming there was nothing of relevance when you looked into it?'

Still not saying a word, Derrick got up and closed the blinds to his glass fishbowl of an office. Then he crossed to a cabinet, took out a bottle of Johnnie Walker Red Label Whisky, and poured himself at least a triple. He held up a second glass towards Joseph and raised his eyebrows.

'No, thank you. Still a bit early in the day for me.'

The superintendent nodded, sat back down, and then emptied his glass with one large gulp.

Joseph was so unsettled by the DSU's uncharacteristic behaviour, he actually felt a vague stirring of concern for the man.

'Is everything alright?' he asked.

Derrick fixed his gaze on the DI, then finally spoke. 'Don't act so bloody innocent, Joseph. You know full well you've got me bang to rights.'

A sense of confusion filled Joseph's head. 'I do?'

'Come on, at least have the decency to tell me to my face that you're going to drop me in the shit. Or is this something else, like blackmail, where you expect me to suddenly promote you to the role of DCI that you've been after all these years?'

Joseph stared at the man as though he'd gone stark raving mad. 'Derrick, I think we've got some very crossed wires here. All I wanted to know was what Joanne...' Then his gaze tightened as a cog deep within his brain began to turn. 'You didn't follow up on this message and talk to her, did you? That's what this is all about.'

As Derrick grimaced, Joseph realised he'd hit the nail on the head.

'You have to understand, I had a lot on my plate with a promotion in the offing. So when Joanne's call came in, I just didn't have the time...' He met the DI's gaze.

'You're telling me that you knowingly left a potential lead sitting on the table?'

'Look, you've seen the transcript from the phone call. It was probably nothing.'

'Probably isn't the same as definitely,' Joseph said, feeling an ember of anger beginning to burn. 'Permission to speak freely?'

Derrick gave him the barest of nods.

'For feck's sake, you could have offloaded it to me as your errand boy, and I would have gladly checked it out. Or...' A darker motive suddenly occurred to him.

The superintendent grimaced as he realised where the DI's line of thinking was about to lead him.

Joseph's mind travelled back four years to when Derrick had been on the verge of being promoted to DSU. The man had done everything in his power to be noticed, making sure he was involved in every case that looked likely to be solved. And he had bathed in the reflected glory when that happened. He had been all puffed-out-chest and the *big I am* back then, and still was, but maybe with less of the youthful arrogance he'd once had in spades.

As for the less promising cases, DCI Walker, as he'd been then, was careful he didn't touch them with a barge pole, particularly after the Hannah Emmerson case. After all, who wanted to be burdened by the lead weight of unsolved cases when they were trying to climb up the slippery pole of promotion?

Joseph thought of Derrick's behaviour after Chris's briefing when, back in this office, he'd had his head in his hands. Now he knew why.

The DI looked at the man like he was a turd he'd just stepped in. 'You deliberately suppressed evidence because you didn't want Hannah's case to be dredged up again? Were you worried that your superiors would have realised that the great DCI Derrick Walker wasn't infallible?'

'Look, Joseph, I know we haven't always seen eye-to-eye over a lot of things. But if this gets out, it could put a huge stain on my career.'

'Maybe you should have thought about that when you sat on a potential lead,' Joseph replied, trying to keep the anger out of his voice.

'Look, I know more than anyone that I got this wrong. But I'm pleading with you as an old mate, we need to keep this between ourselves.'

'An old *mate?* That's a fecking good one from the man who has taken every opportunity to stab me in the back.'

Derrick held up his hands. 'I realise I could have been a better friend...' He shrugged, his neck going red, obviously realising just how hollow those words sounded. Then he looked at Joseph like the DI was his executioner. 'So what are you going to do now?'

'To start with, I'll begin with what you should have done three years ago. I'm going to track down Joanne Keating and find out everything I can. As for you, I'm going to have to think on this, Derrick.'

'I need your word, Joseph, that this stays between us.'

'You'll get no such thing, and you'd better not say another word, because right now I'm very much inclined to head straight out of this office and report you to the Independent Office for Police Conduct.'

Derrick went to say something else, but thought better of it, and shut his mouth again. Then, as though someone had let the air out of him, he didn't so much crumple as deflate into himself.

Joseph turned on his heel and headed out of the door. But he already knew that, however pissed he was at the man, he was unlikely to actually use this against the DSU. No, that would be to lower himself to Derrick's level, which resided firmly in the gutter. Everyone made mistakes occasionally, even Joseph, and he had no actual intention of hanging the boss out to dry. The truth was, he would probably end up saying he spotted the report misfiled under the wrong investigation. However, Joseph wasn't going to let the little bollox know that just yet. Much better to see him squirm like a worm on a hook for a while longer.

The DI headed back into the incident room with a fresh sense of purpose in his step.

'You look in a better mood, Joseph,' Megan said the moment she saw him.

'I am indeed. We have a possible lead. I want you to arrange a meeting with Joanne Keating as quickly as possible.'

Ian's ears perked up. 'I know that look—you're onto something.'

'Possibly, but it could still turn out to be nothing.'

'I think we'd all take any lead, however tenuous, right now,' Megan replied.

Joseph nodded and tore off the bottom of the transcript that mentioned Derrick by name, handing her the rest.

Sitting back down, he noticed the rapidly cooling mug of tea, Ian had left out for him. The DI was in such a good mood he could have almost taken a sip, and that was seriously saying something.

CHAPTER SEVEN

JOSEPH THOUGHT the big man upstairs was obviously smiling down at him today. Not only had Megan discovered that Joanne Keating was still in the country, but that she was also in her final year at Oxford, completing her Masters Human Science degree in Psychology, Philosophy, and Linguistics.

When he pictured her, it was hard for Joseph not to imagine a woman in a trouser suit peering over her specs at her client on her couch, no doubt as they divulged their darkest inner secrets. The added bonus for her patients, with the degree Joanne was studying, was she could not only debate the meaning of life with them, but also pick them up on their grammar whilst doing so. He could imagine a lot of the well-heeled Oxford set definitely signing up for that sort of psychology boot camp.

The significant thing for the investigation was if Hannah really had been starting to lose her mind, Joanne might be just the woman in the right place and time to make an informed judgement about it.

That was why he and Megan were currently heading along St Clements Street, which was lined with dozens of independent shops, from vintage clothing to alternative health. When they reached a former pub at the turning onto Cave Street, which had been converted into a Sri Lankan restaurant, Megan stopped and sniffed the fragrant curry-ladened air.

'That smells so good,' she said.

'You can't still be hungry?" Joseph asked. 'I watched you eat at least two bacon sandwiches in that café less than an hour ago.'

Megan shrugged. 'My mother always used to say that I had hollow legs.'

'Aye, it certainly sounds like it,' Joseph replied as they began to walk down Cave Street, with its rows of terraced houses crammed in together.

The DC's gaze ran over the house numbers as they passed them. 'I can't believe that this lead was missed.'

Joseph shrugged. 'It happens. Small details sometimes get overlooked or lost in the system like on this occasion. The important thing is it's come to light now.'

'I suppose you're right, but I'm surprised you haven't reported this to DSU Walker. It's exactly the sort of thing he loves to roast an officer over the coals about.'

Oh, the irony, Joseph thought. Out loud he said, 'Everyone makes mistakes, Megan. And don't worry, I've already had a quiet word with the offending officer. I'm certain they've learnt their lesson.'

Megan gave him a small smile. 'You really are one of the good ones, aren't you?'

If only she knew how good.

'Shush, don't tell anyone. It would blow my surly old detective cover story.'

'Surly, yes, but old I'm not so sure about.'

'Oh, you sweet talker,' Joseph said as they came to a stop in front of a brick house with a white door. He double-checked the address he had for Joanne. 'Yes, this is the one.'

The small drive was empty of cars. That would have been

great if the detectives had known they could have parked here, rather than in the dodgy public car park off the high street. Trying to park anywhere in the city was always something of a lottery unless you were prepared to use your blue lights. That was less than ideal when you didn't want to draw the attention of neighbours to you trying to have a discreet chat with a potential witness.

An impressive collection of weeds was growing between the paving bricks in front of the house, indicating that maybe dealing with them was not a high priority for the current occupant.

Joseph tried the bell on the door, but when there was no hint of a chime they could hear inside the house, the DI tried three sharp raps with the knocker.

A few moments later, they heard the clatter of feet coming down the stairs. The door was opened by a woman in her late twenties. She was wearing the tattiest of patterned wool jumpers, holes everywhere, and pink elephant-print leggings. Just to complete the effect of the ensemble, her hair was going every which way as though she'd just been scooped up by a tornado. This was not, by any means, the soon-to-be professional psychologist, Joseph had pictured in his head. The woman wasn't even wearing glasses.

'Joanne Keating?' Megan asked with uncertainty.

The woman nodded.

'I'm DC Anderson and this is DI Stone. We spoke on the phone.'

'Yes, I've been expecting you. You'll have to excuse my appearance. I've had my head buried in books.'

'Then thank you for letting us interrupt you,' Joseph said, as though he hadn't even noticed the general state of the woman's attire.

'No problem. Please come on through, but sorry for the

mess. I've never been the most organised of people when it comes to my own home.'

Joanne wasn't exaggerating, either. Not only did the two detectives have to pick their way past a bicycle and a folded-up treadmill crammed into the hallway, but there was also an enormous teetering pile of unopened junk mail stacked next to the bottom of the stairs that would have given the Leaning Tower of Pisa a run for its money. The final part of the obstacle course challenge was a sideways shuffle past a clothing rail crammed with at least a dozen coats.

Joseph had always thought a person's home said a lot about them. He just hoped for her sake that if one day Joanne did end up having clients, they never got to see how she lived on her days off.

His mind travelled back to his own brief encounter with the psychologist who had tried to help him deal with his PTSD following the death of his baby son, Eoin, in the car crash. Despite the fact the accident had been indirectly caused by a stag startled by the Midwinter Butcher, Joseph had always blamed himself. He hadn't been able to sleep without nightmares for several months after it had first happened, reliving the events of that night over and over again.

Eventually his then-wife Kate had told him he really needed to see someone. He'd decided to go to a private shrink to avoid tipping off anyone on the force he was having issues. A psychologist friend of Kate's had turned out to be the real deal. Her garden office had come complete with a leather couch, tasteful sculptures, and plants everywhere. She even had a tropical fish tank. No doubt everything in that environment had been designed to instil a sense of calm in her clients, but it hadn't helped a lot during his own therapy sessions. Joseph eventually ended up going to his GP to get sleeping pills, which had helped. Eventually, his nightmares had subsided, or at least been pushed down deep enough into his subconscious to not make a nightly appearance.

Joseph stepped over a half-full bin bag left in the doorway. The state of Joanne's chaotic lifestyle was also evident in the condition of her kitchen. Dirty plates were piled high in the sink and takeout boxes spilled out of the bin.

'Tea?' Joanne said brightly, like this den of squalor was a perfectly normal way to live.

The DI glanced at the sink area. It didn't take much of a leap of the imagination to determine that if he tried her brew, he might actually catch some disease that would give even the Oxford teaching hospitals a run for their money.

Megan, who had obviously come to the same conclusion, quickly shook her head. 'Not for me.'

'No, I'm grand, too, thank you,' Joseph said.

Joanne's eyes immediately locked onto him like he was an exhibit in a zoo. 'That's a Dublin accent, isn't it?'

'Born and bred there,' Joseph replied.

'I've always been a fan of foreign languages. That's part of the reason I chose a degree that included linguistics.' Her eyes widened. 'Sorry, I'm not saying that you're a foreigner or anything.'

Joseph smiled. 'Don't worry yourself. As an Irish man, I'm indeed a foreigner and proud of it among you Sassenachs.'

'Of course you are.' Joanne blushed so hard that it almost reached her ears, obviously believing she'd managed to put her foot in it, which she really hadn't with him. This lass had a lot to learn if she was ever to going to work in psychology.

'Anyway, you wanted to talk about Hannah,' Joanne said, quickly changing the subject.

'That's correct, we would appreciate it if you could tell us more about Hannah telling you that things had been moved in her flat?' Megan said.

Joanne nodded, quickly scooping up a pile of books that had been piled on the kitchen table. She cleared a space and gestured to the chairs.

A moment later they were sitting at the table, Megan's note-book already open and her pen poised.

'So first of all, I must apologise about the police not following up on your phone call three years ago,' Joseph said.

Joanne waved her hand in the air. 'No problem. I realise how busy you all are, and you probably didn't think it was worth following up on, anyway.'

'We try to follow through on all leads, because even what might seem trivial could lead to a major breakthrough,' Megan said.

'Of course, I didn't mean to imply...' Joanne gave them a slightly helpless look as her face flamed again.

If only Joanne knew how right she was, that someone at St Aldates station had cocked up. Joseph still couldn't quite believe he was covering for Derrick, but here he was doing exactly that. So it was important to steer the conversation away before she asked any more questions about the delay that would be difficult to explain. Thankfully, Megan was already primed to do just that.

'So, if you don't mind us asking you a couple of questions before we go over your phone call?' Megan started.

'Yes, fire away, you can ask me anything,' Joanne said.

Megan referred to her notes. 'First of all, why did you wait a year after Hannah disappeared to come forward with your information?'

'Oh, that's easy to explain. I was on a sabbatical travelling through India for a year. Before I headed off, Hannah told me she was worried about the state of her mental health. But it was only when I got home that I found out she had disappeared. That's when I rang the police station.'

Fecking Derrick, not following this up, Joseph thought to himself, making sure his expression revealed nothing.

'Were you close to Hannah?' he asked.

'Not really. We had a sort of on-off casual friendship from the very start.'

'I see. So how did you know each other?'

'I was looking into sports psychology as part of my research. We were interviewing members of the rowing team to see if there was a way to help improve their mental performance. Hannah and I hit it off straight away, although we never went out of the way to look for each other. But if we ran into each other, we were more than happy to spend time together.'

Joseph nodded. 'So, your phone message about Hannah worrying about the state of her mental health?'

'As I mentioned in the phone call, it all seemed to happen over a period of several months while I was still in Oxford. At first, it was minor things, like her leaving a light on when she headed out to class. But then she started to find that things had been moved from where she thought she'd left them, like tea bags being put back in a different cupboard, or her textbooks on the table instead of where she remembered putting them on the shelf. One night, Hannah even came back to find her home smart speaker blaring rave music at full volume.'

'She thought she was doing these things, but just couldn't remember?' Megan asked.

'Yes, and there was a plausible explanation for why she might have been doing that. You see, she was under a lot of pressure with all the training for the Women's Oxford Boat crew. Hannah often complained that the coach piled on so much pressure that it was enough to break a person. And that was on top of all the studying necessary for her degree in Ancient and Modern History. Even though she was a cox, she trained every bit as hard as the rowers. She was both mentally and physically exhausted. That's why she believed she was having memory lapses.' Joanne pulled a face.

'You're not convinced?' Joseph asked.

Joanne looked into the middle distance. 'To be honest, I'm highly sceptical. Yes, Hannah was under a lot of pressure, but she never once buckled. Like so many do, she certainly never turned to drugs or alcohol as a way to cope. The only thing she used to do was vent to me about the coach, who was, if you'll pardon my language, an a-hole. But apart from that, she was as mentally sound as anyone could be in that situation, even if she had started to doubt herself.'

'So, what about these incidents that happened at her house?' Megan asked.

'I can't be sure, but I think she was the victim of some sort of prank, even though there was no sign of any break-ins. Maybe it was someone who had got hold of her key somehow, had a copy cut, and wanted to mess with her mind—especially when one of the rowing medals went missing from a display case on her wall.'

Joseph immediately sat up straighter. 'Sorry, you're saying something was actually taken from Hannah's flat?'

'That's right, although she still managed to convince herself that she must have taken it out to clean or something, and had forgotten where she put it.'

'That sounds like a bit of stretch,' Joseph said.

'No need to tell me. That's what I told Hannah, and that she should contact the police. But she just laughed it off.'

'In that case, do you know of anyone who might have wanted to deliberately upset her by breaking into her flat and moving things around?' Joseph asked.

'Not to my knowledge. Hannah was always the first person to say she didn't have time for relationships because of everything that was going on in her life with rowing and her studies.'

What Joanne was saying certainly rang true for Joseph. He

had heard countless times from the other members of the women's and men's Oxford Boat teams during the original investigation that the coach, Charles Norton, had been a real slave driver.

'What about any other friends who might have held a grudge against Hannah?' Megan asked.

'*Friends?* Hannah was the very definition of a loner when she wasn't on the team coxing.'

Joseph dragged his teeth over his lip and nodded. There was a definite lead here, possibly even an MO for Hannah's murderer, deliberately targeting her home before eventually snatching her.

'Is there anything else that you can tell us?' Megan asked.

'No, that's it really. But hopefully this all has a happy ending, and it turns out she's doing okay wherever it is that she took herself off to. After all, she wouldn't be the first person to drop out of Oxford and go dark on everyone who knew her.'

Joseph was impressed that Megan didn't so much as give him a sideways glance as Joanne had been speaking. As Chris had said, they needed to keep Hannah's death out of the public's attention for as long as possible, until they were ready to reveal the truth.

The DI made sure his own emotional mask was well in place. 'So that's what you think happened to her—she did a flit?'

'Maybe...' Joanne replied, her tone uncertain. But then she forced a smile. 'Of course, it is. Hannah is the very definition of a people pleaser, who would want to harm a hair on her head?'

'I see.' This time Joseph did trade a look with Megan. 'I think we have everything we need, DC Anderson.'

She nodded and closed her notebook.

As they stood, Joseph reached out and shook Joanne's hand. 'You've been very helpful, Miss Keating.'

'I just hope it's useful,' Joanne said as she shook Megan's hand as well.

Joseph handed her his card. 'Very, and if you do hear anything else that you think is relevant to Hannah's disappearance, please get in contact.'

'Don't worry, I will.'

'So what are your thoughts, Joseph?' Megan asked as they headed back up the road towards the car park.

'I think Hannah had some sort of stalker who broke into her home before her disappearance, one who was deliberately playing mind games with her. I also wonder if the rowing medal that vanished was taken as some sort of trophy.'

'I agree. Do you think the fact that the missing medal was connected to rowing is significant? Maybe someone on the boating crew?'

'This is all old territory that we looked at four years ago, Megan. We didn't manage to come up with anything then, and I'm not sure we'll find anything now that four years have passed. However, this is the first real evidence that someone may have had Hannah in their sights before she was murdered.'

'So what's the next step?' Megan asked.

'First, we report back to Chris to get him, and the rest of the team, up to speed with what we just discovered. After that, I need to fly solo briefly as there's someone's brain I need to pick.'

'Dylan's, by any chance?'

'No, not on this occasion. I was going to ask Kate if there were any reports that didn't make it into the papers. I'm wondering if any other students at the time also experienced things in their homes getting moved, or even going missing entirely.'

'You think the murderer may have been targeting more than one person?'

'We won't know until we do a bit of digging.'

'But what about tipping Kate off about this case being a live investigation again? Do that, and she's bound to want to know why.'

'Leave that to me. She and I may be divorced, but we still have an understanding when it comes to active police investigations. Kate would certainly never jeopardise a case by leaking a story, at least until she gets the nod from me or Derrick that it's alright to do so.'

'I just hope you're right about that.'

'Trust me, I am,' Joseph said. The smell of exotic curry caught his nose as they wandered past the Sri Lankan restaurant. The DI turned to his colleague. 'What do you say to two takeaways, on me?'

'Bloody hell, I know everyone warned me about the bad habits I would pick up from working with you, but no one said anything about the weight gain. You, Joseph Stone, are bad for my waistline.'

'Says the woman with the hollow legs. Anyway, if you don't want any...'

'Hey, I didn't say that.'

'That's what I thought,' Joseph said, winking at her and leading the way, headed into the restaurant.

CHAPTER EIGHT

BRIEFING CHRIS about the information Joanne had provided required all Joseph's skills in lying to cover up Derrick's mistake. Unfortunately, Chris had been like a tenacious terrier, determined to deal with whoever was responsible for *misfiling such a fucking important piece of information!* Although Joseph had quietly tipped off Derrick that Chris was on the warpath, how the superintendent was going to avoid landing himself in a cesspool's worth of shite, he had no idea. He certainly wasn't going to lose any sleep over it. Any sense of goodwill, which wasn't exactly a lot to start with, had long since evaporated towards the festering armpit of a man.

When Chris had heard a possible MO for the murderer included stealing a trophy from the victim, he'd ordered everyone available to search through the database for similar incidents around the time of Hannah's disappearance. After giving Megan the nod, Joseph had finally managed to slip away for a secret meeting with his ex-wife, Kate, at a wine bar on a corner of Little Clarendon Street. The bar also served excellent no-nonsense arabica coffee, without a Frappuccino in sight.

Although the DI's beverage was strictly caffeine-based, Kate was nursing a glass of Pinot Grigio, even though it was only eleven am.

'It's not like you to be drinking this early in the day, Kate,' Joseph observed as he sat across the table from her.

'Hey, it's been a long day already, and it's wine o'clock somewhere in the world,' she replied with a tired smile.

Joseph had already taken in his ex-wife's generally exhausted demeanour. It was emphasised by the lines radiating from around the eyes of someone who'd been staring at screens for too long. Also, going by the way she was slightly hunched over her wine, it was obvious she was more than a little stressed.

'Is everything okay?' he asked gently.

She nodded. 'Work's just been a bit full-on recently. You know what it can get like sometimes.'

'I remember far too well. Ellie said you'd sunk your teeth into a major news story?'

Kate tilted her head to one side as she looked at him. 'Good to see the family grapevine is working as well as always. But yes, she's right, and it's become something of an obsession...' She glanced distractedly out of the window as though she was looking for someone.

But when Joseph looked outside, he couldn't see anyone other than a woman hurrying past, holding up an umbrella as it started to rain again.

Kate's gaze slid away from the window and back towards him. 'I think I'm onto something really big, Joseph.'

Despite her exhaustion, he immediately recognised that glint in her eyes. 'How big exactly?'

'A major organised crime syndicate that has its fingers in lots of pies, big.'

He sat up straighter. 'Okay, now you've got my attention. What sort of thing are they into?'

'In a word, everything. Extortion, blackmail, bribery, arms

and drugs smuggling, even trafficking women from Eastern Europe for prostitution.'

'Wow, talk about a full house. Is it one of the major players we already know about?'

'No. This group seems to be new and is far more clandestine than your run-of-the-mill criminals.'

'I know I may be a bit biased here, but in that case, shouldn't you be getting the police involved?'

'Not yet. I haven't got any real evidence, just a lot of signs that point towards a syndicate that's going out of its way to keep off the radar. It even includes a guy who runs a classic car showroom.'

'That doesn't exactly sound like a major crime, unless he charges extra for the floor mats?'

'Oh, his showroom is just a legitimate front to disguise what he's really up to. I'm up to my neck tracking his and his associates' fingerprints across a whole range of crimes. I've even had to pull in Callum to help me at work, because there's so much to sift through.'

'I don't suppose I need to tell you to be careful? You can guarantee that a group like that won't take kindly to a journalist poking their nose into their business.'

'You don't, but I'm a big girl now, and I can look after myself. Anyway, the moment it gets too hot for me and Callum to handle, or when we have any real evidence, I'll hand the lot over to you. As long as I get the exclusive when the story eventually breaks.'

'Of course, but why not Derrick?'

'We both know that he's about as discreet as a priest in a bar at happy hour.'

Joseph smiled at the mental image, but then he caught the slight flicker in Kate's eyes as she looked down at the table. It was quickly gone again, and she glanced up to give him a bright, if forced, smile.

'Anyway, enough about me, to what do I owe this impromptu meeting and this rather nice glass of Pinot Grigio?' Kate asked. 'Are you trying to butter me up for something?'

Joseph gave her his best winning grin. 'Am I that obvious?'

'You are and always will be, at least to me. So, what is it I can help you with this time?'

He glanced over his shoulders to check no one had wandered into hearing range, and then leant in conspiratorially towards her. 'You remember we investigated that case four years ago? When that Women's Oxford Boat Team's cox went missing?'

'Oh, you mean the Hannah Emmerson case, of course I do...' Then her eyes widened. 'Is this discussion anything to do with the body that you found on the embankment of the Isis?'

Joseph stared at her. 'Pillow talk with Derrick?'

Kate pulled a face at him. 'Oh, come on. Unlike certain people I could mention, my husband doesn't always tell me everything about his work.'

Now Joseph had a chance to engage his brain, that actually made sense. Derrick would try to keep his involvement with the Emmerson case as low-profile as possible, especially as he'd been the one responsible for sitting on evidence. That would certainly include not telling his wife about it. Joseph also knew Kate would take a very dim view of that sort of thing, and it would sit badly with her—just like it did with him.

'So how the hell do you know about the body?' Joseph asked.

'You forget newspapers have eyes everywhere.' She fluttered her fingers in the air like a person manipulating a puppet. 'Anyway, in this case, it was a dog walker who saw the forensic tent being set up.'

'Yes, I suppose that is the equivalent of a big neon arrow

saying, *Dead body found here*. But Chris is going to be spitting bullets when I tell him word of this has got out.'

'Don't worry, I managed to get my eye witness to give me his word to keep it to himself for the time being, at least until I give him the nod when I publish the story. But you know how these things go—I can only sit on this for so long until it eventually gets out, regardless.'

'Then you best talk to Derrick tonight and give him a heads up with that pillow talk you guys allegedly never have.'

Kate chuckled before leaning in again and lowering her voice. 'So, I'm assuming from this conversation that this is Hannah's body we're talking about?'

He knew there was no point in trying to lie to Kate, as she would see straight through it.

'Aye, so it is.'

She gave him a grim look and nodded. 'That poor woman. I'm guessing foul play, based on the fact everything is being kept so hush-hush?'

'Yes, unless Hannah found a way to bury herself under six feet of earth, everything is pointing towards murder.'

Kate leant even closer, so their hands were almost touching. 'You have a suspect yet?'

'No, and that's where I need your help. New evidence has come to light, and it looks like Hannah's murderer may have been stalking her before she disappeared. It also appears that before she was abducted, her killer may have broken into her flat.'

Kate took a sip of her wine. 'To do what, exactly?'

'They deliberately moved things around—nothing major, but enough to mess with her mind.'

'Right. And you think this is something that I can help you with?'

'Like you just said, the Oxford Chronicle has eyes everywhere, including close links with all the colleges.' Joseph made the puppet master mime, making Kate smile. 'We're obviously already looking into it, but I was wondering if you could also put out some extra feelers to see if anything similar was happening to anyone else four years ago? I'm trying to work out if this was a pattern of behaviour with the murderer, or it was just a one-time deal with Hannah.'

'In case the killer had a close relationship with her, you mean?'

Joseph smiled at her. 'You could be doing my job with those deduction skills, Kate.'

She laughed. 'And vice versa. That's one of the many reasons we always made such a good team. We always got each other, and understood each other's obsession with work.' Her gaze met his and lingered.

What was that about? Suddenly, Joseph was very aware of the tiny space separating their hands. It would take the barest effort to reach out and take hold of her hand. But Kate was already blinking as though awakening from a dream and sitting back, taking her hands well out of his reach. Because that was exactly what it was, an impossible *dream.*

'I'll see if there's anything I can find out for you,' she said.

'Thank you, Kate, you're one in a million.'

'Flattery will get you everywhere,' she replied.

If only that were true, Joseph thought to himself.

Kate's gaze sharpened on him. 'So what's this I hear about Ellie fixing you up on a blind date?'

Joseph groaned. 'She hasn't been talking about that nonsense with you as well, has she?'

'She might have...' Kate raised her eyebrows at him. 'But for what it's worth, I actually think it's a good idea. It's long past the time that you should have started dating again, Joseph.'

He shrugged. 'Maybe, or maybe not.'

'Oh, come on. It would do you good to be seeing someone.'

'You do know that this is starting to sound like a family conspiracy against my bachelor lifestyle?'

The quickness of Kate's grin told Joseph all he needed to know.

'God, you two have been hatching this bloody plot together, haven't you?' he said.

'Whatever makes you think that?' Kate's grin widened, then her expression became serious again. 'Joseph, I just want to see you happy again. We both do. You deserve it after all the years of torment you put yourself through after Eoin's death.'

She wasn't wrong, either. The shadow cast by that event had been a long one, spread out across the rest of his life. Joseph had been too broken to even contemplate getting involved with anyone else after he'd separated from Kate. But now, with the Midwinter Butcher case finally closed, maybe she had a point. It was time to start looking forward again and building dreams with someone new.

'Yeah, it's been a long winter, so to speak.'

'Then, you'll give this dating game a whirl,' she said, not so much as a question but as an order. 'If there's a man who won't have any problem having a woman fall into his arms, it's you, Joseph, with all your bloody Irish charm. I should know.'

He shrugged. 'But not, it seems, enough to hang onto the woman that I will always love...' The words were out before he could stop them. He shook his head. 'Sorry, ignore me, I'm an old romantic fool of a man.'

Kate gave him such a kind and understanding look, it almost broke his heart. Then she went to say something, but with the barest headshake of her own, stopped herself.

Instead, she finished her wine with a gulp. 'Right, I better get back to it. That research won't get itself done with me sitting here.'

Before Joseph could even reply, Kate had stood and was leaning over to kiss him on the head. 'I'll be in touch as soon as I find out anything.' Then, in a handful of seconds, she was slipping her coat on and was out of the door without a backward glance.

Joseph sat back, gazing at his now-cold cup of coffee, and wondering what it was they'd really been discussing.

CHAPTER NINE

JOSEPH HAD BEEN LOST in the murk of his own thoughts since heading out of the police station. Megan kept casting sideways glances at him, but picking up on his current need for silence, had respected it and hadn't asked any questions.

They were now walking along the edge of Christ Church Meadow, which was covered in a patchwork of puddles left behind by the recent flood. The bright blue sky was dazzling, its reflection distorted in the rippling puddles. Unfortunately, it was accompanied by a freezing northerly wind that seemed intent on sucking the heat from the marrow of Joseph's bones. That was despite him wearing a jacket from an outdoor sports shop, that was supposed to be rated for minus ten degrees. Based on the Trade Descriptions Act, the DI could foresee himself demanding his money back in the near future.

At least it seemed like they were both in Chris's good books now, after unearthing the information about Hannah's stalker. He'd tasked them with talking to the Oxford Boat coach, Charles Norton. Even though the DCI hadn't come out and said it exactly, it certainly felt like the boss was giving Joseph a second chance after the failure of the original investigation.

As was the case for so many officers, unsolved cases were the ones that kept Joseph awake at night. Even if they hadn't crossed his mind in years, out of nowhere, he could suddenly find his thoughts returning to a cold case. Then he would end up looping over the evidence again and again, trying to spot something he hadn't before. The unspoken fear was he'd screwed up somehow, and because of that, a murderer might slip through the net to strike again.

He sometimes pictured his anxiety as an actual thing, a shadowy creature, one he carried on his back. The burden of the beast always lurked there, but ever since Hannah's body had been found, it had been getting heavier by the minute.

They passed a small gaggle of tourists taking selfies with Christ Church College in the background. Joseph thought it was the grandest of all the Oxford colleges. Its warm-coloured Cotswold stone was currently glowing in the sunlight, accentuating the Gothic pointed arches and intricate carvings. The shadow of the college's cathedral tower almost reached all the way to the St Aldates Police Station next door. Yes, it was a grand bit of architecture by any measure.

Joseph often came to the meadow next to the college to decompress during his lunch breaks, listening to some Einaudi or Max Richter as he watched the deer graze. But today, as he and Megan turned onto a wide, gravelled avenue lined with bare winter trees, he didn't feel the usual sense of peace in his sanctuary.

What did we miss? he wondered as they walked between the towering line of trees, the branches reaching over them like an echo of the vaulted arches from the college cathedral behind them.

They reached the end of the avenue and turned left to walk along the embankment of the River Isis. Ahead of them, on the edge of the river, stood a long row of the Oxford University Boat

Clubs' boathouses. Joseph had learned during the original inves-tigation the two and three-storey rectangular buildings contained the Eights—racing boats—the best of which were used in the Oxford and Cambridge Boat Race.

It was hard for Joseph not to look at the river where Hannah had first disappeared off the face of the planet, whilst running circuits of Christ Church Meadow.

'You're quiet,' Megan finally said, after glancing at him for the umpteenth time.

'Just mulling things over,' he replied. 'I keep thinking if we hadn't given up on the case, then Hannah might still be alive.'

'Life's often filled with what-ifs and maybes. But it's what we do now that counts, or as Yoda might say, now is what matters much.'

Joseph raised his eyebrows at her. 'Aye...'

A line of Canada geese, honking to each other, landed in the Thames just outside the boat club's buildings.

'Power ten,' a male voice called out.

Both detectives turned around to see a female boat crew speeding along the river in an Eight, with a small male cox sitting in its stern, steering the boat and calling out instructions. They overtook the detectives at speed, making a group of ducks who'd been paddling across the river scatter from their path with indignant quacks.

With one look, Joseph could tell the crew was a well-oiled machine, their oars perfectly synchronised and doing a mesmerising figure-of-eight movement as they dipped in and out of the water.

The small male cox then called out, 'Length.'

Immediately, the women extended the strokes of their oars. Seated facing backwards, as they passed by, he could clearly see the sheer grit and determination on their faces as they gave it everything. The boat streaked away with the soft creak of the oars in their gates, leaving the barest ripples behind the craft as it sped away.

Unlike the rest of his crew, the cox had a cosy bobble hat pulled down over his head, and a scarf wrapped several times around his neck. He probably also had a hot water bottle tucked somewhere in there too, to keep out the biting, freeze-your-nads-off wind blowing over the river.

On the opposite bank, a man on a bicycle was keeping pace with the boat, calling out instructions to increase their pace as they headed towards some imaginary finish line on the river.

Joseph had witnessed this many times whilst cycling along that same footpath himself, but this was obviously new territory for Megan. She watched it all with the fascination of a tourist on their first visit to Oxford.

'Talk about hard training in freezing weather,' Megan said, with a look of admiration for the crew.

'Oh, this is nothing,' Joseph replied. 'They are out here in all weather, come hail or shine. Driving themselves to their absolute limits as you can see for yourself.'

'The things people do to have'—Megan made air quotes—'*fun.*'

'Yep, each to their own. And their training regime is just as hard off the water as on it.' Joseph jutted his chin towards one of the structures ahead of them.

Some serious money had obviously been spent on this particular boathouse. It was all stainless steel and glass balustrades. Hardcore techno music pumped out from a balcony area on the first floor. On it, a group of men were using a variety of gym equipment, unsurprisingly including a line of rowing machines.

Someone blew a whistle, and everyone jumped up and moved to the next piece of equipment, and began exercising on that. Not circuit training in a casual, *I'm going to keep fit*, sort of way, but more legs and arms pumping as fast as possible, teeth bared, muscles straining to the maximum.

Joseph gestured towards them. 'The one thing you can say about the Oxford crews is that they're certainly dedicated.'

'Yes, and you can almost smell the sweat from here,' Megan said, maybe allowing her gaze to linger on the men's well-toned bodies a bit longer than was strictly professional.

'Aye. They really don't muck around. Every member of a boat team is expected to be at peak physical fitness.'

'And if they're not?'

'Then they're quickly shown the door because, as we heard from Joanne Keating, there's always someone keen to take their place.'

Megan nodded as they headed across the front of the boat club, towards the building where all the techno music was coming from. The female crew that had just passed them were now pulling up to the slipway in front. People in wellies had already emerged from the open garage door beneath the training balcony.

As they neared, Joseph could see at least a dozen other Eight boats were stored inside, many of which appeared to be made from carbon fibre. The detective was pretty sure no expense had been spared when it came to competing against Cambridge in the famous Boat Race, pitting both universities against each other.

As the team disembarked from their boat, one of the women was rotating her arm in its socket and grimacing.

A man in a dark blue tracksuit was already heading out of the garage towards her, shaking his head. Despite the four years since Joseph had last spoken to him, he immediately recognised the man as Charles Norton, the Oxford coach.

'Don't bloody tell me that you've damaged your shoulder

again, Mary,' they heard the man say as he approached the woman.

She cast him a pale look. 'Honestly, I'll be fine,' she replied. 'I just need a session with the physio to sort this out.'

Charles narrowed his eyes at her. 'Then, let's hope for your sake that it's nothing serious, or you'll be out on your arse. You know I'll replace you in a heartbeat with someone from the reserve Osiris squad.'

Joseph gave Megan an, *I told you so look*, as they neared.

The blond cox, who had been standing next to one of the female rowers, headed up to the man, his eyes blazing. He had to be all of five foot two.

'Leave her alone, Charles,' he said. 'We need Mary if we're to have a chance against Cambridge. If she says she'll be fine, she will be.'

The far larger man glared down at the cox as though he were a particularly annoying gnat to be squished.

'I've told you before, Craig, keep your nose out of other people's business.'

Megan shot Joseph a look, but he shook his head. They came to a stop behind the altercation, waiting for it to blow itself out.

When he'd interviewed the rowing teams four years ago, Joseph had learnt Charles had something of a reputation for being a bully. Unfortunately, it seemed the years hadn't softened the man. Joseph hadn't been a fan back then, and based on his current performance, it wasn't looking like he was going to be a fan now. It was no wonder he'd immediately warmed to Craig, who had squared up to the man like a Pit Bull Terrier, his chest puffed out and his fists clenched. There was no doubt how an actual fight would end up if the smaller man tried to land a punch, but the DI still had to admire the lad's spirit.

Craig narrowed his eyes at the coach. 'Then stop making it

my business by being such a—'

The woman from the rowing team who'd been whispering to him, had quietly walked up behind the cox. She put her hand on his shoulder and shook her head at him.

'Leave it, Craig. He's not worth it.'

The lad's shoulders, which had risen around his ears, sagged. Then he nodded. 'Yes, you're right, Joanna. I wouldn't give *him* the satisfaction.'

'But, I haven't finished with you yet,' the coach said, crossing his arms.

Joanna glared at him. 'I think you have, don't you, Charles?'

The coach met her eyes, then he blinked and said nothing.

The woman's expression hardened. 'Let this drop now,' she said with a tone of iron.

That seemed to well and truly take the wind out of the coach's sails, because he gave her the barest nod before turning back to the cox. 'Okay, no need to take this any further, just don't do it again,' he said.

Not that the cox paid any attention to the coach because at least five of the women from the squad had surrounded Craig, and were escorting him into the boathouse, nearly all of them casting narrowed-eyed looks back towards Charles. It seemed the coach was as popular as ever with his students.

Megan leant in towards Joseph and whispered, 'Wow, what a cock.'

Despite them still standing a good ten feet away, the man obviously had far sharper hearing than he had empathy for his students, because he whirled around to face them. The lines of annoyance that had already appeared around his eyes quickly smoothed out as his gaze latched onto Joseph.

'DI Stone?' the coach said.

'In the flesh, Mr Norton. I hope you don't mind us interrupting your training session, but DC Anderson and I would like to have a quick word. Is there somewhere private where we could talk?'

The man visibly paled. 'Yes, of course,' he said in a soft voice, which was in stark contrast to the fire and brimstone version of the man from just a few moments ago. 'If you'll follow me, we can use my office.'

The detectives walked behind the coach into the boathouse, as the Eight boat that had just been in the water was lowered by four of the female crew onto a cradle stand. All of them looked curiously towards the detectives as they headed past with Charles.

The detectives followed him up a staircase and entered a glass-walled corridor. On the other side of the glass was an indoor gym leading to an outside balcony where the men's team was currently exercising.

Joseph was no slouch himself when it came to keeping fit, thanks mainly to cycling, but these people put him in the shade. Every single one of them was dripping with sweat, all working flat out and all with a laser focus. One giant of a blond guy was lifting a bar loaded with enough weights to rival a small car, every single sinew in his arms and neck standing out. The DI could see this was definitely an extreme training regime by any measure.

They followed Charles into an office where the rear wall was filled with photos of the winning Oxford teams, both male and female, holding up their medals and cups. It was hard to miss the fact there were no images of the losing Oxford sides over the years. Presumably, they had been determinedly forgotten by this particular coach, who had held his post for ten years now.

Thankfully, as soon as he closed the door behind them, the headache-inducing thumping music from the gym was reduced to a muffled beat.

The coach pointed to two chairs in front of his desk, and as they sat down, Joseph took in the three live-feed monitors mounted on another wall. They seemed to cover what was happening, both in the gym and also on the external balcony. This man obviously kept a tight eye on exactly what was going on within his training kingdom.

Charles headed over to a small fridge and took out a sports drink. He held it up to Joseph and Megan. 'Fancy one?'

'No, I'm grand,' Joseph replied.

Megan shook her head. 'No, thank you. Caffeine is more my usual poison.'

'Right...' Charles replied.

As he pulled the tab on the can and took a long gulp, Joseph noticed the slight tremble in the coach's hands. The detectives' presence had obviously rattled him, and that was of immediate interest. The question was, why?

'So what's this all about?' Charles asked, doing his best to put on the pretence of being relaxed by leaning back in his office chair.

'We're following up on a new line of enquiry regarding Hannah Emmerson's disappearance,' Joseph replied.

The coach's eyes grew larger. 'You have new information about her?'

'Yes, actually, we do.'

The man's gaze flicked to Megan as she took out her notebook and pen.

'Is this a formal interview, then?' Charles asked, his jaw tightening.

Megan held up her hands in a placatory manner. 'No, I'm just taking notes so we don't forget anything useful you might be able to tell us.'

'Such as?' The coach's eyes darted back to Joseph like he was a cornered dog.

Interesting, very interesting, the DI thought to himself.

'It's come to our attention that Hannah may have had some sort of stalker before she vanished,' he said.

'A stalker...' Charles repeated like a bloody parrot. 'I don't know anything about that.'

Joseph gave Norton his best attempt at a reassuring smile. 'I didn't think you would, because I'm sure you would have told me four years ago if you had.'

'Yes, of course I would have.'

Joseph nodded, but from where he was sitting, he could see the coach's leg jiggling under the desk. If the DI could arrest someone based on body language alone, he would have. The problem was he doubted a *jiggly leg* would be seen as sufficient evidence by a judge to prove this man had anything to do with Hannah's murder.

The DI narrowed his gaze on Charles. 'Did you have any concerns about Hannah's mental health?'

'Only that she became rather withdrawn during training sessions. But that's not unusual as the whole team comes under a lot of pressure during training, including the cox.'

Nothing to do with you being a bully then? Joseph thought to himself. Out loud, the DI said, 'But you didn't witness anything to cause you any real concern?'

Norton stared at him. 'Hang on, you're not saying she took her own life, are you?'

Megan stopped writing. 'That's a bit of a leap, isn't it?'

'I just meant that was one of things that we originally discussed when Hannah vanished, DC Anderson. But I said then, and I say it again now, I don't think Hannah was the type. Enough students have passed through this boat club for me to be able to spot the signs and, if necessary, get the University Counselling Service to talk to them.'

Joseph nodded as Megan began taking notes again. But it

was certainly interesting Charles had so quickly locked onto the idea of suicide before denying Hannah would ever take her own life. But now, to steer things back to what Joseph really wanted to know.

'We were wondering if you knew of any other women, or men for that matter, on the rowing teams, who mentioned anything unusual happening in their flats or homes while they were living in Oxford?'

'What sort of things?' Charles said, a confused expression crossing his face.

'Like things being moved while they were out—that sort of thing.'

The coach shook his head. 'Not that I recall. Why, did that happen to Hannah, then?'

'I'm afraid I can't divulge anything to do with an ongoing investigation,' Joseph replied.

The coach blinked. 'So, you've reopened Hannah's case?'

'We have, but that's as much as I can tell you for now. I was wondering, have you remembered any more details, no matter how minor, since Hannah's disappearance?'

'Sorry, absolutely nothing comes to mind.'

'I see. If anything does occur to you, will you contact us?'

'I will,' Charles said.

The man visibly relaxed, obviously thinking he was off the hook. Of course, he absolutely wasn't until Joseph had hard evidence one way or the other.

'Then we will take up no more of your time, and thank you for your help.' Joseph stood, and having shaken the coach's decidedly clammy hand, the detectives let themselves out.

If the coach had a bottle of the hard stuff in there, Joseph suspected he was already knocking it back.

'Talk about looking guilty as hell,' Megan said, as they headed back down the stairs.

'Unfortunately, that's not enough to convict a man, and he may have been worried about something else. One thing's for sure, that man has a secret he doesn't want the police to know about.'

Megan nodded as they walked outside. It was then a whistle was blown and the techno music came to an abrupt and relieving halt.

'Ending of training,' a man shouted from the balcony above them, followed by the relieved groans of people finally able to catch their breaths.

Craig, the cox who'd been on the slipway, hurried over to Joseph and Megan.

'Good, I was hoping to catch you before you left, Detectives,' Craig said.

'Detectives? And how would you know that?' Joseph asked.

'Let's just say I have very good hearing. I overheard when you introduced yourself to Charles Norton; no thanks to that bloody racket they love to play upstairs.'

'Aye, not exactly the most relaxing music,' Joseph said, smiling at him.

'Yes, tell me about it, and we're not allowed to even use headphones to listen to our own stuff. It's all groupthink round here and no room for individual tastes.'

'Because of the coach's training regime?' Megan asked.

'You could say that. It's his way or the highway round here. Do what he says or you're out.'

Joseph could already tell this lad might provide useful insight into the coach, who already felt like he might be a suspect.

Megan looked at Craig. 'Then it must have taken some real courage to stand up to him like you did when he was picking on that rower.'

The cox shrugged. 'I just did what had to be done. The

others are terrified of him, although I keep telling the women that they should make a formal complaint against Charles. That's why I wanted to have a word.'

Now Joseph's interest was well and truly alight. 'Why's that, exactly?'

Craig shook his head. 'Let's just say that if you have the time, you really need to interview the rest of the women's crews, both on the Blue boat and the reserves, the Osiris teams. It's not my place to tell you things that have been confided in me, but some of them will have a lot to say about our illustrious leader. If I were you, I'd start with Millie Dexter, who dropped out only a few days ago.'

'Okay, but you really can't tell us any more?' Megan asked.

'I would if I could, but a gentleman never reveals the secrets that a woman confides in him.' A smile flashed across his face. 'Just, please don't let Charles know that I put you on his trail. If he found out he would do everything in his power to make my life a living hell.'

'Of course; you can rely on our discretion,' Joseph replied. 'But just one quick question. You weren't a member of this club four years ago, were you?'

Lines spidered from the corners of Craig's eyes. 'No, I wasn't even in Oxford back then. Why?'

'Don't worry about it. Anyway, thank you for the information, and I'll personally make sure that I follow through on it.'

'That's good to hear. It's long past the time that Charles should have faced the music.'

At that precise moment, the techno music started again upstairs.

'Well, maybe not *that* music,' the cox said, winking at Megan, which made her grin. 'Anyway, must dash. It never stops round here, and I have a paper to write for tomorrow.'

With a nod to the detectives, the cox headed over to a bicycle inside the boat shed and unlocked it.

As Megan and Joseph headed across Christ Church Meadow, she turned towards him. 'What do you think Charles has been up to?'

'Nothing good, that's for sure, and I doubt that Craig would have tipped us off if it had just been bullying.'

'So, what then?'

'Oh, I have some ideas, as I'm sure you have. But let's check our facts first before jumping to any conclusions. That's why I would like you to pull up the details of the Oxford women's crews, and see if you can arrange some meetings, especially with this Millie Dexter. Then hopefully, we'll find out exactly what we're dealing with here. Meanwhile, let's get back to Chris, and suggest we do a lot more digging into the coach's background to see what we can unearth.'

'So he's a potential suspect, then?'

'Maybe, but at the very least, his photo certainly needs to have a bloody great question mark above it on the evidence board. But who knows, maybe we really do have our murderer in our sights already. However, as always, we need evidence rather than suspicions to prove it.'

Megan nodded. 'You'll get no argument from me. We need a cast iron case if we want to secure a conviction here with the CPS.'

'Aye, that we do.'

One thing Joseph knew for certain was the sooner he found out what Charles had been up to, the happier he would be. There was a renewed sense of purpose in his stride as the two officers headed back to St Aldates station, along the path where Hannah had vanished.

Joseph already had in mind someone who might be able to lend their assistance in looking into the coach's background.

CHAPTER TEN

LATER THAT EVENING, back on board *Tús Nua* for a much-needed rest, Joseph invited Dylan over for a drink so he could ask the professor for his own special brand of help on the case. To tempt his neighbour, he'd bought a bottle of the rather poetically named Crofter's Tears Highland Gin. For Joseph, that name conjured up a mental image of a Scottish man standing by a loch, his hair and kilt tussled by the heather-scented wind. No doubt the marketing team would love Joseph's interpretation, although he wasn't quite sure if he was their target market.

A knock came from his cabin door, and he opened it to see Dylan standing with Max and White Fang at his heels. He was also holding a small wooden tray with some upmarket tonic bottles, along with twists of orange peel, and blackberries on a small plate.

Joseph gave the berries a suspicious look as the man and his dogs made themselves at home in his cabin. 'Surely there aren't any blackberries on the hedgerows in March?' he asked.

'They're not,' Dylan replied. 'These are the supermarket's finest. I was doing my research. Apparently, blackberries with a twist of orange are just the thing to set off Crofter's Tears, and of course, not forgetting exactly the right sort of tonic.'

'Has anybody ever told you that you take your gins far too seriously?'

'Nonsense, if anything, not seriously enough.'

'If you say so,' Joseph said, shaking his head at his friend.

Dylan began to root through the cupboards and took out two glasses. 'I take it by the summons, you've had one of your more interesting weeks?'

'*Interesting* is one way of putting it,' Joseph said as he opened the bottle and poured them both a double measure, leaving the scientific part of adding the right amount of tonic and aromatics to Dylan.

The professor set to work with exactly the sort of effort Joseph expected from him, eyes squinting as he poured the tonic. If he'd brought a pipette and a set of scales, Joseph wouldn't have been surprised.

'So are you going to tell me about your latest case?' Dylan asked, working with the precision of a scientist trying to split the atom with a scalpel.

'What makes you think that I'm working on anything in particular?'

In the way of answer, his friend just peered over the top of his glasses at the detective, holding his gaze.

Joseph grinned at him. 'Yes, alright, you know me way too well.'

'Correct, and I'm basing that on the fact you invited me over for a far too nice bottle of gin, which is what you always do when you want to discuss a case with me.'

'Bloody hell, am I really that transparent?'

'Do you really need me to answer that?'

Joseph chuckled. 'Probably not. Anyway, I need you to be

my unofficial consultant, but what's said between the walls of this cabin must stay between us.'

'As always,' Dylan said, apparently satisfied with his gin efforts as he handed Joseph a glass of the expensive spirit.

The detective went to pick up some cubes from the bucket of ice he'd already prepared, but the professor immediately covered his glass with his hand.

'Don't you dare. Gin is best appreciated without ice to dilute it. Besides, I've already chilled the tonic.'

'In that case, I had better follow your lead, maestro.'

The professor made a show of inhaling the scent rising from the glass. 'Yes, heather with a hint of cinnamon, maybe even nutmeg.'

Joseph did the same, the scent scratching at the back of his nose. 'That reminds me of the bowl of potpourri that my nan used to keep in the lav.'

Dylan just scowled at him. 'What happened to that inner poet all you Irish chaps are meant to be born with?'

'I must have missed the handout on that one,' Joseph replied.

The professor shook his head, but then a slow smile filled his face as he tasted his drink. 'That, my friend, is gin perfection in a glass.'

Joseph took a sip, but it was still a bit too floral for his taste. 'That's grand,' he said, trying to put as much enthusiasm into his voice as he could muster. No doubt for a connoisseur like Dylan, it tasted great, but for him it was just a bit too much. Joseph made a mental note to make sure he gave his friend the rest of the bottle when he left. When it came down to it, he was a single malt man first, second, and probably third.

Dylan settled into his chair, resting the glass on the arm. 'So, tell me all about this latest case.'

Joseph nodded. 'You remember that incident with Hannah Emmerson, four years back?'

'Of course, the Oxford Boat Blue team student who disappeared while out jogging. So all your current frenzy of activity has something to do with a new development in the case?'

'It has. Her body turned up last Sunday from where it had been buried in the embankment of the Thames near Iffley Lock. That's what I was called in for. But the forensic examination suggests she was held somewhere else before she was eventually buried there.'

'I see, and do you have any suspects yet?'

'Maybe... The Oxford coach, Charles Norton, has come into our sights. The team at work is currently looking into his background, but I know when it comes to research that you can often turn up things everyone else misses. So I was wondering...'

Dylan waved his hand through the air like a thespian getting ready to take a bow before the final curtain fell. 'I'd be delighted to help, dear chap. If nothing else, it helps me to keep my grey matter sharp, and is much more interesting than doing *The Guardian* cryptic crossword.'

'I knew I could rely on you,' Joseph said, raising his glass to the professor's. This time he took a much larger sip and, to his surprise, discovering he actually rather enjoyed it the second time round.

The professor could obviously tell by his expression that Joseph was starting to appreciate the gin. 'It's a grower, isn't it?'

'Aye, a bit like the bloody bramble patch that those berries probably came from,' Joseph said.

White Fang barked, followed a few seconds later by a knock on the door.

'Expecting anyone?' Dylan asked.

'Not when it's meant to be my night off,' Joseph said, rousing himself from his chair and heading to the door.

Joseph opened it to find Megan standing there. 'Sorry to disturb you after a long day,' she said.

'Not at all, but do come in and have a drink with Dylan and me. We're trying another one of the professor's favourite craft gins.'

'You have no idea how tempting that sounds, but I think you'll want to come with me. I was putting in a late one at work and managed to track down Millie Dexter. I gave her a ring, and she's happy to see us right now, although we can postpone it until morning if you prefer?'

Joseph was already putting his glass down and grabbing his coat. 'Oh, no way. If we're about to dig up some dirt on Charles Norton, I'd rather do it sooner than later.' He turned back to Dylan. 'Looks like we're off to the races again, but help yourself to the bottle and lock up here when you're finished.'

'Of course.' Dylan raised his glass to them. 'And good hunting to you both.'

Millie's flat turned out to be over one of Oxford's finest fish and chip shops. Far from being a run-of-the-mill establishment, it served up some of the very best battered fish in a wide area. Joseph put it down to whatever magic they did to the batter that made it so crispy. It was certainly light years above the usual armour-plated, coated offering most chippies served up. The kind that made you feel three stone heavier just by inhaling its scent.

With a mental note made to introduce Megan to the height of fish frying cuisine after they finished talking to Millie, Joseph scanned the numbers on the door and pressed the button for flat 5A. A short while later, a woman in her early twenties was standing before the detectives, her dark shoulder-length hair hanging limp, eyes hollowed out with exhaustion.

'Millie Dexter?' Megan asked.

The woman nodded.

'I'm DC Anderson and this is DI Stone,' Megan said as they both showed her their warrant cards.

'Oh right. What's this all about?'

'I think this is a conversation probably best had inside, rather than on your doorstep,' Joseph said. 'Your friend, Craig, at the boat club said you might want to talk to us.'

Her gaze immediately widened. 'Bloody hell, he had no right to talk to anyone about my private business.'

Joseph shook his head. 'He'd didn't. In fact, Craig insisted he couldn't tell us anything, because you'd confided in him. The only thing he mentioned was that it was something to do with your coach, Charles Norton.'

'Ex-coach. I dropped out of the team a few days ago. But I don't want to discuss this with you or anyone else.' She got ready to close the door in their faces.

'Please, Millie, we really need to talk to you about this,' Joseph said. 'It's far more important than you realise.'

She held his gaze for a moment and then finally her shoulders dropped. 'Okay, you'd better come in.'

They followed Millie up the stairs into an almost empty living room, where cardboard boxes filled the floor space. Books, photos, and the rest had been crammed into them and were poking out of the top. There were also the tell-tale rectangles of blue stickers on the wall where posters had been removed. Through an open door to the kitchen, Joseph could see similar packing boxes in there.

'Are you moving out?' he asked, not that he really needed to ask.

'Yep, out of Oxford. I'm going home to Nottingham. My dad's coming to get me tomorrow.'

'That sounds pretty final,' Megan said.

'That's because it is. I've had enough of the university and this city. That's why I'm getting out of here before I lose my mind.'

'Sorry, what do you mean?' Joseph asked.

'It's just all too much. When I was offered a place at St Mary's, I thought I was living the dream. But the reality is anything but that. I'm drowning here and need to put this place as far behind me as possible.'

'Is that anything to do with Charles Norton?' Megan asked.

Her face became an instant mask. 'I didn't say that.'

The DC frowned at the woman. 'But Craig said—'

'I don't fucking care what he or anyone else said. This is my business, and I don't want anyone else sticking their nose into it. All you need to know is that I'm going home.'

Joseph traded a look with Megan. Even though this woman was throwing up walls, he needed to push a little harder to see if he could persuade her to open up.

'So this has nothing to do with Charles Norton abusing his position of trust with his female students?'

Millie wrapped her hands around herself and then gestured with her chin towards the stairs. 'Please go, I've said all I'm going to. What happened is history and I need to move on with my life.'

Joseph gazed at her. 'But, Millie—'

Her eyes flashed with anger. 'Fucking get out of here,' she shouted, spittle flying from her mouth.

Joseph immediately held up his hands at the sudden change in her mood. 'Okay, message received loud and clear.'

The DI shook his head at Megan, who was opening her mouth to say something, but then closed it again.

Slowly, like he was dealing with a skittish animal, Joseph reached into his jacket pocket and withdrew his card. 'Just in case you change your mind,' he said, laying it down on a sideboard.

The student clenched her hands and cast him a withering look, leaving the DI in little doubt his card would be in the bin the moment they left.

Millie didn't say a word as she escorted them back down the steps.

As they stepped out onto the pavement, Joseph turned to make one last-ditch attempt to plead with her, but was met by the door being slammed in his face. A moment later, they heard suppressed sobs as Millie headed back upstairs.

'Well, that was about as useful an interview as a one-legged man in an arse-kicking contest,' Megan said.

'You think?' Joseph replied. 'Although she didn't actually come out and say it, Millie's reaction clearly implies that Charles Norton has been abusing his position. You don't need to be a detective to work out what way.'

'You mean sexually?' Megan asked.

'Aye, and I'm sure that's what you've been thinking, too. Am I wrong?'

'No, I definitely picked up that vibe from the way the women on the boat team were looking at him. My hunch is that Norton, someone who is a married man, probably fancies himself as a bit of a player.'

'Or something far worse.'

'A sexual predator who crossed the line into murder?' Megan asked.

'That's exactly what we need to find out,' Joseph replied. 'Anyway, it's about time I introduced you to the best fish and chips in Oxford.'

'You really are a terrible influence, even if I don't take much prompting,' the DC replied with a grin.

Joseph winked at her as they headed towards the chippie, feeling they were definitely on the right track with the investigation.

CHAPTER ELEVEN

MILLIE WAS FINDING it hard to sleep after the detectives' visit. She was lying on her lumpy mattress, staring up at the ceiling of her bedroom. The same thought was churning through her head on a spin cycle.

How could Craig have done that to me?

The cox had been the one person she'd confided in about Charles. As much as she detested that man, how much he made her skin crawl, she certainly didn't want to end up testifying against him.

Millie felt numb to her core about the events of the last few months. They'd wrecked her spirit and her will to cling on. She had been under so much pressure that all she wanted to do now was to crawl home, into the comfort of her family's embrace, and lick her wounds. She already knew she would need months, years even, to heal from what had happened. Even then, the events of that night would probably haunt her for the rest of her life.

Even if she had the emotional strength to take Charles on, it would be her word against his. She'd watched enough TV dramas to know how that would pan out. Millie mentally kicked herself for being so naïve about being flattered by the coach's attention.

Stupid, stupid, stupid, she thought to herself as she remembered how he'd invited her back to his house, only for her to discover that his wife was away. The oldest married man trick in the bloody book.

Millie rolled over and looked at the alarm clock display: 1:23 am. The hours had crawled past, her mind too wired to shut down. But at least now she was in the final countdown to escaping all of this crap. By this time tomorrow, she would be back at her parents' place, catching her breath and putting her shattered life back together.

Her dad had promised her that he would arrive promptly first thing to help her pack her stuff into the back of his SUV. It really wasn't long until she escaped this life and was able to hit reset on everything and start over.

When she'd rung her dad to say she was coming home, he hadn't laid any sort of guilt trip on her about the tuition fees they'd covered so she could pursue what she'd thought was her dream. If he'd been disappointed at the news, her dad had masked it well. She was certain he would already be fiercely defending her choice to drop out of Oxford with her mum, and would support her in any way he could. Millie sometimes thought her mum was a bit jealous about how close her relationship was with him. Maybe that was why she'd become increasingly distant from her over the years. Yes, she would always be *daddy's* girl, even if she'd let him down.

The stupid thing was, so many women on the rowing team had tried to warn her about Charles. She'd stubbornly ignored them, seeing the older man's attention towards her as flattering. That the prick had done what he had made her sick to the core of her being. It was certainly going to be a long time before she ever trusted any man ever again, at least apart from her dad.

With a click, she heard the fridge in the kitchen hum to silence. At the same moment, the glowing numerals of her alarm clock face went out, plunging her bedroom into darkness. Millie could still see the glow of the streetlight creeping beneath the curtains. That meant that her flat's pay-as-you-go electricity meter she'd been trying to eke out without topping up before she left tomorrow, had finally run out.

That was no biggie. As long as Millie had her phone she had an alarm clock, and there was only a bottle of milk left in the fridge to go off. Besides, Millie knew for certain that the first thing her dad would insist on doing before loading the car with her stuff, was treat her to a slap-up breakfast at the Scandinavian café in the shopping mall. And who was she to argue? Especially now she didn't have to worry about her diet and the exercise regime the coach subjected all the rowers to.

Millie took several deep breaths, trying to use a meditation technique to empty her mind, and surprisingly it actually began to work. It was then, at last, she felt the knot of muscles her body had become start to relax. Yes, as awful as the past few weeks had been, this was the beginning of the end. Once she got over the trauma of what had happened, she might be able to start looking forward again.

As her body settled into her mattress, lumps and all, she felt the weight of a real weariness take hold to the depths of her bones. Her mind began to tilt gently towards sleep.

With a start, Millie sat up, disorientated. It was still dark outside. She hadn't even been aware she'd fallen asleep. She could have been out for minutes or hours, but something had awoken her. Probably a drunk staggering home from one of the clubs. The students who lived in the accommodation blocks over the row of shops were the worst when it came to that. Whatever courses they were doing at Oxford, it was obvious they weren't fellow sufferers on the rowing team, where you were encouraged to think of your body as a temple.

The truth was, Millie didn't have the time or energy for nights out. The training regime she and the others had been subjected to was a strict seven days a week, two sessions a day affair, and lasted for the seven months up until the Oxford and Cambridge Boat Race. Many on the team said it was like being in prison, and that was putting it mildly.

God, she wasn't going to miss any of it.

Millie's thoughts were interrupted as she heard the softest creak of a board in the darkness of her bedroom. Adrenaline immediately surged through her body, her mouth going dry. She reached out and grabbed her phone, the light from its screen blinding her, so it took her a moment to register the lack of signal reception bars.

What?

A second board creaked and Millie's body tensed, her heart thundering, her vision swimming with the afterglow from the phone's screen as she tried to see who was there.

'Charles, if that's you, you can stop playing fucking games now. How the hell did you get in here, anyway? If you've broken down my door...'

Millie strained her ears. She could hear the telltale whisper of someone breathing quietly. Suddenly, a hand shot out and seized her phone. The intruder threw it at her bedroom wall, and with the sound of cracking glass, it tumbled to the floor.

Fury blazed through her. 'Bloody hell, this is going way too far, Charles. Isn't it enough that you ruined my life, including making me think I was losing my mind? So help me, if you don't get out of here right now, I'm going to scream my lungs out. Then we'll see what the police say when they come and arrest you. You know what, maybe Craig was right, and I should let them know about the real Charles Norton and how he likes to prey on young women.'

Another creak of a board.

'I bloody warned you!' Millie sucked in a big lungful of breath, getting ready to give the scream everything she had.

Then she heard the hiss of air and instinctively ducked. She was too late. Something hard crashed into the side of her head with a brutal bone-jarring force. The blow whipped her head sideways, and her skull crashed into the wooden headboard with another sickening impact slamming her jaw shut.

As shocking pain burned through Millie's head, she felt the trickle of blood running down her temple. Before she'd even had a chance to recover, her hands were seized in a crushing grip and were lashed together with something that bit into her wrists. Although dazed, she tried to kick out at her invisible assailant, but then her legs were grabbed as well and tied together.

Millie knew she was in real danger, and she had to get help before it was too late.

She tried to scream again, but something was already being pressed into her mouth. She gagged as it was tied tightly to her face. In the next moment, something was pulled over her head, and the last sliver of light beneath the curtain vanished as the cloth fell over her eyes.

As an instinct for survival kicked in, Millie fought with everything she had, thrashing on her bed like a wild animal.

But then a hand clamped round her throat. For a moment she thought her assailant was going to strangle her, but then the sharp prick of a needle was buried into her neck. Part of her mind registered warm liquid being injected into her. Almost instantly, Millie felt her thoughts begin to slide, as whatever she'd been drugged with took hold.

'Don't do this, Charles. I promise I won't tell anyone,' she said, her voice slurring.

'Shush,' a man's voice whispered in her ear.

Then she was being hoisted onto his shoulder. As oblivion washed away her thoughts, the last thing Millie was aware of was being carried down the stairs.

CHAPTER TWELVE

JOSEPH WAS STANDING in the incident room with Chris. He moved Charles Norton's photo to the top of the evidence board, now their one and only suspect. The DCI then linked the coach's photo to Hannah's with a piece of red string.

With those sort of craft skills, the boss could have been a presenter on Blue Peter, Joseph thought.

'You do realise that this is still all conjecture at this point, and we don't have any actual proof that the coach was responsible for her murder?' Chris said as he gazed at the board.

'Oh, I know, but what we do have is a possible pattern of behaviour from the coach towards the female crew members that he preys on.'

'*Possibly* preys on,' Chris corrected him.

Joseph shrugged. 'Either way, it's just a shame that Millie isn't prepared to make a statement. If anyone could tell us categorically whether he's a sexual predator, it's her.'

'Yes, but having a roving eye for the students isn't the same thing as abducting and murdering them. So we're just going to have to keep an open mind towards Norton and keep digging until we find some real evidence.'

'You don't need to tell me, Boss,' Joseph said. His gaze slid across to the photo of Hannah's decomposing body, among the other photos of her burial site on the river embankment.

Chris's expression softened as he saw where the DI's attention was focused. 'Don't sound so despondent. This is a good start, Joseph. Even if Millie wasn't prepared to talk, then maybe someone else on the women's boat crew will be. If we can prove there's a pattern of behaviour here with Norton, even if it isn't damning evidence in itself, it certainly strengthens the case for him being a person of significant interest in our investigation.'

'Aye, you're right, and at least it's a step in the right direction, especially when we have no other leads.'

Chris shrugged. 'We do what we can with what we're given.' He dipped his chin towards Joseph and headed back to his desk.

Megan appeared by the DI's side out of nowhere. Then, keeping her back to the room so no one else could see, she showed him the cardboard box she had in her hand.

A Krispy Kreme logo was printed on the lid.

Megan cast a furtive glance around them, before opening the box to reveal twelve assorted doughnuts, all covered with different toppings.

'Bloody hell, what's the occasion?' Joseph said.

She leant in conspiratorially. 'My birthday, but don't tell anyone. Having said that, I don't want to be totally sad by letting the day pass without marking it in some way. So I thought I'd get some doughnuts for us both. My treat.'

It's said that police officers have an instinct for certain things, like when a suspect is lying. However, that's nothing compared to the ability of an officer to smell out a cake or pastry, but especially a doughnut, at a hundred paces at least, or probably a mile if the wind is blowing in the right direction.

Before Joseph could warn Megan to put the box away, Ian

had materialised at her elbow and was gazing down into the box doing a reasonable impression of Gollum finding one the One Ring in that Lord of the Rings film.

'Bloody hell, those look delicious. Are those for us?'

Joseph felt a pang of sympathy for Megan as she met his gaze. After all, what can you say when you've been put on the spot like that?

So the DC did what anyone would, she just nodded.

Ian didn't even pause and grabbed the epic-looking chocolate one that Joseph already had his eye on.

Just to rub salt into the wound, the DI then turned to the room. 'Megan's brought doughnuts.'

As a boy, Joseph had once had a bag of chips ripped out of his hand by a Herring Gull in Dún Laoghaire Harbour. That beast had nothing on the pack of hungry police officers who now descended.

Megan barely had a chance to blink before she was surrounded as people helped themselves, and within what seemed like milliseconds, the box had been emptied.

'So any special reason you brought these in?' Ian asked as he munched on his delicious-looking doughnut.

Once again, before Joseph could stop her, Megan uttered those three words that should never be uttered in a police station.

'It's my birthday,' she said, like a lamb to the flipping slaughter.

A cheer immediately went up around the room.

'Then we'll see you down the pub after work,' Ian said, grinning as though this day couldn't get any better.

Megan looked at her empty box and then at Joseph. 'And I'm going to be buying, aren't I?'

'How did you guess? But don't worry, I'll buy you another

box of doughnuts, my shout. Just let's maybe not bring them in here.'

A smile filled the DC's face. 'I think that might be a wise move.'

As they returned to their desks, Chris raised one of the chocolate sprinkle doughnuts to Megan and gave her a thumbs up. The man must have moved like greased lightning because Joseph hadn't even seen him pounce on it. Perhaps that was one of the skills you needed to become a DCI these days.

Mid munch, Chris's desk phone rang and he picked it up. As he listened to the caller, his eyes widened. He ended the call a few minutes later, then stood and clapped his hands.

'Can I have everyone's attention? The front desk rang through to say that Geoffrey Dexter, Millie's father, just rang from her flat.'

'Yes, she mentioned that he was going to take her home to Nottingham today,' Joseph replied. 'Why, what's happened?'

'Her father arrived at her flat this morning, but when Millie didn't answer the door, he let himself in. There was no sign of her anywhere inside, but when he checked in her bedroom, he found blood on the headboard. Also, when he tried her mobile, it went straight to voicemail. Needless to say, he's worried that something's happened to her, and he doesn't even know about our investigation yet.'

A churning feeling was already spinning through Joseph's gut as he grabbed his coat from the back of his chair. 'Then we need to get over there right now.'

Chris nodded. 'As you and Megan spoke to Millie, it makes sense that you investigate her disappearance,' the DCI said as though he was giving the orders, and that Joseph wouldn't have gone anyway. 'I'll alert Amy to head over there as well with her team, and uniforms are already en route. Also, in light of the context of Millie's disappearance, until we know otherwise, we're going to assume the worst. I need someone to check the whereabouts of Charles Norton over the last twelve hours.'

Ian put his hand up. 'Leave that to me, Boss.'

'Good man. Right then, everyone, let's get to it, and hope there's a perfectly innocent explanation waiting at the end of this.' The only problem with the SIO's last statement was that there wasn't any conviction in his voice, and they all heard it. Or rather, they didn't.

Joseph rushed out of the room with Megan close behind. She was as grim-faced as he felt.

Joseph and Megan arrived to discover Amy had somehow managed to beat them to it, her forensic van already parked up outside.

Megan gestured at a man with the first tinges of grey in his dark hair talking with two uniformed officers as they got out of the Peugeot. 'Millie's father?'

Joseph looked across and guessed him to be in his mid to late forties. He had his hands clamped around the back of his head. Some curious passersby hovered a short distance away, desperate to find out what was going on. At least none of them had their phones out to take photos. Yet.

'Based on his, worried out of his mind, expression, I'd say that's a safe bet,' Joseph said.

He also recognised the two police constables. The shorter one was Paul Burford, as good a guy as you could ever hope to meet. The second man was Greg Robson, who was relatively new to the force. The two of them were trying to calm the father, who was pacing and casting constant looks towards the door of Millie's flat, which had been cordoned off with blue and white perimeter tape.

Spotting the detectives, Paul headed straight over.

'What's the situation here?' Joseph asked as he reached them.

'SOCOs are already on the scene. However, we're still not certain there's been any foul play. None of the flat windows or the door appears to have been forced. The only sign of any trouble was the blood on the headboard.'

'Which is not insignificant. It could mean that Millie knew the person who may have abducted her, and she let them in,' Joseph replied.

'But there's also still a chance that she could have just banged her head and took herself off to hospital, or even had a friend drive her,' Megan added.

Paul shook his head. 'The dad, Geoffrey Dexter, is ahead of you there. He's already rung round to all the local hospitals. Apparently, there's been no report of his daughter being checked in to any of the casualty departments.'

'Right, but if you could liaise with the station, just to double check that, I'd be grateful,' Joseph said. 'It wouldn't be the first time that someone has slipped through the net by having their name misspelled when it was entered on a computer.'

'I'll get on that straight away, sir.' Paul headed back to his patrol car.

The detectives walked over to the father and a pale-faced Greg, who was watching the other man pace up and down.

'We can take it from here, PC Robson,' Joseph said.

The young officer shot him a relieved look. 'Yes, sir.' Without another word, he walked away with the briskness of a man who didn't know the first thing about how to calm a father on the verge of tears.

Mr Dexter was now looking down at the ground, his shoulders rising and falling, taking in rapid hyperventilating breaths. Far too easily, Joseph could imagine what was going through his head. As a parent, your mind always went to the worst-case scenario, and in this case might actually be justified. Hannah had disappeared suddenly, and this was already an uncomfortable echo of that former cold case.

'You must be worried sick,' Joseph said to the father as they headed over.

The man's gaze slowly came up to meet the DI's, and the detectives showed him their warrant cards.

'That doesn't even come close,' Mr Dexter replied. 'Please tell me you have some idea where she might be?'

'I'm afraid we have nothing yet, but an alert issued across the entire Thames Valley Police Force has only just gone out.'

Megan nodded. 'We've also contacted St Mary's College and the Oxford Boat Club she belonged to, to see if anyone has any ideas where Millie might be.'

'Yes, that makes sense,' Mr Dexter said as his breathing decelerated and he began to look less like a man on the edge of a panic attack.

His gaze pivoted between the two officers. 'I know you probably think Millie has just taken herself off somewhere, like to a friend's or to get her cut bandaged, and that I'm over-reacting. But I must stress how uncharacteristic of her this is. My daughter is normally the most organised person in the world, and always punctual. I only spoke to her yesterday to confirm the time I was arriving to help move her things back home. For her to not even leave me a note is totally out of character.'

'I see, and what time did you talk to her yesterday?' Joseph said, nodding to Megan, who immediately took out her notebook.

'Around 9 pm.'

'I see...' Although the man was in a real state, Joseph still needed to press him to try and find out what he could. 'Do you happen to know why she wanted to abandon her studies and leave Oxford?'

'How do you know about that?' Mr Dexter asked, narrowing his eyes at the DI.

'Because DC Anderson and I were here around seven o'clock last night, asking her some questions.'

Geoffrey's eyes widened. 'Oh God, is she in some sort of trouble? Is that why she wanted to leave Oxford? That would certainly explain why she refused to talk about it to me or her mum.'

'No, nothing like that, Mr Dexter. However, I'm afraid I can't say any more as it's part of an ongoing investigation.'

The father gave him an intent look. 'But this somehow relates to my daughter's disappearance?'

Joseph held up his hands. 'Let's not get ahead of ourselves. It will probably turn out to be totally unrelated,' he said, although he was already thinking exactly the opposite. 'But as soon as we have any real information, you'll be the first to know.'

Mr Dexter drew in a shuddering breath and nodded. 'Thank you.'

Megan, her pen poised, gazed at the father with a sympathetic expression. 'It would be a real help if you could tell us exactly what you found when you arrived here this morning.'

'As I told the officer over the phone, when Millie didn't open the door, I let myself into her flat as I have a spare key.'

Joseph glanced over at one of the SOCO team, Shaun Adams, who had emerged from the flat and was taking close-up photos of the door lock. No doubt he was looking for any unusual scratch marks to indicate the lock had been picked.

'Then what happened?' Megan asked.

'The first thing I tried to do was turn on the lights because it was so dark in there. When the switch didn't work, I assumed that Millie hadn't topped up the meter. But when I glanced up at the fuse box next to the front door, I noticed someone had turned it off at the mains.'

'That's odd,' Megan said, looking up from her notes.

Mr Dexter nodded. 'The only explanation I can think of was that Millie was getting ready to hand the flat back over and had turned off the power in readiness. She mentioned something about someone from the agency popping over to pick up the keys sometime this morning.'

Joseph glanced at Megan. 'Make a note to contact the agency, just to see if they've already been here; they may have seen Millie.'

The DC nodded, and scribbled something down in her notebook.

However, a more obvious, darker thought had already entered Joseph's mind. If there had been an intruder, maybe they killed the power when they'd entered Millie's flat. That might have added to the element of surprise when they attacked her. But Joseph kept that thought to himself rather than rattle the father any more.

'So what did you do next, Mr Dexter?'

'Obviously, I called out to Millie to see if she was there, but when I didn't hear anything, I went upstairs. Then, thinking she might have overslept, I headed for her bedroom.' His face paled further. 'That's when I saw the blood—' His voice caught and he stared at the pavement, breathing deeply again.

'This must be so hard for you,' Megan said, her eyes filled with sympathy for the broken man before them.

Mr Dexter raised his gaze to hers and nodded. 'Millie's our only child. If anything has happened to her...' He wiped away the tears that had flooded his eyes.

Joseph patted the man on the shoulder, over the years having seen that same expression on far too many faces of parents who had lost a child. 'We're going to do everything we can to find her. You can be sure of that.'

He nodded. 'Please, and if there's anything I can do, just ask.'

'We will,' Joseph replied. 'Has anyone offered you a cup of tea or coffee?'

'No, but they've all been so busy.'

Joseph raised his eyebrows a fraction at Megan, and she nodded.

'Let me take you to a deli just down from here and give you a chance to catch your breath, Mr Dexter,' she said. 'This has been a huge shock.'

He gave her a desperate look. 'I just don't know what I'm going to tell Millie's mum.'

As the two of them headed off together, Joseph walked over to the van and helped himself to a forensic suit.

Shaun Adams was dusting black powder over the tiled floor as Joseph approached.

'How's it going?' Joseph asked, fully kitted out in his PPE.

'Just seeing if we can get any footprints that didn't belong to Millie in the entranceway. I've already taken a print of her father's shoes so we can eliminate him. But you never know, we may get lucky and come across a match on the database.'

'That's always worth a go,' Joseph replied, knowing that was a long shot at best that there would be a record of a shoe print in the database. 'So where's Amy?'

'Upstairs taking photos and samples of the blood.'

'Thanks, I'll head on up to see how she's getting on.'

Even though Joseph had the white overshoes covering his boots, he made sure to keep to the edges of the entrance, before making his way up the carpeted stairs.

Signs that the forensic team had already been hard at work were everywhere. There was more of the black powder on every shiny surface in the kitchen, as the team hunted for prints. Not that Joseph held out much hope, as anyone with any sense would have worn gloves.

A pool of bright light was visible through a doorway at the end of the kitchen, and he headed towards it like the proverbial moth. Joseph entered a bedroom where several portable lights had been set up, bathing the room in dazzling white light. Amy was in there taking photographs of a blood splatter mark on the headboard.

'This doesn't look good,' Joseph said.

Amy turned round, and seeing him, nodded. 'It's not, Joseph. Looking at the spray pattern and the height, my best guess is that Millie was assaulted whilst she was sitting up in bed, probably startled by the intruder.'

'That suggests she didn't let him in through the front door, so somehow he managed to break into her flat.'

Amy nodded. 'There's no sign of forced entry, suggesting it might be someone who had a key. Unfortunately, there's no sign of the object she was struck with. But the good news is there's not enough blood here to suggest it was a fatal blow, especially as we haven't found any bleach residue to indicate that someone tried to clean it up.'

'So, if an intruder really did abduct her, there's a chance that Millie may still be alive?'

'Quite possibly. Obviously, I need to confirm that this is Millie's blood, but the father has already volunteered to give a blood sample so we can check it for a DNA match at the lab. Of course, there's always an outside possibility that this is someone else's blood.'

'I strongly doubt that.'

Amy nodded. 'Me too. But we have these procedures in place for a reason, so if nothing else we can at least challenge our assumptions.'

'Aye, but I've already got a bad feeling that this might be linked somehow to Hannah's murder. If so, we could be looking at a possible killing spree. If they follow the same MO of the first murder, that could mean they're currently holding Millie prisoner somewhere.'

Amy's brow furrowed. 'Based on the postmortem report, maybe somewhere with lots of rats.'

Joseph tried to ignore the nightmare image of Millie's current situation threatening to overwhelm all his other thoughts.

'What about her mobile? Any sign of that?' Joseph asked, trying to keep focused.

'None. We've already contacted the phone company to run a trace. We did find an impact point on her bedroom wall though, along with some glass shards, indicating that someone may have thrown the phone at it.'

Joseph scratched his chin. 'The intruder might have snatched it from her. You should ask her mobile company for any texts or phone calls she might have attempted to make before the intruder assaulted her.'

'I've already submitted the request. We're also going to start checking footage of any cameras in the area, in case they caught something useful. But I'm sure that I don't need to tell you that we may have a very small window of time to find Millie, if she isn't already dead.'

Joseph blew out his cheeks. 'I know, but let's not go there just yet.'

Amy nodded, and as she returned to her work, Joseph took a moment. He took in the scene, imagining the absolute terror Millie must have felt when an intruder appeared in her bedroom. He made a silent vow to her then, whatever it took, he would catch the bastard.

'Right, I'm going to leave you to it, and head back to the

station,' Joseph finally said. 'If we're lucky, we already have our man in Charles Norton, so we have a distinct chance of rescuing her. I, for one, can't go through all this again, especially after Hannah's murder.'

Amy looked up from the camera, her eyes softening. 'You know that there was no way that anyone could have solved that case with the information you had back then?'

'That's what I keep trying to tell myself. The only problem is that part of my mind never got the memo. I still feel personally responsible, even though I wasn't the one running the investigation.'

Amy reached out and squeezed his shoulder. 'I know, but every officer feels like that.'

Joseph nodded, and patted her gloved hand. Turning, he headed for the door, already worried to the core of his being they might be too late to save Millie, and she would be added to the long list of those he hadn't been able to save that weighed down his soul

CHAPTER THIRTEEN

LATER THAT DAY, Joseph was back in the incident room waiting for Chris's latest briefing about the case. Amy was also going to be presenting her preliminary report on the forensic team's findings so far.

Joseph stood before the evidence board, where Millie's photo had now been placed alongside Hannah's at the top. Below them was a map of Oxford, a length of blue string stretched from Millie's photo to a pin in St Ebbes Street where the abduction from her flat had happened.

A similar blue string ran from Hannah's photo to a pin on the footpath next to the River Isis that ran along the bottom of Christ Church Meadow, indicating the spot where she'd vanished four years ago. There was also a length of red string linked to where her body had been found buried in the embankment to the south of Iffley Lock.

Joseph stared at it, as he considered the implications. How long did they have left until they added a second length of red string to where Millie's body would be found?

Megan appeared next to him. 'It can't just be down to

chance that both abductions were so close to one another,' she said.

'Yes, within less than a mile of each other. The ironic thing is that St Aldates Police Station is right in the middle, which you think would have at least given Hannah's murderer pause for thought. But they're obviously arrogant enough to believe they can act with impunity.'

Megan's eyes widened. 'You don't think one of our own could be responsible?'

'I certainly pray not, although nothing should be ruled out just yet. But such a small radius is certainly a bit too much of a coincidence. That tells me it could be someone very local to both abduction sites.'

'Or maybe someone who works close by. The other thing, and I hate to voice this, do you think we're potentially dealing with someone who is on a murder spree?'

Joseph rubbed the back of his neck as he contemplated the board before them, then nodded. 'I'm afraid there's every chance, especially when you consider the similarities of both cases.'

'But even if that's true, if the killer is following their previous MO, hopefully there's a good chance that Millie is still alive, at least for now.'

'It's the *hopeful* part of that statement that worries me. If she turns up dead, especially at the hands of the same killer who slipped through our fingers last time, it will be my worst nightmare come true.'

'I know, but as long as we haven't got a body, there's still cause for optimism.'

Joseph knew the DC wasn't wrong, and as a younger officer, he'd once allowed himself the luxury to think like that. Unfortunately, bitter experience had taught him that in an abduction case, things rarely turned out for the best. So it was better to get that straight in your head, rather than cling to false optimism.

He turned to Megan, intending to put her right, but then he saw the small reassuring smile on her face she was attempting to give him. Just like that, Joseph didn't have the heart to shatter her illusions. Experience on the job would eventually do that to her, grind her soul down like it had with the rest of them.

With no hint of his internal dialogue, Joseph just nodded. 'Aye, you're right.'

It was at that moment that Chris, his face drawn, walked into the incident room along with Amy. Derrick was just a few steps behind them, and once again he peeled away to take up a position at the back of the room, in an, *I'm here, but not here,* move. Everyone stopped what they were doing as Chris and Amy headed towards the front of the incident room. But Joseph could already tell by their expressions they didn't come bearing good news.

'Okay, everyone, we need to give you an update about Millie's disappearance. Amy is going to kick things off by giving you a quick briefing on Forensics' side of the investigation.'

Amy nodded and stepped forward. 'We're still waiting for a match on the blood sample to come back from the lab to confirm whether the DNA is a match to her father's. However, I think it's safe to assume that it will be. As regards shoe prints, unfortunately, nothing of use was recovered. There had been too much corruption of the crime scene by Geoffrey Dexter, when he entered the flat to check on his daughter.'

Amy scanned through her notes. 'Fingerprints across the flat predominantly matched those of one person, almost certainly Millie. We also found some of DC Anderson's and DI Stone's prints on the scene as per their interview with the victim yesterday evening. A further set matched her father's prints.'

Joseph's gaze travelled to the board where Mr Dexter's

photo had been added. Even though he was Millie's father, no one was above suspicion until it was proven otherwise.

'Have we been able to eliminate him as a suspect yet?' Megan asked, as though she'd been reading his mind.

'Not completely, although his wife has already confirmed that he was with her at the time we believe the abduction occurred. For now, we're assuming that it wasn't Millie's father. So, on that basis, it would be safe to conclude that the intruder was wearing gloves.'

'Was there any other DNA evidence retrieved?' another officer asked.

'Everything we were able to recover is at the lab for analysis and we won't know for a while yet.'

'What about her mobile, any joy there?' Ian asked.

'We're still waiting for the phone company to come back with details of Millie's texts because, as usual, they're dragging their heels,' Amy replied. 'However, we do have a triangulation report for the last time it was connected to the cellular network. Millie's phone was turned off whilst still in her house. According to the mobile company's records, that was uncharacteristic of Millie, who apparently was someone who always kept her mobile turned on. The last reported connection to a cellular mast was just before one-thirty this morning.'

'In other words, this confirms our assumption that her abductor seized her mobile so she couldn't ring for help,' Chris added. 'However, that also means we know the likely time when the intruder gained access to her flat.'

'Nothing from any CCTV footage in the area, I suppose?' Ian asked.

Amy shook her head. 'We retrieved smart doorbell footage from a few adjacent properties, along with other camera footage, but have nothing for that period. There wasn't so much as a car, let alone a person picked up during the time frame in question.'

'Hang on, how is that even possible?' Megan said. 'If the intruder moved Millie, they couldn't have just vanished into thin air with her.'

'Yet, that's exactly what seems to have happened, DC Anderson,' Amy replied. 'And before you ask, there's no way to get to the roof from street level.'

'Maybe Millie's abductor took her to a nearby flat or house,' another officer suggested. 'That could explain why no one was spotted by CCTV.'

'That's certainly one scenario, which is why I've got a search warrant for all the properties in the immediate area,' Chris said. 'As we speak, uniforms are going door to door in the surrounding area.'

As Joseph knew someone would, they stated the other obvious possibility. And of course, that someone was Ian.

'What if the intruder has already killed Millie and dumped her body, say, in a rear garden?'

Everybody traded tight frowns. It would certainly be easier for one person to do a flit that way, rather than someone trying to carry an unconscious victim away on foot. In that context, getting rid of Millie's body as fast as possible would certainly make sense.

'Until we know differently, we won't assume that's happened,' Chris replied. 'That's part of the reason I've assigned a dog team to the case, to see if they can pick up any trail. But based on the fact she was a member of the women's Oxford Boat crew, and the nature of her disappearance, I'm sure it's not lost on any of you that this bears a striking resemblance to the Hannah Emmerson case. That suggests that these are indeed connected abductions, possibly by someone known to both women. With that in mind, what's the update on interviewing Charles Norton, Ian?'

Ian looked distinctly uncomfortable. 'I haven't been able to get hold of him so far, Boss.'

Chris stared at the DI and was about to speak, when Derrick beat him to it.

'What do you mean you haven't got hold of our chief suspect?' the DSU asked, his tone icy.

'Apparently, he's out on the Thames on a launch shadowing the men's Oxford Blue Team, right now,' Ian replied. 'Unfortunately, there isn't a way of getting hold of him as he always makes a point of leaving his mobile behind during practice sessions.'

'*Unfortunately?*' Derrick replied, his eyes slitting. 'Are you bloody incompetent, Ian? You're not arranging a fucking tea party invitation here. There's a good chance that man is our killer and he could be holding Millie somewhere, even as we speak. So we have a very narrow window of time before our murderer decides to dispose of her, just like they did with Hannah. So I don't care what you have to do—arrest the coach if you bloody have to—but I want him inside this station within the hour.'

Ian looked like he wanted the ground to open up and swallow him where he sat as he nodded.

It was as much as Joseph could do as he clenched his jaw not to verbally lay into Derrick.

But then Chris, who was staring across the room at the DSU, spoke up. 'With all due respect, sir, I'm the SIO assigned to this case, and that will be my decision.'

The way Derrick's face went scarlet, Joseph honestly thought the man was about to burst a blood vessel as he locked eyes with Chris. 'Then I might have to reconsider my decision to hand this case over to you,' he muttered.

Everyone in the room was trading shocked looks. It was rare to see Mummy and Daddy arguing openly like this. The senior officers might not see eye to eye, but that's what offices with closed doors were for.

Joseph didn't know quite what possessed him, but for some reason part of his subconscious thought it was necessary to stick his nose into their business.

'With all due respect, DCI Faulkner has handled this case with absolute professionalism, and hasn't put a step wrong. I think I can speak on behalf of every officer on this case and say that he has our full support.'

Derrick's pupils were like pinpricks as he turned towards Joseph. It was then the DI noticed the redness ringing his eyes, and the slightly unfocused way he was glaring at him. Even though the man hadn't slurred his words, Joseph was pretty sure if he'd been close enough to smell his breath, he would have picked up the strong fragrance of whisky on it. Yes, the man was definitely feeling the pressure.

'What did you say?' the superintendent demanded, his volume dropping to a threatening whisper still loud enough for every single person in the room to hear him.

Joseph met the glare with his own and was just getting ready to tell the steaming turd exactly what he thought of him when Chris got in there first.

'I actually believe there is sufficient cause for concern to pull Charles Norton in for a discussion.' He nodded to Ian. 'Just do whatever you have to, and get him here quickly for questioning.'

'Of course,' Ian replied, not quite managing to make eye contact.

Chris's gaze met Derrick's again. 'If I think there is even a hint that we have our man, I will hold him for the maximum twenty-four-hours whilst my team searches for evidence.'

Joseph was impressed at the not-too-subtle way the DCI

was making a very direct statement to Derrick with just his use of the word, *my*.

'If Millie is still alive and being held captive somewhere, we will leave no stone unturned trying to track her down,' Chris continued. 'That all begins with the interview with Charles Norton, and that will initially concentrate on his whereabouts when Millie went missing last night.'

Not too shabby, Chris, Joseph thought to himself, really impressed with how the DCI was conducting himself against his senior officer, someone who had always been a bit of a bully. But if the man was going to act as a lightning conductor for Derrick's wrath, Joseph would be damned if he'd let him do it alone.

'Maybe because of the time-critical nature of finding Millie, the time has come for us to go public,' Joseph said. 'We could tell the press that we found Hannah's body, and we now believe Millie's life is in danger, too. We could also ask Geoffrey Dexter to make a plea. After all, we need all the help we can get to track her down before it's too late.'

Suddenly the anger that had filled Derrick's face melted away, and he blinked rapidly. 'Call a press conference and openly link this to Hannah's murder?'

Joseph could see the fear in the man's eyes as he faced what he believed might be a career-ending revelation.

'Maybe, maybe not, because with no hard evidence, all we have to go on at this point are our suspicions that these events are linked.' Joseph then gave Derrick a very pointed look. 'The priority here is to save Millie's life, something we failed to do with Hannah.'

Although there wasn't an actual sharp intake of breath as Joseph suggested the original investigation had come up short, he could still feel the tension as almost tangible static crackling in the room.

As the officers looked between him and the superintendent, they obviously expected Derrick to lay into him. What they didn't expect was for the big man just to nod meekly, then turn and head out of the room, closing the door quietly behind him.

Then everyone's attention was solely on Joseph as if to say, *What the feck just happened?*

The DI simply shrugged. 'The man obviously got out of bed on the wrong side, this morning.'

There were a few chuckles at that, but also a few questioning looks, wondering if he knew something that he wasn't letting on. Not that Joseph was going to tell anyone. At least, not as long as Derrick didn't screw things up by trying to cover his tracks. If he crossed that line, Joseph would more than happily blow the whistle and bring the entire edifice of his career crashing down on his head.

Chris was one of the officers staring at him, then he returned his attention to the rest of the room. 'Okay, we all have jobs to do. Millie is counting on us, so don't let her down. Let's get to it, people.'

There was a murmur, most of them returning their attention to their screens. Ian stood up, grabbed his coat, and headed for the door like his arse was on fire.

'Wow, what was all that about, Joseph?' Megan asked as conversations started up all around them.

Joseph just tapped the side of his nose. 'That's for me to know and for you to wonder about.'

'Right...'

'Coffee?' he asked, trying to change the subject.

'Yes, thanks,' Megan said distractedly.

Joseph was heading out of the room when he felt someone tap him on the shoulder.

The DI turned, expecting to see Megan, but instead, he found himself looking at Amy.

'That was quite the performance, Joseph. I have to say, I never thought I would see you standing up for Chris, especially with Derrick.'

'If I'm honest, I'm as surprised as anyone. I hate to admit it, but I'm starting to have a grudging respect for the man.'

'I agree, but what possessed you to take Derrick on like that? You know full well he's been looking for a reason to sack you for years, so what happened to your keeping your head down strategy?'

'You do actually know me, right?'

She chuckled. 'Okay, you might have a point there. Anyway, I know how this case has been weighing you down, so I have a proposal if you're up for it. It's a way to take your mind off things, even if it's for a short time.'

Joseph gave her a mystified look. 'Such as?'

'Such as, I was wondering if you would like to join me at a free swimming event next weekend. Ellie's also a member, and I've even persuaded Megan to join us. It turns out, she's a keen swimmer, too.'

'Whoa there, me freezing my nads off in the river during what is still technically winter? I don't think so. That appeals about as much as drilling a hole through my forehead.'

Amy chuckled. 'Then, how about acting as our support crew, with towels and a flask of hot coffee at the ready?'

'Now that, I can do,' Joseph replied with a smile.

'Excellent, then put it in your calendar for next Saturday at 9 am. I expect to see you there bright-eyed and bushy-tailed.'

'I'm not sure about the bushy-tail part, and it will probably be more bleary-eyed on one of the few days I'm meant to get a lie in, but that aside, I'll be there.'

'Excellent. Anyway, I must shoot. People to chase, lab reports to acquire.'

With a backward wave, Amy headed past Joseph and down

the corridor, with what he would swear was an extra bit of hip swing he'd never seen her use before. What the hell was that about?

Slightly confused, Joseph turned away to make some extra strong coffee as he worked out what his next step should be.

CHAPTER FOURTEEN

It had been a frustrating week for everyone at work. Ian and Chris's interview with Charles Norton hadn't yielded any results. Not only had the coach told the detectives that he'd been away in Manchester at a conference when Millie had been taken, but a colleague had also confirmed his story.

Even the one thing Joseph thought they had on the man had led nowhere. When Norton was pressed about why Millie had an obvious issue with him, he'd admitted to being a ruthless bully when it came to training. According to Ian, the shite had even been proud of it. He saw it as a badge of honour that he was prepared to do anything to push the students to deliver their absolute best.

On hearing that, Joseph, along with Megan, had made a point of interviewing the rest of the women's boat team to find out if Charles was the sexual predator they suspected he was. But if he was, then none of them were saying anything.

Once again, just like with the original investigation, Joseph was painfully aware they seemed to have reached something of a dead end.

In previous cases when he'd been stuck like this, and had

been trying to work out exactly what had happened, he often returned to the scene of the crime, trying to visualise it.

So it was little wonder that Joseph kept heading to the one place that might still offer up a clue. For the last four days, he'd made a point of making a very minor detour whilst cycling into work.

Almost on autopilot now, he pulled up outside Millie's flat and leant his bike against a lamppost. He stood there, gazing up at it, trying to work out how the intruder had been able to spirit Millie away without anyone spotting them.

What are we missing here? he thought.

Joseph was surprised to see Dylan rounding the corner onto the street, with Max and White Fang in tow on their leads. On seeing the DI, the dogs gave him a waggy-tail welcome.

The DI gave the professor a questioning look. 'Fancy running into you here.'

Dylan raised his shoulders. 'Well, if you spill your heart out to me about this case, what else is an old man who's had his interest well and truly piqued to do? That's why I wanted to see the crime scene with my own eyes. I keep finding myself wondering how Millie's abductor pulled off this disappearing act with her.'

'You're not the only one. That's the same reason I'm standing here. It just doesn't make sense, does it? How can one, let alone two people, vanish into thin air?'

Dylan gestured towards the flat. 'Is there any rear access into the property?'

'Just a small, high-walled garden with no way in or out of it. The intruder must have entered the property through the front door, and the fact that there doesn't seem to have been any scratch marks on the lock, suggests that either Millie knew her abductor, or they got hold of a key somehow. Even so, the bigger question is how did they then spirit her away without ever getting spotted?'

'I hate to be pessimistic, but I assume you've already checked the sewers in case they might have escaped through them?'

'Megan already came up with the idea. It turns out, the sewers here aren't big enough for a person to crawl through.'

The professor grimaced. 'What if the abductor chopped her body up?'

'I suppose that's a possibility, and if they disposed of her via a sewer, we haven't been able to find any remains in them so far. We've already had sniffer dogs check every single bin and dumpster in the immediate area, but they've picked up nothing, either.'

'Okay, that's at least cause for some optimism that Millie might still be alive. What about the nearby student accommodation block in Cambridge Terrace? That isn't too far away and even if we can't work out how she was moved, maybe Millie is being held there by another student?'

'That already occurred to us and two of the team have checked, even doing a room-to-room search. Apart from one solitary blonde woman who returned to the block around 3 am, who was picked up by their CCTV, there was absolutely nothing else. Just to make sure that it wasn't someone wearing a wig, we even tracked the woman down. Turned out to be a student returning from her boyfriend's flat on the other side of town. So, as you can see, there are no easy answers, Dylan. That's why I keep returning here. I can't help the feeling that we're missing something that's right under our noses. Discover what that is exactly, and maybe then we'll have a chance at solving the case.'

Dylan nodded. 'I agree, and now it seems you have me at it too, trying to work out how they did it. I was barely able to sleep last night wondering about how Millie's abductor pulled this off like some sort of magical act. I'm going to put all my effort into solving this, Joseph, if only so I can eventually get some sleep again.'

'You and me both,' the DI replied. 'That aside, any joy finding any women who had their flats broken into and had their things moved around?'

'Nothing so far,' Dylan replied. 'I've asked all my contacts across the Oxford colleges, but no students reported anything like that happening to them when Hannah was abducted four years ago.'

'So maybe she was a unique case until now, suggesting that she was deliberately targeted. Interesting. But if you unearth anything relevant, call me immediately, Dylan. If ever a case urgently needed a breakthrough, it's this one. The clock is ticking and the whole team is feeling the pressure. Anyway, I'd better get going, so I don't give Derrick another reason to sack me.'

'Then I'll see you later when you get back to your boat, and you can debrief me with all the latest titbits about the case.'

'I sometimes wonder why we don't be done with it and just put you on the payroll.'

Dylan smiled. 'A good glass of gin is all the payment I require, and your own excellent company, of course.'

'You, sir, are a grand man.' Joseph cast his gaze over the property again, hoping the answer might just leap out and hit him. But like always, it didn't. 'Okay, I better get going to see if anyone has unearthed any other leads.'

'Then, as always, good hunting,' Dylan replied. 'I'm heading home to try out your mother's Irish stew recipe that you shared with me last week.'

'Make sure you make enough for both of us, because hers is

one of the very best on the planet and will leave you licking your plate.'

'Don't worry, I was already planning to with my own spin, maybe using a certain famous Irish stout for the stock.'

'Good man, now you're talking my language, and I think even my ma would approve of that addition.' With a wave, Joseph mounted his bike again and set off to the St Aldates Police Station only a few streets away.

As he cycled away, he looked back to see the professor still gazing at the flat and scratching the back of his head.

The DI was having an increasingly uneasy feeling the murderer was someone who lived close by. Could they even be watching him now, laughing to themselves because, for all their best efforts, the police were just as clueless this time round as they had been with Hannah's case?

To say there was an air of despondency hanging over the incident room would have been a serious understatement. The usual banter had all but evaporated, and the long faces were almost dragging on the floor. It was obvious to Joseph he wasn't the only one feeling the pressure of the invisible clock counting down to what felt like the moment of Millie's inevitable murder. It was certainly a bad sign that even Chris had dipped into his pocket, which was why there was a box of Danishes they'd all helped themselves to.

Joseph glanced at Megan, finishing her second custard-filled pastry, and shook his head. 'I honestly don't know where you put it.'

'That will be all my nervous energy, currently burning off these extra calories,' the DC replied.

He sighed. 'Aye, me too. I still can't believe the public statement Chris eventually decided to okay hasn't yielded any results yet.'

'Tell me about it. Not so much as a crumb of information. You'd think someone would know something relevant, but if they do, they're very much keeping it to themselves.'

The DI nodded. 'I tell you now, Megan, this is feeling uncomfortably like a rerun of the Hannah Emmerson case. The worse thing is we could already be too late, and it might take another four years or more until we find her body.'

'Don't even entertain that thought, Joseph. At least, not yet.'

'Aye, but it's hard not to. One too many cases like this, and you'll find yourself wired the same way.'

Megan frowned, but said nothing else, obviously realising words alone wouldn't help persuade Joseph otherwise.

The DI returned his attention to the map, now littered with red circles. They showed the sites that had already been searched, anywhere it was possible that someone could be kept captive. That list was an extensive one, and included every single abandoned building and lock-up they could think of. The list had only grown as the public had also rung in with no end of suggestions, from disused warehouses to a rusting railway wagon a man had used as a shed. That one had been flagged by a neighbour, who'd told the investigating officers, 'He's just the sort to abduct a woman.' Of course, the man had been nothing of the sort, and was using the wagon as nothing more than a storage space for his old garden tools.

The sum of all this influx of material meant the entire team had been working flat out, checking every single lead, however unpromising. It was little wonder everyone looked wrung out. At least no one could accuse them of not putting their backs into it.

Chris appeared next to Joseph's desk, looking as knackered as the DI felt, and wearing what the DI was pretty sure was the same shirt from the day before. That meant he'd probably slept at his desk.

'So how did you and Megan get on with checking that old grain silo yesterday?' Chris asked.

'As usual, no sign that anyone had ever been held captive there,' Joseph replied.

Chris clicked his tongue and nodded. He had the despondent look of a man who'd heard similar from far too many officers today. 'Then maybe it's time to see if we missed something obvious.'

The DCI headed over to a clean whiteboard and picked up a marker pen. Then he turned to face the room and clapped his hands.

'Okay, can I just have everyone's attention for a moment? First off, I wanted to say no one could have worked any harder than you all have, trying to piece together what little information we have about this case. That said, I know I don't need to tell anyone, barring a sudden breakthrough, we seem to have stalled on this investigation, and worse still, we don't currently even have a suspect after Charles Norton proved to have a credible alibi. So, maybe we need to roll things back to the basics. To start with, let's brainstorm what relationship the murderer might have to their victims?'

Chris wrote Hannah and Millie's names on the board, followed by *Murderer* beneath them, and ringed all three with arrows linking them. Then he wrote a question mark in the middle.

Joseph nodded. 'Okay, let's start listing possible relationships. But it has to be someone that could be linked to both victims despite the four-year gap between the abductions.'

'Boy or girlfriend,' someone called out.

Chris nodded, writing that down beneath the names. 'Yes, someone could have dated both women.'

'You should still have the coach on there,' Megan said.

'Even though he's been cleared?' Chris asked.

'Yes, he had a direct relationship with both women, so on that basis alone, his name should still go up.'

'Fair point,' Chris said, adding it to the list. 'Keep them coming, people.'

'How about a random stranger who gets their kicks out of killing women on the Oxford Boat team?' Ian suggested.

'Yes, we certainly can't rule that out.' He added *Stranger with a fixation on the women's boat team* to the board.

Megan's eyes unfocused as she looked into the middle distance. 'A fellow crew member?'

'We've already ruled that out, because no one who was on the team four years ago is on it now,' Chris replied.

'But if the coach is up on that list, I don't see why a team member shouldn't be as well,' Joseph replied, giving Megan a small smile of encouragement.

'Okay, that's a good point,' Chris said, adding it. 'Anymore?'

Everyone shook their heads.

'Then let's pick up on something else.' The boss then wrote on the board, *Why the Four-Year Gap?*

'A copycat killer,' a detective at the back of the room said.

The DCI nodded and added it.

'Maybe, they were just taking their time selecting a new victim,' Ian said. 'Or possibly, they just had a change of heart, saw the light, so to speak, but then have slipped back into their old ways.'

Chris wrote both ideas down on the board.

'What about it being more than one person responsible, like during the Midwinter Butcher case?' Megan suggested.

Joseph nodded to Megan, liking the way she was thinking, as that was added.

When there were no more suggestions, Chris turned to the golden nugget Joseph had known he would eventually come to.

'Then how about the motive for killing Hannah, and now possibly Millie, too?' Chris said.

'Trying to silence someone who had it in for the murderer,' Ian said almost too quickly, leaving them all in no doubt he was thinking about the coach.

That went straight on the board without any argument from their SIO.

'Revenge—someone that both women managed to cross,' Megan said, who was obviously on a roll.

'And let's not forget the classic psychopath, just doing it for kicks,' Joseph added.

'Bloody hell, give me a chance,' Chris said, writing down both suggestions they'd just thrown at him.

'If we're going for golden oldies, then extortion has to be up there,' Sue, a DS that had recently transferred over from the Cowley station, added. 'Maybe the women were trying to black-mail someone who didn't take kindly to it.'

Chris added *Extortion* to the list. Then his gaze swept the room, but when no one said anything else, he nodded.

'Okay, this is not an exhaustive list and if you think of anything relevant, please feel free to add it. But somewhere in there is the profile that fits our murderer. I realise the answer isn't going to leap out and announce itself, but in my experience, just going back to basics like this helps to clarify thinking, especially when it feels like we're chasing our tails. Anyway, I'll leave this up for you all to think about.' Chris put down the marker pen and returned to his desk.

Megan was already copying the contents of the board down into her notebook.

'Doing your homework?' Joseph said.

'Something like that, but he's right, it really helps to lay it all out like this.'

'You're not wrong. It's a technique as old as the hills, but that doesn't mean it can't help bring something into focus.'

Megan took a bite of her next custard Danish pastry and nodded.

Joseph leant back in his chair, gazing at the information on the whiteboard. Somewhere on that list were the signposts to why the killer had done what they had. Then his gaze flicked to the window, and his mind once again returned to how they had spirited their victim away. The DI once again had the distinct feeling that if they could work that out, it would be the key to unlocking the whole case.

CHAPTER FIFTEEN

THE THING about the city boundaries of Oxford was one moment you could be strolling through its streets, and the next you would find yourself out in the wilds of the countryside. Right now, Joseph was standing less than half a mile away from the edge of the city in an expanse of green fields next to a river. He was also freezing his nether regions off, as he watched a group of obviously insane swimmers getting ready to take the plunge.

The weather wasn't exactly what the detective would call ideal for throwing yourself into the freezing water. It might be March, but there was a distinct arctic chill, thanks to the bitter northerly wind currently whistling over the fields and doing its best to turn him into a human ice statue.

But his discomfort was nothing compared to the men and women, including Ellie, Megan, and Amy, who'd now stripped down to their swimsuits on the bank of Wolvercote Mill Stream. The waterway, a tributary to the Thames, was easily large enough to qualify as a river in anyone else's book, apart from the person who'd actually had the audacity to call it a mere stream.

Joseph watched the swimmers, including his daughter,

limber up. *What some people do for pleasure never ceases to amaze me...*

'A hot chocolate?' suggested Kate, who was also supporting their daughter in her latest hobby. She'd helped Joseph put together the provisions for their idiot family and friends, who were prepared to bare flesh in these near-frostbite conditions.

'Damned right,' he replied. 'I think I'm already losing the feeling in my fingers.' Then he produced his hip flask. 'Maybe a shot of Irish whiskey in that hot chocolate?'

'Now you're talking my language,' Kate said, as she poured them each a mug.

Joseph did the honours with the alcohol and soon it was doing wonders for warming his body and soul.

'Our daughter is obviously built of sterner stuff than us,' Kate said, gesturing towards Ellie, who was standing next to Amy and Megan. The three of them didn't even have the decency to be shivering as they adjusted their goggles and swimming caps.

'It must be your family genes somewhere along the line, because mine have always felt the cold,' Joseph replied. 'If you forced me to go for a swim in these conditions, I'd only do it with a wetsuit and having slathered at least ten pounds of lard all over my body.'

Kate laughed. 'Now there's a grim mental image.'

'Oh, you love the idea of it, really,' Joseph said, winking at her.

The sharp trill of a whistle, blown by a bearded man who would have given Father Christmas a serious run for his money, drew their attention back to the imminent river race. Two dozen fully grown adults, including their three ladies, who really should have known better, all dived into the water without so much as a squeal between the lot of them. This group was seriously hardcore.

The pack of wild swimmers headed downstream towards where the Wolvercote Mill Stream met the Thames. Ellie had already told Joseph during his and Kate's *parent briefing* the group would be turning around there. Then they were going to race back to the finish line, where the spectators, including them, would be waiting with blankets to stop hyperthermia from setting in.

The swimmers pulled away, most with a crawl stroke. With considerable pride, Joseph noted their daughter was holding her own in the middle of the pack, along with Amy. The chief SOCO had a really graceful swimming style, and both of them were cutting through the water efficiently and quickly. But it was Megan who was the real surprise. She was right at the front with the leading pack as they pulled away from the rest of the group, her crawl stroke incredibly powerful and controlled.

'Good grief, with that sort of form Megan should consider applying to become an Olympic swimmer,' Kate said, a look of admiration on her face.

'She's certainly impressive, I'll give her that,' Joseph replied.

They watched the slower group splashing away along the river. A few spectators kept pace with them by jogging along the embankment, shouting encouragement with a couple of dogs barking excitedly.

'Should we be doing that as well?' Kate asked, gesturing towards them.

'After the week I've had, I am almost too exhausted to even think about a brisk walk, so I'm grand, thanks all the same.'

'To be honest, I'm surprised to see you here with everything that's going on at work. From what Derrick has been saying, it sounds like you've all been burning the candles at both ends.'

'Has he now?' Joseph asked.

Kate immediately shot him a questioning look. 'What's that mean?'

'Just that he's been like a bull in a china shop lately, laying into anyone on the case given half the chance. Meanwhile, all he's done is keep holed up in his office, at least when he hasn't emerged to bellow at people.'

Kate looked away to the receding pack of swimmers, but didn't say anything as she wrapped her arms around herself.

'What's wrong?' Joseph asked gently.

When she turned back towards him, he was surprised to see tears in her eyes. 'Derrick's taken the whole thing with Millie really badly, and is now blaming himself for not doing more to try and crack the Hannah Emmerson case.'

'Right...' Joseph said, trying to keep his tone as neutral as possible.

'And he's drinking again. I'm worried about him, Joseph, I really am.'

Quite how he was meant to respond to that, he wasn't sure. The gobshite certainly deserved to be putting himself through hell about deliberately suppressing evidence. But this was also having an impact on Kate, a woman Joseph would always care about, even if she had shown remarkably bad taste in men when she'd chosen the DSU to be her new husband.

'That's not good,' Joseph said, with his best attempt at a sympathetic face.

'It's certainly not. But you must be feeling it, too, having worked on the Hannah case with Derrick.'

'Aye, I am. I wouldn't have come here at all if Chris hadn't insisted that some of us take time off to recharge our batteries. You see, for now, we've run out of leads about where Millie could be held.'

'*Chris* is it? Whatever happened to his nickname *Fucker?*' Kate asked with a small smile.

'I hate to admit it, but the guy is actually alright. Yes, some-times he walks around like he has a stick up his arse, but he's a good copper underneath all that pompous exterior. He certainly knows how to lead a team.'

'Wow, that's high praise from you. Are you sure you're feeling okay?' That wonderful smile of Kate's flashed across her face again. It always made his heart skip several beats, like it had from the first day he'd met her.

Joseph laughed. 'Obviously not. But how are you keeping, yourself?'

She shrugged. 'Apart from what's happening with Derrick, I've been better.'

'Kate?' Joseph asked when she didn't elaborate.

She waved her hand at him. 'Don't worry about it. Anyway, I meant to say that, sadly, I haven't been able to dig up anything about students having to deal with intruders, or anyone playing mind games with them by breaking into their homes.'

Joseph sighed. 'It was a long shot, but thank you for trying. What about your own secret investigation?'

'Still digging, but getting nowhere fast.'

Joseph nodded.

The Father Christmas lookalike who'd been watching the swimmers recede into the distance raised his hand to get people's attention. 'The leaders have just reached the Thames and have already turned back,' he announced to the gathered spectators.

Kate and Joseph looked along the river, trying to make out the swimmers, but they were nothing but specks at that distance.

'I wonder how Ellie and the others are doing?' Kate said.

'Knowing our daughter, really well. But it's Megan that I'm most intrigued about. Whether she's been able to maintain that blistering pace she set off with.'

Kate nodded. 'Yes, she even seemed to match the speed of Joanna from the Oxford Women's Blue Boat team.

'Sorry, you're saying there's a member of the Oxford women's crew taking part in this?'

'Yes, she's a regular in these wild group swims.'

'I don't suppose that means that Ellie knows her by any chance?'

'They're not that close, if that's what you mean. But I think they share the same circle of friends and certainly know of each other. Why?' She looked at him and frowned. 'I recognise that look. You're hatching something.'

Kate was absolutely right. The DI could already feel a plan forming in the back of his mind. So far, the women on the boat club teams had refused to say anything about the coach, but maybe if he could get Ellie to have a quiet word...

His thoughts trailed away as he spotted PC John Thorpe from the Cowley station. He half expected him to head over to tell him he was needed back at the station. Instead, the young officer went over to join the group of onlookers.

'Why is John here?' Joseph said, almost to himself.

Kate turned to him with a surprised look. 'What, you don't know?'

'Know what?'

'He's dating our daughter.'

Joseph stared at her as though he'd just fallen into a parallel universe. 'How long has this been happening, exactly?'

'Three months now. They hit it off when John was standing guard at our house. That was before those psychopaths knocked him out and abducted our daughter.'

'And why is this the first I'm hearing about *him* dating our daughter?' Joseph asked.

'This isn't the nineteenth century, when a young man has to ask the father for permission to step out with his daughter, you know?'

'More's the pity,' Joseph muttered as he shot the back of John's head *the look*.

Kate rolled her eyes at him. 'Will you listen to yourself, Joseph? Don't tell me you have a problem with our daughter going out with a police officer.'

'Of course not, it's just...' He waved his hands around and gave Kate a hopeless look.

'Seeing you react like this, no wonder Ellie wasn't keen to tell you. She's a grown woman now, if you hadn't noticed.'

Joseph sighed and nodded. 'Sorry, just me being overprotective.'

A second sense must have kicked in for John, because he glanced around, caught the DI's dagger-like gaze, and quickly looked away.

Kate raised her eyebrows at Joseph. 'The poor man looks petrified now. Maybe try dialling the non-verbal hostility down from an eleven to a five?'

Before Joseph could respond, the spectators around them suddenly began whooping and clapping.

They turned to see two swimmers, far ahead of the rest of the pack, were approaching fast and matching each other stroke for stroke. It was only when his ex-wife's clapping grew even more frantic, Joseph realised one of the women was Megan.

'Talk about having a serious talent for this,' Joseph said, really impressed now at the DC's prowess in the water.

'She looks as at home as a fish in that water,' Kate replied. 'She's certainly giving Joanna a stiff run for her money.'

Joseph watched, transfixed as the two women powered towards the finish line. He would expect the Oxford boat crew woman to be at the peak of physical fitness, but Megan? Although she was slim despite whatever food she shoved into her mouth, he'd never seen her anywhere near a gym.

But then, with less than five metres to go, he saw for himself why Joanna had been selected for the Oxford crew. She dug deeper and began to accelerate, arms and legs suddenly moving at twice the speed of Megan's, sending spray flying as she shot through the water like a human torpedo.

There was nothing Megan had left to respond with. Joanna cleared the makeshift finish line strung over the river with a clear three-metre lead over her opponent.

A cheer went up, with Joseph and Kate clapping with the best of them for Joanna, but also especially for Megan as she crossed the line a close second.

'We're up, fellow crew support member,' Kate said.

They gathered up the towels and the hamper containing two flasks of hot chocolate, minus the whisky, and headed over to the shore.

Megan followed Joanna out of the water, breathing hard, but also looking as lit up as Joseph had ever seen her. Megan hugged her chief rival before she peeled away and headed towards them.

'Wow, that was fun,' she said, as she accepted a towel from Joseph and began drying herself.

'I have to say I'm impressed, Megan,' Kate said. 'I'd no idea you were such an amazing swimmer. You seem to have a natural talent for it.'

'That's because I grew up on the Isle of Wight. Swimming is part of my family's DNA. My sister and I swam in the sea every single day, come hail or shine. But these days, I keep fit by using Rosenblatt Pool most mornings, before heading to work.'

'You're definitely a dark horse,' Joseph said.

'Don't I know it,' Megan replied, grinning at him.

Kate nudged Joseph in the ribs. 'Will you look at our daughter go?'

He looked back to the river to see Ellie was having her very own race with Amy. The two women were neck and neck in the middle of the pack as they headed for the finish line together.

'Come on, Ellie!' Joseph found himself shouting.

Both women definitely had their own private competition, neither cutting the other any slack. They literally crossed the finish line with absolutely nothing to separate them.

'Wow, talk about a photo finish,' Kate said.

Joseph was about to head over to offer Ellie a towel as she climbed out onto the embankment when John beat him to it. The next thing the DI knew, John was drying his daughter and kissing her neck, all in plain bloody sight of him.

Kate just gave Joseph a sideways glance. 'Whatever you're thinking, don't.'

'I wasn't thinking anything,' Joseph said, trying to expel the mental image of shoving John's head into the river and holding it beneath the surface for a good five minutes.

'Young love, eh,' Amy said, joining them and tussling her hair in a towel as she dried it.

Kate smiled at her, pointedly ignoring Joseph. 'Yes, it's great to see,' she said, before heading off to join their daughter.

Joseph turned to Amy intending to come up with a wise-crack response, but when he actually looked at her properly for the first time, he completely lost his train of thought. Amy was positively glowing after her swim, not to mention the way her eyes seemed to shine when she looked at him. Her whole appearance was more than magnified by the swimsuit, which really showed off her figure.

Her gaze caught Joseph's and she flashed him a smile that positively matched Kate's in brilliance. 'Quick, hand me over that hot chocolate before I freeze,' she said.

'Yes, of course,' Joseph said, not quite able to tear his eyes away from her face as he handed her a mug.

She took a sip and pulled a face. 'What, no schnapps?'

Whatever spell she was currently casting over him lifted a fraction, allowing Joseph to produce his hip flask. 'Will Irish whiskey do?'

Amy smiled at him. 'Always.'

He poured her a generous measure while she watched him with an unreadable look.

'What?' Joseph asked.

'Oh, nothing,' she replied, taking a sip of her now alcohol-laced drink. 'Much better, although I should get some clothes on.'

With a hip swing, she walked back to her gym bag. For years, Joseph and the SOCO officer had been friends, but something told him that maybe for the first time, she was considering something more than that between them.

With a bemused expression he watched her head away, not quite sure how he felt. He noticed in the distance, the dark storm clouds rolling in and squalls of rain were already falling from them. The last thing they needed was more water to swell the already swollen river again.

Kate came back over to him with the broadest grin. 'Seems like your luck is in there, Joseph.'

'What, already?'

'Oh, don't act all innocent with me. For Amy, that was downright flirting.'

'It was?'

'God, you can be slow on the uptake sometimes, but yes, that's exactly what it was. I don't remember you being like that when we started dating.'

Joseph shrugged. 'What can I say? Maybe the ravages of time have taken their toll on my perception skills when it comes to women.'

'Bloody hell, sometimes you make yourself sound like a hundred and three, rather than a guy in his forties.'

Ellie came over, practically dragging John by the hand behind her.

'Hello, sir,' John said stiffly to the DI, before nodding to Kate. 'Ma'am.'

'It'd better be Joseph when we're not at work, especially as you're now apparently' —he tried not to grind the word between his teeth— '*dating* my daughter.'

'Yes, sir, I mean, Joseph,' John said, almost stammering.

Ellie's eyes sought her mum's. 'You told Dad before I had a chance to?'

'I think he was going to work that part out for himself when he saw you both together,' Kate replied.

She grimaced. 'Sorry I didn't tell you sooner, Dad.'

John very wisely chose to stay mute as Ellie looped her arm through her dad's. 'Can I have a quick word?'

'Of course,' he replied, letting himself be towed away, and mentally preparing himself for whatever she was about to hit him with next. After the week he'd had, she was probably about to announce she was pregnant, giving up university, and...

'Dad?' Ellie said, interrupting his runaway train of thought.

'Sorry, zoned out there for a moment. What did you want to have a chat about?'

'You see that woman over there?' Ellie said, gesturing towards Joanna, who'd just beaten Megan.

'Yes, she's on the Oxford Blue crew isn't she?'

'That's right. Well, I heard via a mutual acquaintance of ours that she's been having some trouble with the coach. Her friend wouldn't tell me what exactly, but it sounded like he was sexually harassing her.'

This was not the conversation Joseph had been expecting, but his daughter had his full attention now.

'Really? Someone from our team has already spoken to all the female crew members, but no one is saying anything.'

'They're all terrified of the coach, because he's so well-connected at the university. Apparently, he once claimed that a woman who'd accused him of sexual harassment had made it all up, and got her slung out of college for slander.'

'Jesus, so that's why they're all keeping their mouths shut.' Joseph glanced over at Joanna, who had finished changing into a tracksuit, and was now walking towards a parked Mini.

'Do you think she'll talk to me off the record, or even on it?'

Ellie pulled a face. 'I'm not sure, but knowing how important this is to you, I've already arranged to meet her for coffee tomorrow, between her training sessions. I'm going to try to persuade her that someone needs to speak up, and it should be her.'

'I was actually going to suggest something along those lines, but you beat me to it. You really are a policeman's daughter at heart.'

'I must be, as I seem to be going out with one.'

Joseph shook his head at her. 'Steady there.'

She mock-punched him in the arm. 'Right, where's this alcohol-laden hot chocolate Mum told me about?' she said, steering him back towards the others, as John gave him a worried look.

As well he should, Joseph thought.

CHAPTER SIXTEEN

JOSEPH WAS STILL WAITING in the incident room for Ellie to contact him to say Joanna had agreed to chat with him about Charles Norton, when the phone call everyone on the team had been dreading finally came in.

When Chris's desk phone rang, the DI had been examining the proliferation of red dots that had spread like an outbreak of measles on the map. They showed all the searched sites that had come up empty so far. Maybe police officers have an instinct for bad news, because almost instantly all conversations fell away and their collective gazes turned towards the DCI as he picked up the handset, his face paling as he listened.

That was why, as the rain hammered down on them, Joseph was currently walking with Megan towards a lock in Abingdon where a body had just been discovered.

A deep sense of dread had already taken hold of the DI.

Ahead of them were a scrum of press being kept back from the outer perimeter tape surrounding the incident scene by at least ten uniformed officers. The moment the press spotted the warrant cards hanging from the lanyards around the detectives' necks, a barrage of questions was fired at them.

'So do you believe this to be the body of Millie Dexter?' a woman with a hawkish face and purple-framed glasses shouted louder than the rest.

'No comment,' Joseph said as one of the uniforms raised the tape for them to pass under.

'Do you believe she was being kept captive somewhere in Abingdon?' another man called out.

'Again, no comment,' Joseph replied with his most measured tone as they headed towards the inner perimeter of the cordoned-off area.

'In that case, do you have a statement regarding the failure of the police to find Millie before she was murdered?' another reporter called out. 'Especially after the similar failure during the Hannah Emmerson case?'

Of all the things that might have been asked, that was the one that ignited a cold fury in the DI. When Joseph spun round, he spotted the little fecker who'd asked the question. It was Ricky Holt. He was the sort of journalist that even Kate referred to as a *prize prick of the highest order*. The guy was in his thirties and looked exactly as one might imagine him to, with greased down dark hair, a stupid little quiff at the front, and a permanent expression stuck somewhere between a leer and a sneer.

The bag of snot of a man raised his eyebrows when he realised he'd managed to bait the detective. He thrust his voice recorder towards him with a look that said, *go on then, you know you want to.*

Joseph had clenched his hands into fists when Megan, who had quickly doubled back, appeared before him and gave him the barest of head shakes. That was enough to clear the red mist that was descending. It seemed this little toerag was going to live to see another day. At least Joseph wouldn't be giving Derrick the opportunity of a lifetime to fire him, if he'd punched this arsewipe all the way across the county border in front of a pack of journalists.

'Don't let that bastard bait you,' Megan whispered.

'Aye,' Joseph replied, and with a deep breath, he turned around and headed towards the lock with the DC.

It was a hive of activity, with a fire engine, ambulance, and crews all parked up. The rain somehow managed to grow in intensity, with apparent delusions of becoming a waterfall, as they drew closer to the crime scene.

Joseph braced himself and looked down into the lock. Two divers were sliding a woman's bloated naked body onto a submerged red stretcher. The victim might have once been Millie, but it was hard for Joseph to tell. Her once slim and toned body had become badly swollen, the tongue a sickly grey balloon pressed forward and filled her mouth. It was hard to reconcile the corpse with the woman they had spoken to such a short time ago.

Megan sucked air in between her teeth. 'Bloody hell.'

'I know. I can't help but think that gobshite reporter might have a point. It seems we've let Millie down, just like we did Hannah.'

The DC shook her head. 'With no leads, all we could ever hope to do was get lucky and find her. We certainly tried every-thing we could.'

'Maybe, but even so...' Joseph said, spotting Doctor Jacobs on the other side of the lock, who raised his hand in greeting.

Joseph dipped his chin in acknowledgement as two firemen lowered a line, using an electric winch that had been mounted on the side of the lock.

As the hook lowered towards the body, a collective silence descended. The diver connected the hook to the straps on the stretcher. With a whir, the winch began to slowly haul the woman's body up the wall, the corpse trailing a stream of water from it and sending ripples across the lock to merge with those of the falling rain.

The stretcher was received by the waiting firemen, who placed it on the ground before Doctor Jacobs.

The two detectives crossed the closed lock gate to the other side, and as they neared the body, Joseph saw the angry line cut deep around her neck.

'Oh, bloody hell, it's the same MO as Hannah's murderer,' Megan muttered.

'Yes, and that's a detail we never told the press, meaning this is unlikely to be a copycat,' Joseph replied.

'So you're saying Hannah's murder definitely wasn't a one-off?'

'Yes, which suggests we're indeed dealing with someone on a killing spree.'

Megan shot him a tight-eyed look as the paramedics took hold of the stretcher, and under the watchful eye of Doctor Jacobs, carefully loaded it into the waiting ambulance.

A few moments later, blue lights off, the vehicle headed away along the access road, the scrum of reporters stepping aside to let it pass. Some even had the decency to lower their heads. As Kate kept telling him, not all reporters were like that scumbag Ricky Holt.

Doctor Jacobs headed over to the detectives. 'Do you want to join me to get the results of the autopsy, first-hand?'

'Absolutely. If there is so much as a tiny clue as to who the sick bastard is that did this, I want to know it as soon as possible,' Joseph replied.

'In that case, give me an hour and then head over to the lab. Bring coffee.'

'We'll see you there,' Joseph said, giving Megan a sideways look as he tapped his pocket to check he had a fresh supply of Silvermints on hand.

The sickly sweet smell that had been absent with Hannah's body hit Joseph as they walked into the autopsy room where the victim's body had been laid out on a stainless steel table. The extraction fans were running at full speed, but were doing little to reduce the smell. It reminded the DI of a rotting leg of lamb he'd once had to deal with when his mam's chest freezer had broken down. But this was worse, much worse, and had more than a hint of human faeces to it.

Over the years, Joseph had learnt to suppress the gag reflex triggered by the smell of a dead body, especially one several days dead, but he was already popping a Silvermint into his mouth. He quickly offered Megan one too. Her face had gone pale. Without any argument, she accepted it. Then they both tied their masks as tight as possible to try and keep the stench out.

'Oh good, you're here,' Doctor Jacobs said, looking up from the skin abrasions around the victim's neck he'd been examining with Doctor Reece.

Joseph was relieved to see whatever internal rummaging they had been up to must have been completed, because the woman's chest cavity had been neatly sewn up.

'Those look like the same wire marks around her neck,' Megan said, as she handed over the enormous cups of coffee they'd brought the pathologists.

'That's because they are,' Doctor Reece replied. 'It appears that the victim has been strangled to death with a ligature in exactly the same way that Hannah Emmerson was.'

Joseph nodded as he approached the body, trying to make himself as emotionally detached as possible. 'Is there any confirmation of her identity yet?'

'I already had Millie Dexter's dental records at the ready,

just in case she turned up like this,' Doctor Jacobs said. 'I'm afraid they're an exact match. We also have the father, Geoffrey Dexter, who is coming over to identify his daughter's body.'

'Is that strictly necessary?' Megan asked, staring at him.

'No, it's not. However, like many parents who find themselves in this awful situation, he insisted. There will certainly be no pressure from me to go through with it when he arrives. But as distressing as it is, I suppose confronting death in this way has a finality to it, and actually can be a form of closure. No false hope that we have the wrong person, and all that, so they can get on with the grieving process.'

'But Mr Dexter has no idea what he's letting himself in for,' Megan said.

Doctor Reece shrugged. 'Sadly, the relatives rarely do, especially when the victim has gone through a violent death like this one.'

Joseph gazed at Millie's bloated face, and tried not to imagine it was Ellie on that slab.

As the DI's gaze swept over the woman's body, he noticed for the first time her skin had become transformed into a mosaic of colours, from deep scarlets to yellows and greens, the patterns resembling some sort of exotic marble. There was an almost macabre beauty to it. But then any sense of detachment vanished, and he unexpectedly felt a lump in the back of his throat that he had to swallow down. First Hannah and now Millie...

With considerable effort, he tried again to bury the emotions threatening to erupt, attempting to focus his thoughts. 'So what have you been able to find out so far?'

'It appears that the victim was assaulted, probably more than once, with blows from some sort of blunt object to the body that were hard enough to crack several ribs,' Jacobs replied.

Megan grimaced and wrapped her arms around herself

almost as though she was protecting herself from those imagined blows.

'You can wait outside if this is proving to be a bit much,' Joseph suggested gently.

But the DC shook her head. 'No, I'm good.'

Joseph nodded and proffered her another Silvermint. He knew from experience just how easy it was to picture this sort of violence happening either to yourself or to someone you knew.

Megan took two, slipping them beneath her mask and into her mouth.

'Okay, if we're ready to continue?' Doctor Jacobs asked.

'Go for it,' the DC replied.

'The chest cavity had only just started to fill with gas after being submerged,' he continued. 'That's why it floated back to the surface and was carried down the Thames to the lock.'

Doctor Reece nodded. 'That theory is also supported by the abrasions on the limbs, probably caused by being dragged along the bottom of the river as the corpse gained buoyancy. My current estimate is that the victim died around three days ago. There is also a lack of fluid collection in the pleural cavities, suggesting the victim was dead long before the body was disposed of in the water. Also, the victim's face was discovered in the upwards position, indicating that she didn't die from drowning. The cutaneous changes from immersion—wrinkly skin, before you ask—aren't as pronounced as they could be either. Once again, suggesting that she wasn't in the water for anything longer than seventy-two hours. That's also confirmed by the level of vascular marbling, dark discolouration of the skin and soft tissue, and internal putrefaction of the organs.'

Joseph gestured towards a missing patch of skin about ten centimetres long on her thigh. 'Is being dragged along the riverbed what caused that?'

Jacobs shook his head. 'No. If you look closely, there is a lack of any scratch marks around the edges. It's also far too clean a cut, suggesting that the murderer sliced it off with a very sharp knife. See this scabbing? That proves this was done to the victim whilst she was still alive.'

Megan shuddered. 'Bloody hell, what a fucking monster.'

'I don't think there was ever any question about that,' Joseph replied.

The DC nodded as a phone on the wall chirped. Doctor Reece immediately headed over to it, removed her glove, and picked up the receiver.

'Just give us another five minutes,' she said, before replacing the handset.

Doctor Reece turned back to them. 'Mr Dexter is in reception, ready to identify his daughter.'

Megan's face paled. 'Surely you're going to do something. No father should see their daughter in this state.'

Doctor Jacobs nodded and grabbed a folded sheet from a trolley. He drew it over the corpse leaving only the head exposed, the material high enough to hide the ligature marks on her neck. The face of the woman who had once been Millie was still a gruesome sight, but it was certainly a lot better than exposing the poor man to the full extent of what had happened to her.

Doctor Jacobs turned back to the detectives. 'Okay, that's pretty much the summary of what we've been able to discover so far. As always, if we find anything else out from the lab analysis, it will be in my full report.' He glanced at the wall clock. 'You'll probably want to get out of here before Mr Dexter arrives.'

'Are you sure you're both okay to deal with him, alone?' Megan asked as she closed her notebook.

'Unfortunately, and as difficult as this awful situation is, I've got a lot of experience in dealing with grieving relatives, so leave this to us,' Doctor Reece replied.

Joseph stood for a moment, looking at the covered body. He thought of the hundreds of difficult conversations he'd had over the years, as he'd broken the news to families that someone they loved had been killed. Witnessing someone else's life imploding never got any easier.

Now, somewhere beyond the autopsy room, Geoffrey Dexter would be waiting, a parent whose life was about to be destroyed by a coldhearted killer who had shown his daughter no mercy. As God was his witness, Joseph intended to make the bastard responsible pay for what they'd done.

CHAPTER SEVENTEEN

When an event as awful as Millie's death happened during an ongoing investigation, there was inevitably a moment when the team took a moment to catch their collective breath. There was also an old tradition, where everyone gathered in The Scholar's Retreat. It was a pub that was a straightforward choice for any officer at St Aldates because it was just over the road from the police station. In its way, this was their version of a wake for the victim, where all the officers silently vowed to do better next time.

The pub was filled with most of their investigation team, and also a good number of students. Those were presumably from Christ Church College, which was also over the road, hence the name of the pub. Quite what the scholars there had to retreat from, Joseph had no idea.

There was also the inevitable handful of tourists in the pub, whom you could always spot as they were the ones taking photos of everything with their phones. The Scholar's Retreat was one of the oldest pubs in the city.

Despite the rain bucketing down outside, which hadn't eased up since they'd discovered Millie's body in the lock, it was very cosy inside the pub thanks to the press of bodies filling it. To Joseph, the whole thing felt suffocating. The volume of conversation wasn't exactly helping the headache that had been threatening him all day, either. He felt wrung out to the core of his being. All he really wanted to do was crawl into his bed and sleep. But a tradition was a tradition.

'I still can't believe that we didn't find Millie in time, even after everything we threw into it,' Megan said, nursing a vodka and soda that Joseph had just bought her.

'Unfortunately, that's just part of the job,' Ian said, who had joined them, along with Sue.

Ian's new partner nodded. 'As much as we all would have dearly loved to, as they say, you can't save them all,' Sue said.

'Yes, but still...' Joseph said, finishing the last of his beer.

Ian's gaze tightened on him. 'This must be especially hard on you after the Hannah Emmerson case.'

'Isn't that the truth? Talk about history repeating itself. This is certainly the sort of thing to grind a man's soul down. The one small mercy was, this time I wasn't the one who had to break it to the victim's father.'

Ian sighed. 'I feel for you on that one. That's always one of the worst aspects of the job. But I have to give our DCI his due. Although he didn't have to, Faulkner insisted on taking on that job personally.'

'I have to say the man is doing alright,' Joseph said.

Megan gestured across to Chris nursing a pint in the corner by himself. 'Not that you would know it to look at him.'

Joseph glanced over to see that their SIO was looking as despondent as it was possible for a man to look.

Ian pulled a face. 'Yeah, Chris has obviously taken it badly. That can't have been helped by DSU Wanker laying into him.'

Sue sat up straighter. 'You have gossip?'

Ian leant in conspiratorially towards the group. 'Even

though Wanker's office door was shut, it was hard not to hear. The superintendent was tearing the DCI a second arsehole, so much so that I'm surprised he's here at all.'

Joseph immediately felt a pang of sympathy for the DCI. He knew from bitter experience just what a shite Derrick could be when his back was against the wall. That was when he was at his most dangerous.

'Yes, that's the problem with being in charge of an investigation, the buck stops with you, even if it's not your fault,' Joseph said as he stood up.

'Will that be you getting another round in?' Ian asked, tapping his empty pint glass.

'All in good time, my friend. But first I'm going to have a quiet word with our illustrious leader.'

'Go easy on him, he's probably had a worse day than the rest of us put together,' Megan said.

'Oh, don't you worry about that,' Joseph said, giving her a small smile.

He headed to the bar, quickly scanning the selection of single malts and choosing one of his favourites, a Highland Park, and then ordering two doubles. With drinks in hand, he arrived at Chris's table. He handed one of the Scottish whiskies straight over to the DCI.

Chris gave him a surprised look. 'What's this for?' he asked, as though he suspected Joseph might have spat in it.

'Let's just say, I know exactly what you're going through. May I join you, Boss?'

The DCI nodded, and pointed to the vacant seat opposite him.

Joseph sat down. 'So, how are you doing here?'

Chris sighed. 'As well as you might expect, Joseph, and the superintendent wasn't exactly happy either.'

'I wouldn't take that personally. He's pretty much a shite

with the rest of us most of the time as well.'

That elicited a grin from Chris who nodded. 'Good to know.'

'Anyway, as people keep reminding me, I just wanted to say that we only had the cards that we were dealt on this case. We never had enough to secure Millie's freedom, let alone capture her murderer. So far, at least. At best, we were relying on either getting very lucky, or the killer making a slip-up.'

Chris sighed. 'I know you're right, but it doesn't make this any easier to deal with.'

Joseph sighed. 'Based on personal experience, I have to agree.'

The DCI nodded, then gave him a questioning look. 'Look, I know we haven't always seen eye to eye, but I'm surprised you weren't promoted to DCI years ago.'

Joseph shrugged. 'Enemies in the wrong places, and all that.'

'You mean our mutual friend, the superintendent?'

'I never actually said that, did I?' Joseph asked, raising his eyebrows at him.

Chris chuckled. 'Understood. That aside, I'm someone who likes to make up their own mind about people. So despite what a certain individual told me about you, in my opinion, you're an excellent copper. I'm certainly glad to have you on my team for this investigation.'

'Then that makes two of us,' Joseph replied, raising his glass to Chris's and clinking them together, before taking a sip of the excellent whisky from the distant Isles of Orkney.

A loud bang sounded from the front of the pub as the doors were thrown open, and a burly athletic guy charged in. He was quickly followed by two other men who were unsuccessfully trying to stop him.

The newcomer was so enraged, it took Joseph a moment to recognise him as a rower from the men's Oxford Boat Team.

He'd last seen him training in the gym, lifting weights, during his and Megan's visit to the boat club.

The blond-haired man scanned the room, and spotting Ian and Sue, headed straight over to them.

'I hope you're bloody pleased with yourselves,' he shouted at the detectives, his hands balled into fists. 'Because of your fucking incompetence, Millie is dead!'

The whole pub fell silent, and everyone turned towards the commotion.

Chris and Joseph traded looks as they both stood and squeezed through the crowd towards the brewing altercation.

Ian raised his hands. 'Look, Brian, calm down. I'm really sorry, but there's nothing more we could have done.'

The rower, his jaw set, looked as though he was getting ready to punch the DS's lights out. However, before he had time to lay so much as a finger on Ian, Craig Franks, the cox for the women's team, seemed to appear out of nowhere to stand right in front of the towering Oxford rower.

'Brian, please stop this,' he said, squaring up to the much bigger man. 'Millie wouldn't have wanted any of this.'

The rower stared down at Craig, someone he could easily have thrown aside with just a flick of his hand. But much to Joseph's surprise, the rower's shoulders suddenly dropped and tears filled his eyes.

'But it's all their bloody fault,' Brian said, all the fire and brimstone now completely drained out of his voice.

The cox shook his head. 'No, it isn't, and you know it. It's the bastard who did this to her. And they can't very well arrest them if you've punched their lights out, can they?'

The smallest smile appeared then on the rower's face. 'Yeah...'

Craig patted his shoulder and nodded to the man's two mates, who'd followed him in.

Without a word, they both draped their arms around Brian's shoulders, then gently turned him around, and led him away and out of the pub.

Like this was some sort of Wild West bar, albeit one deprived of a juicy fight, conversations immediately struck up again like nothing had happened, everyone returning their attention to the important matter of drinking.

Craig turned to the gathered detectives. 'I'm really sorry about that, everyone. As you saw, Brian took the news of Millie's death badly. He actually used to be her boyfriend before she broke it off with him.'

'A boyfriend, and why is this the first we're hearing about him?' Megan asked, her eyes narrowing.

'Because the boat crews keep their dramas to themselves, and besides, that was ancient history.'

'Bloody hell, we really could have done with knowing about that sooner rather than later,' Joseph said.

Craig shrugged. 'You would have jumped to the wrong conclusions. Anyway, Brian has moved on and is dating someone new, even if Millie, who dumped him, wasn't.'

Chris raised his eyebrows at the cox. 'You do realise that this could be vital information to our investigation?'

The cox thinned his lips and nodded. 'I know, and I understand now that I should have come forward sooner with it.'

Joseph peered at the lad. 'Aye, you absolutely should have. But that aside, thank you for stepping in with Brian just now. That could have turned ugly real quickly, and at the very least, could have ended up with Brian in a cell to cool his heels.'

'Just as well I intervened, because if Brian had punched a detective, let alone what you would've been forced to do, that would have left the coach with no choice but to sack him from the team. So it wasn't entirely altruistic, Inspector Stone. We need Brian if the men's team is going to have a chance of beating

Cambridge. Anyway, I'd better shoot off and see how he's doing.' With a dip of his chin, Craig turned and disappeared out of the pub in pursuit of his friends.

Chris shook his head. 'That lad really has no idea that he's just dropped Brian in the shit, has he?'

Joseph sighed. 'Not one iota. As a former boyfriend, Brian definitely has to be considered a person of significant interest, and also one with a motive since Millie dumped him.'

'But surely, if he had anything to do with her murder, he would have just kept his head down, rather than charge in here like a bull in a china shop,' Sue suggested.

'Unless he thought someone else was about to tell us that he was her ex,' Megan said. 'This could all have been a performance to put us off the scent.'

Chris scratched the back of his neck. 'It sounds to me like we need to pull him in for a formal interview.'

Joseph nodded. 'I think you're right.' Then he gestured to their table. 'Maybe you would like to join us, Boss, and brainstorm how we handle things from here?'

Chris gave him an unreadable look, then smiled. 'Okay, who needs a fresh drink then? Because technically we're still off duty.'

'Now you're talking,' Ian said, pushing his empty glass across the table towards the DCI.

CHAPTER EIGHTEEN

JOSEPH'S DAD had an old saying, that if you got knocked down you only lost if you stayed down. So it was with the investigation team the following day. Certainly the discovery of Millie's body had been the worst sort of setback, and questions were already being asked in the press about the competency of their investigation. But despite all of that, they were still standing and ready to do whatever they could to bring the murderer to justice. Having a new potential suspect in the form of the Oxford rower, Brian Reed, had also injected fresh vigour into the team. If there had been a determination to catch the murderer before, that drive had been magnified tenfold by the discovery of Millie's body.

That was why they were going over all the evidence again with a fine-tooth comb. No one was giving up just yet. Although no one came out and said it, Joseph suspected part of the major motivation was no one wanted to end up in the same situation they had four years ago with the Hannah Emmerson case. He certainly wouldn't wish that weight of guilt on any of their souls.

As the rain relentlessly poured down outside, Joseph stood with Chris in the incident room, their attention currently focused on the evidence board.

'I got that river current modelling data back from Thames Water,' Megan said, joining them. 'Amy has already had a look at it and according to her analysis of the river speed, the body could have entered the water up to five miles upstream, before being carried down to the Abingdon Lock. According to the lab analysis, the body would have become buoyant because of the gases building up inside it around twenty-four hours before it was carried away by the current.'

Chris studied the map on the board and made a clicking sound with his tongue against his teeth. 'That means the murderer could have disposed of the body by throwing it into the river upstream anywhere within Oxford, or in the surrounding area.'

'I think it could also be significant that the murderer didn't have enough time to dig a grave first, unlike for Hannah Emmerson,' Joseph added.

'So you're saying they were in a hurry to get rid of Millie's body?' Megan asked.

'I think that's a reasonable assumption. Another thing we shouldn't overlook is the autopsy didn't reveal any rodent teeth marks on Millie's body. That suggests to me the time of her death to the disposal of her body was far shorter, compared to Hannah's abduction four years ago.'

'So that once again supports the theory that the murderer was in a hurry, and if so, why the rush?' Chris asked.

'Perhaps they felt under real pressure because of the current investigation?' Megan suggested. 'But that was probably true with Hannah's case, so what's different this time round?'

Joseph turned the thought over in his head. 'Maybe they didn't think it was worth the risk of trying to bury Millie. Especially with the public being on the lookout for any suspicious activity, thanks to the appeal.'

Megan nodded. 'That makes sense. The other possibility is

that maybe one of our searches got closer to where Millie was being held than we realised at the time.'

Joseph studied the map that had been extended to include the location of where Millie's body had been discovered in the Abingdon section of the river.

'There is one common denominator for both murders, and that is the river itself,' he said. 'Both victims were abducted near the Isis, and both of their bodies were recovered near or in it, too. That can't just be a coincidence.'

The DCI narrowed his gaze at him. 'What are you thinking, Joseph?'

'As someone who lives on the canal, I'm wondering whether our killer might do the same. We've thought about that before, but maybe we need to give it a bit more serious consideration. After all, that could explain an awful lot if they can travel up and down the Isis and the Thames on their boat. No one would even notice them. They could have been travelling past when Hannah was out running that morning, and saw an opportunity to grab her from Christ Church Meadow.'

'Okay, but that still doesn't explain how Millie was taken from her home, which is a good half mile from the river,' Chris said. 'Also, why the connection of both murders to the Oxford Boat Team?'

'Then let's try looking at this with fresh eyes,' Joseph said.

He headed over to the whiteboard and picked up a marker. First he changed, *Relationship to Victim?* to *Relationship to Victims?* He tapped on *Boyfriend or Girlfriend?* written beneath it.

Chris nodded. 'Okay, we obviously have a clear lead in Brian Reed, especially since Millie dumped him, but surely he wasn't on the boat team four years ago when Hannah was seized?'

Joseph nodded, and let his gaze travel down the other

options listed beneath it—*Stranger with a fixation on the women's boat team? Fellow team crew member?* And last but definitely not least, *The coach?*

'There is still another possible lead that's worth following up, which could throw up some answers,' the DI said. 'My daughter Ellie has a connection to one of the rowers on the women's Blue team, Joanna Keene. I'm waiting to hear back from Ellie, as she's trying to persuade Joanna to come in and make a statement about Charles Norton.'

'Confirmation that the man is a sexual predator, by any chance?' Megan asked.

'That's what I'm hoping to find out.'

'Certainly any insight we could get into the coach would be incredibly useful, even if we end up eliminating him from our enquiries,' Chris replied. 'You should chase your daughter up as a matter of priority, Joseph.'

'Don't worry, I intend to.' The DI's gaze returned to the evidence board, specifically to the course of the river on the map. 'Also, based on the idea our killer might live on a boat, we should build up an exhaustive list of anyone with moorings along the Isis and Thames, in or near Oxford, and to play things on the safe side, probably now Abingdon as well. Then we could try cross-referencing them to anyone with a connection to the women's boat team. We should include everyone from support staff to the cleaners, but specifically Brian Reed and Charles Norton.'

'Good thinking,' Chris said. 'I'll put people on that straight away. Also, as you suggested, Megan, maybe we got close enough to rattle the murderer during our original searches, so we should send teams out to recheck all the locations we've already covered.'

'Definitely worth a shot,' she replied. 'But what if our killer has already gone to ground?'

A terrible sense of déjà vu took hold of Joseph. 'You do both realise that sounds like a rerun of the Hannah Emmerson case? Maybe that's why there's a four-year gap. So the murderer makes sure that any trail has gone cold, before they strike again.'

'You mean that if we don't catch them this time round, we could be looking at a rerun of this case four years down the road?' Megan asked.

'It's a chilling thought, but there's certainly a chance.'

Joseph's mobile warbled. He fished it out of his pocket to see Ellie's name on the screen.

'It's my daughter,' he said to the others. 'Let's just hope she has good news about Joanna.' He pressed the call-accept icon. 'Please tell me Joanna has agreed to make a statement, Ellie?' he said straight away.

'You can relax. She's going to see you tomorrow, Dad,' Ellie replied. 'It didn't turn out to be too hard to persuade her.'

'Why's that?'

'Apparently, all of the women on the boat teams have been rattled by Millie's murder. From what I can gather from Joanna, quite a few are close to coming forward about Charles Norton themselves. Joanna didn't come straight out and say he's a sex pest, but she talked about the strange mind games he seems to be playing with her. Get this, Dad, that included things being moved around in her flat when she's not there, and items even going missing.'

The tension tightened in the DI's chest as the others stared at him. 'What sort of things exactly?'

'A TV remote went missing, and then appeared in the fridge three days later, something Joanna is adamant she didn't do. She also lost one of her rowing medals.'

Joseph gripped the phone harder in his hand as the magnitude of what his daughter had just said hit him. 'Okay, I need to see her right now, rather than tomorrow, Ellie.'

'But why the rush, Dad?'

He decided not to pull his punch. 'Because her life may be in serious danger.'

The volume of his voice had obviously increased, because everyone had stopped working and were now all openly listening to his conversation.

'Bloody hell,' Ellie replied. 'Right, I'm going to ring her now and tell her to get straight over to the St Aldates station. She lives near there, anyway.'

'Hang on, where exactly?'

'In Paradise Square near the Westgate Shopping Centre.'

Joseph looked at the map. Joanna's flat was less than a quarter of a mile away from Millie's. Once again, everything in this case seemed to be within a stone's throw of the river.

'Do you know exactly where she is now?' Joseph asked, as a deep sense of foreboding took hold.

'She only just left the coffee shop five minutes ago. I can ring her now if you like?'

'Do it, and give her my number. Tell her we're coming to get her straight away.'

'Leave it to me, Dad,' Ellie said. 'I'll do it now.'

As soon as she'd rung off, Joseph turned to Megan and Chris. 'It seems like our murderer isn't going to wait another four years. It also appears that Charles Norton is back in the frame as being our number one suspect.'

Chris nodded as he turned to face the room. 'Right, Ian and Sue, I want Charles Norton's movements kept under close surveillance, twenty-four hours a day, seven days a week, so we can gather the evidence we need for a conviction. That also goes for watching Brian Reed, the member of the Oxford Boat Team. I don't want either man so much as farting without us knowing about it. Also, the moment we have sufficient grounds to formally interview the coach, I want us to be able to immediately lay hands on him. Meanwhile, I don't want to tip him off that he's a major suspect.'

'Leave that to us, sir,' Ian replied, nodding to Sue.

'What about Brian Reed?' Megan asked.

'I think we should pull him in straight away for questioning,' Joseph said. 'Smoke screen or not, he will expect us to want to talk to him after what he did at the pub last night, so let's not disappoint.'

'Okay, we'll pull him in too. I'll interview him personally,' Chris said. 'Meanwhile, Joseph, I want you and Megan to talk to Joanna. This is your lead, so you should run with it.'

Joseph nodded as his mobile warbled again, this time with an unknown number. He took the call immediately.

'Hello, DI Stone?' a woman's voice said.

'Yes...'

'My name is Joanna Keene. Ellie said I needed to contact you straight away.'

'Absolutely. Now tell me exactly where you are, because I'm coming to get you.' Joseph shot Megan and Chris a relieved look.

If the murderer was about to strike again, this time they had a real chance to not only stop them, but catch them, too. As worrying as this development was, it could also be the breakthrough they'd all been waiting for.

CHAPTER NINETEEN

JOANNA SAT opposite Megan and Joseph in interview room one. She was wearing a dark blue tracksuit with the Oxford rowing team logo of two crossed oars beneath a crown on the breast. Without the swimming cap she'd worn the last time Joseph had seen her during the river race, her curly brunette hair was now revealed.

The rower clasped her hands together as she looked at the two of them with worried hazel eyes. 'Are you seriously suggesting that you think my life is in danger?'

'I wouldn't have pulled you in like this if we didn't,' Joseph replied. 'There are far too many similarities to what happened before Millie's disappearance. Ellie tells me you had your TV remote moved in your flat, and a medal of yours is missing. Is that right?'

'Yes, and the TV remote wasn't just down the back of the sofa, I actually found it in the fridge. And I absolutely swear that when I looked in there the day before, it simply wasn't there. That wasn't the only thing, either. I found a pair of knickers on my bed last night, and I certainly didn't put them there. I can't tell you how much that's spooked me.'

'I'm not surprised,' Megan replied.

Joseph checked the red light for the voice recorder was on. This was already crucial information, and he wanted to make sure they didn't miss a single word of it. Satisfied everything was in order, he then nodded to Megan to take the lead with the interview. This was something they'd agreed on beforehand. That was partly because he was keen to give the junior officer the experience, but also because he thought Joanna might respond better to another female.

Megan leant forward in her chair, clutching her hands together to mirror Joanna's posture. 'Exactly how long has this been happening?'

'For about a month now.'

Joseph traded a worried look with Megan. Yes, the timing was definitely significant. It sounded like the murderer was already lining up his next victim, even whilst they'd been holding Millie prisoner.

'I see,' Megan continued. 'And this all happened at your flat in Paradise Square?'

'That's right, and before you ask, no one else apart from my landlord has a key to my flat.'

'So the obvious question is whether your landlord could have let themself in?'

'I strongly doubt it. I live on the first floor and my landlord is eighty-five and confined to a wheelchair. He couldn't have managed the stairs unless he crawled up them.'

Joseph scribbled that titbit down. They would still need to run a background check on the man, and also any previous tenants who might have had access to the keys.

'Do you have any idea who might be doing this to you?' Megan continued.

Joanna directed her attention towards Joseph. 'I've already

told Ellie this, DI Stone, but I'm certain that it's something to do with our coach, Charles Norton.'

A sense of anticipation filled Joseph, and despite meaning to take a backseat in this interview, he couldn't help but ask, 'Why do you think that, Joanna?'

The young woman cast a wary eye towards the voice recorder. 'Do I need to say this on the record?'

Megan gave her a reassuring look. 'I can't stress to you enough how important this could be.'

Conflicting emotions crossed Joanna's face before she finally nodded.

'Okay...' Joanna took another deep breath. 'To be blunt, it's like this. Charles Norton is a player.'

'You're saying that he approached you for sex?'

She nodded, looking distinctly uncomfortable.

'Sorry, can you give us a verbal confirmation for the benefit of the tape?' Megan said.

Joanna leant closer to the voice recorder. 'Yes, Charles Norton approached me shortly after I first joined the women's boat team. He made it very clear that he fancied me and wanted to take it further.'

'How did he do that exactly?' Megan asked.

'He suckered me in with praise at first, saying that with my rowing form, I could be the president of the women's Blue team. It started innocently enough, him suggesting we meet for coffee. But coffee turned into dinner, turned into me having too much to drink, turned into us ending up in bed together.' She shrugged. 'The same old story, and I'm old enough to know better.'

'You're saying he seduced you?' Joseph asked.

'Yes, basically. But I can't lie—at first, I was flattered by the attention and it was all mutual...' She pulled a face. 'I know what you're thinking. Yes, I knew he was a married man, but I got involved anyway.'

'We're not here to judge you, Joanna, we just want to get to the facts,' Megan said. 'Was this a one-off, or did your affair carry on for any length of time?'

'Oh, it was never about a one-night stand with Charles. At first, it was all champagne and roses, but then he seemed to get bored with me, and even called me his "shag bunny" to my face. Eventually, I came to my senses, but when I told Charles I wanted to end it, that's when things turned ugly.'

'In what way?' Joseph asked, sitting up as he sensed they were heading towards pure gold.

'He started to bully me during training sessions. Then he slowly escalated things, belittling me in front of the others, generally making life unpleasant. But then he showed just what a bastard he truly was. Charles told me that if I breathed a word about it to anyone, especially to you guys when you started asking questions at the rowing club, he would make sure I was not only kicked out of the club but also out of the college. That would have ended any chance of a career for me in quantum computing research before I'd even started. That was too high a price for not keeping my mouth shut.'

'So, just so we can be clear on this, during your affair with Charles Norton, it was consensual sex, and he never attempted to rape you?' Megan asked.

'No, not once, although he was rather a fan of rough sex, but never crossed the line into anything beyond that,' Joanna replied.

'So why exactly are you stepping forward now and making a statement?' Megan asked.

'Two reasons. One is that Ellie can be very persuasive when she wants to be.'

'And the second?' Joseph asked, trying to suppress a smile.

'I learnt Charles had also been having an affair with Millie at almost exactly the same time he was going out with me. The bastard was two-timing his mistresses, along with his wife. Inevitably, I found out, and I confronted Millie. She broke down, saying that Charles had relentlessly preyed on her until she cracked, even though she was going out with Brian Reed from the men's team. That's why she broke things off with both men. She just couldn't handle the guilt. Then she decided to leave Oxford for a fresh start. But like I said, the coach is a player, and this was all part of the game for him, sod the cost to the women's lives he wrecked. I just wish I'd seen him for the misogynist pig he really is. Anyway, when Millie turned up dead, I knew I had to come forward, even if I needed a bit of a nudge from your daughter to pluck up the courage to do so.'

'Because...?' Joseph said, keen not to put words in her mouth because that might one day be seized on by a defence solicitor.

'Because, as crazy as it sounds, I can't help but think that Charles might have murdered Millie to make sure she didn't say anything. I actually admired her for the way she stood up to him, but maybe that's what tipped the coach over the edge, and he silenced her for good.'

Joanna took a long sip of water and the DI noticed just how steady her hand was. Her gaze had also become harder the more she'd spoken. This was a woman on a mission, determined to do the right thing, even if it had taken her a while to arrive at that decision.

'You really believe that Charles Norton is capable of murder?' Megan asked.

'All I know is, desperate people can do desperate things,' Joanna replied. 'Maybe he realised if any of this ever came out, then not only would his marriage be over, but his career here in Oxford, too. The university wouldn't want anything to do with a man who abused his position with students.'

'Yet, despite suspecting that, you've come forward anyway, even though, at the very least, it might cost you your place in Oxford?' Joseph asked.

'In the end, I didn't really have a choice. I owe it to Millie's memory, not to mention that other rower who was murdered.'

'You're talking about Hannah Emmerson?' Megan asked.

'Yes. From what I hear, the coach has been trying to seduce female students like this for years. As I see it, if he murdered Millie, there's no reason to think he didn't kill Hannah as well.'

'But you don't know that for a fact, and this is just a suspicion, correct?' Joseph asked.

'Call it instinct, but it all fits. A bad man in the right place at the right time.'

'If you really believe that, you must be worried about an attempt on your own life.'

'I'd be stupid not to be. As soon as Charles hears I've done this, who knows what he'll do?'

Joseph shook his head. 'We're going to do whatever we have to in order to make sure you're safe.' But even as the DI spoke those words, the seed of a plan was starting to blossom in his brain. 'There's one more thing I'd like to ask you about. What are your thoughts about Brian Reed?'

'Everyone who knows Brian loves him, even if he is impulsive at times. Him charging into a pub everyone knows is filled with police officers, looking to punch one, is a perfect example.'

'Yes, we were both there, and he was clearly upset about what happened to Millie,' Megan said.

'We're all upset, but Brian especially. Even after they broke up, he always held a candle for her.'

Megan nodded. 'So, how did he react when Millie left him?'

'Badly. He went to pieces at first. But his friends rallied round him, and kept him focused on his other true love, rowing.'

Joseph narrowed his eyes at her. 'Okay, but do you think he

was upset enough to do something stupid?'

Joanna looked at him, and then her eyes widened. 'If you mean stupid enough to murder Millie, then absolutely not. No way. I know this will sound out there after what he did in the pub, but that man is a gentle giant and he wouldn't hurt a flea.'

The DI sat back, turning what she'd just said over in his mind. The more Joseph thought about it, the more unlikely it seemed Brian would want to draw their attention to himself, although he still wasn't prepared to rule anything out just yet.

He finally nodded. 'Thank you so much, Joanna, for having the courage to come forward. This has all been a tremendous help to our investigation. I'm just going to pause the tape for a moment whilst I confer with my colleague.' Joseph leant over and stopped the recorder, and the red light blinked off.

'Is there anything we can get you?' Joseph asked, as both detectives stood.

'A coffee would be fantastic, but I really need to get out of here as soon as possible. Our next training session is due to start in thirty minutes. There's only three days left until the Oxford and Cambridge Boat Race on Saturday, and literally every second of training counts now.'

'I had no idea it was that soon,' Joseph replied. 'Anyway, don't worry, we won't hang onto you any longer than we have to.' He nodded to Megan, who followed him into the corridor and closed the door behind them.

'Thoughts?' Joseph immediately asked.

'Despite Charles having an alibi for the time of the abduction, I think he has to be our number one suspect based on what Joanna just told us.'

'Maybe, but we'll need a watertight case for the CPS if we're going to have a chance of prosecuting him. So far, we've only heard Joanna's opinions that he *might* be capable of murder, rather than any hard evidence. We can't even be sure it was Norton who broke into those women's apartments and moved things round.'

'What about Brian?'

'Once again, we're dealing with Joanna's opinion of him. Just because he's a nice guy doesn't mean he isn't capable of murder under the right circumstances.'

'So you're saying we should still treat both men as suspects?'

'Absolutely, but next we get to the thorny subject of what we do with Joanna.'

'Her training be damned. Obviously we can't let her out of this station without police protection,' Megan replied.

'Yes, that would be the sensible option, but I do have an alternative suggestion. We actually let Joanna walk out of here and go to her next training session.'

Megan stared at the DI as though he had a screw loose. 'You can't be serious, Joseph. That could put her life in danger.'

He raised his hands. 'Slow down there and hear me out. I'm going to propose to Chris that we use Joanna to lure the murderer into a trap. We'll have surveillance on her at all times. The moment the killer makes their move, we arrest them.'

'You're seriously suggesting that we use Joanna as bait, and potentially put her life on the line?'

'I know it's not ideal, and we would only do it if Joanna agrees, but this way, we capture this bastard and put them away for a very long time. Trust me, this will work.'

'Bloody hell, Joseph,' Megan said. 'I just hope you're right about your instincts on this one.'

'Not half as much as I do. I know this is a gamble, but sometimes the potential rewards really do outweigh the risks.'

Megan gave him a sceptical look that told the DI she was not convinced, but even then, experience told him this was the right way to proceed if they were to have a chance of catching the murderer. He just hoped Chris would agree.

CHAPTER TWENTY

It was the third night in a row that Joseph and Megan had sat in the unmarked Peugeot on the other side of the road from Joanna's maisonette. Ian was parked around the back in another unmarked car on an access road.

A Ford Transit Cargo Van belonging to the TST, technical surveillance team, was parked further away to avoid drawing too much suspicion. The two officers inside were monitoring the live feeds from the hidden cameras that had been installed inside the flat. The hope was the stalker would make another visit to continue their campaign of psychological games with Joanna, and the moment they did they would catch them in the act.

Despite the rapidly escalating costs, Derrick had signed off on the surveillance operation. But, true to form, the superintendent had insisted that the size of the team Chris had asked for to be cut back. Despite capturing the murderer being an obvious priority, it seemed Derrick was still prepared to penny-pinch.

The number of officers they had on the ground was about half of what Joseph would have liked. But as Chris had rightly pointed out, the more people they used for the operation, the more likely that Joanna's stalker might notice something was off and abort any attempt to enter her flat.

Joseph finished the cold Moroccan meatball sandwich from the provisions he and Megan had stocked up on for their shift of the stakeout.

'Even though the wrap went soggy, that was still delicious,' Joseph said, washing it down with the last of the coffee from his thermal-insulated mug, in his opinion one of the most essential bits of kit for any stakeout

Megan nodded as she finished her green drink with a thoroughly unnecessary loud slurp. 'That smoothie was really good, even if it cost me an arm and a leg.'

'It was certainly a lot to pay for something that looked like pond scum,' Joseph replied. 'I could always dredge the river for you and save you a few quid.'

Megan rolled her eyes at him. 'Ha, ha, ha.'

Joseph grinned as he reached forward to wipe down the windscreen for at least the tenth time that night.

The DC peered out through it at the glistening layer of frost covering everything, and zipped her coat up to her neck. 'Bloody hell, it's nippy in here. It's a shame that we can't run the engine, so we could at least keep warm.'

'Unfortunately, that would only draw attention to our presence,' Joseph replied. 'If we had an electric car in the vehicle pool, it would be a different story. Ian was telling me his dad has one and you can keep the heater on even when the car isn't moving. That would be the bee's knees for stakeouts like this.'

'I'm sure DSU Walker will immediately authorise the purchase of a Tesla when he hears that, just so we can keep toasty warm.'

'If only the big man was wired that way. But knowing how he likes to keep a stranglehold on the budget, he'd probably suggest we use hot water bottles, and only then, if we paid for them ourselves.'

Megan snorted. 'True. So much for me thinking that a stakeout would be glamorous.'

'You, Megan, have obviously watched too many American movies.'

'Guilty as charged. Although, maybe I should put in for a transfer to a Miami Narcotics team.' She made a pretend pistol with her hands, shooting invisible bad guys through the windscreen.

Joseph just raised his eyebrows at her before checking his watch. 'Jesus, nearly 2 am, and not so much as a dog walker.'

'At this time of night, are you surprised?'

The DI shook his head as his gaze travelled to the first floor windows of the maisonette where Joanna would currently be sleeping in her bed. Her windows, as they had been all night, remained dark.

A chirp came from his phone, and he took the call. At the same time, an alert for a message from Dylan popped up on his screen.

'Have you seen anything, Ian?' Joseph asked, ignoring the text message for now.

'Not so much as a rat taking a leak. Also, I just checked in with TST, and they have nothing to report either.'

'So, once again, maybe tonight will be another no show.'

'All I know is I'm looking forward to the relief teams stepping in to take over at 5 am. But what I wouldn't do for a kebab from the Station Grill, right now.'

'Sadly, I don't think even Deliveroo will bring it out to us at this ungodly hour.'

Joseph's phone buzzed as another message came through from Dylan, which he ignored again.

'Oh, don't I know it,' Ian replied. 'Someone should have a

word with the criminal fraternity about the bloody awful hours they keep. They really have no consideration for anyone else.'

Joseph chuckled. 'Isn't that the truth. Anyway, we'll be in touch if we see anything suspicious.'

'Ditto. Now back to the serious business of trying to beat the Wordle score that Sue managed during her shift. Two bloody goes she took to crack it. I tell you, the woman's a flipping cheat and probably looked up the answer.'

'I'll let her know you said that. Anyway, have fun.'

'I'll do my best,' Ian replied.

As Joseph rang off, he read Dylan's first message. *'Call me as soon as you get this. I think I've worked out how Millie's abductor may have broken into her flat.'* The second message contained a map of central Oxford, with a blue line running through it.

Given the late hour, Joseph knew for the professor to contact him, it had to be really important. He pressed the call-back button.

The professor picked up on the first ring. 'Thank goodness! I realise you're staking out Joanna's flat, but this is too urgent to wait until morning, Joseph. I couldn't sleep because I knew I had the answer to this riddle somewhere in this brain of mine. Then I finally remembered.'

'Go on then, tell me how Millie's abductor pulled off their Houdini act?'

'I should have thought of this before now,' Dylan replied. 'He used the sewer.'

'No, don't you remember? I told you we already looked into that. The sewers there are too narrow for a person to crawl through.'

'Maybe the modern ones that run through the area, but not a disused medieval one that still exists today, but isn't on any of the sewer maps. And this is where it gets really interesting. It runs almost directly under Millie's house and opens out back onto the Isis on one end, and a stream is linked to it at the other. Famously, Lawrence of Arabia once kayaked through it, and it's still passable today, at least when the water isn't too high.'

'Hang on, you're seriously suggesting that's how our suspect was able to enter Millie's flat and leave it again, by using this old sewer?'

Megan's eyes widened as she listened to their conversation.

'I can't be sure, but I think it's a good bet. The only fly in the ointment is that I'm not aware of there being any other ways in or out of it, apart from the exits at either end. So I have no idea how the murderer might have been able to enter or exit the stream near her flat. That aside, if you check my other message, you'll see that I sent you a map with an overlay for the course of the ancient sewer.'

'Bloody hell, Dylan, like usual, you're a regular superstar.'

'Anytime, Joseph. But now I really must take to my bed as the dogs will still demand their walks first thing, sleep or no sleep. So good hunting, my old friend.' The call clicked off.

'You caught most of that?' Joseph asked, as he pulled up the second message the professor had sent him.

Megan gave him a sharp nod. 'If the murderer used a small boat, they could have transported Millie away in it.'

Joseph opened up the Google maps image with the blue line for Trill Mill Stream, which was apparently the modern name for the ancient disused sewer, superimposed over it.

'Now, will you look at that,' Joseph said, pointing to where one end came out right next to Christ Church Meadow. 'That's where Hannah vanished when she was jogging.'

'Oh, my God!' Megan said as she pointed to the other end of the blue line.

Joseph peered at where she was indicating, his eyes widening. Not only did the old sewer run directly under Joanna's home, which they were currently parked next to, but it also seemed to open out into one of the many watercourses of Oxford crisscrossing the city. More significantly, that exit was about three hundred metres to the west of where they were parked.

'That's too much to be a coincidence,' Joseph said, shaking his head. 'Using that old sewer, the killer would have their very own secret water highway that they could use to travel around this part of central Oxford, and all totally unseen. Even if they had their victims with them, they could have covered them with a tarp and no one would have been any the wiser when they emerged onto the Isis.'

Megan was nodding when she suddenly pointed to an upstairs window of Joanna's flat.

'What?' he asked, looking up.

'I swear I spotted something from the corner of my eye. Just the briefest movement in the upper-story window. But it's probably just Joanna going to the loo.'

'Better to be safe than sorry,' Joseph said as he punched in the number for the TST.

A woman picked up almost immediately. 'DI Stone, we were about to ring you. We're suffering some sort of technical glitch; all our cameras just went offline.'

The DI's stomach knotted into a tight ball. 'Shite! Alert Ian that we may have an intruder in Joanna's house, and get your arses to the property right now.'

'Will do,' the woman said.

But Joseph wasn't waiting for anyone. He burst from the Peugeot and raced across the street, with Megan close behind him.

As the DI reached the door to the maisonette, he thumped on it and then pressed the doorbell which remained ominously silent.

Megan ducked down to the height of the letterbox and opened it. 'Joanna, are you okay in there?'

They heard a muffled crash coming from somewhere inside the property.

'Help me!' Joanna's voice screamed.

Without hesitating, Joseph kicked at the door once, twice, cracking the frame around the lock. Baton at the ready, he shoulder-charged it and it flew open.

Just behind them, the TST officers arrived at the front door.

Megan tried the light switch behind her. 'Power's out,' she said.

Joseph's blood ran cold. This was already following the same MO that the Millie Dexter case had. Kill the power, but this time they'd also managed to take out the hidden cameras that ran on their own power supply as well.

Joseph hurtled up the stairs into the flat, ahead of the others. The first thing he saw was a wide open back door leading out to a set of steps down to a small garden at the rear.

His chest tightened. 'Joanna!'

'In here,' her voice called back.

The DI burst into the bedroom to see Joanna sitting on her bed, sobbing.

She looked up at the detectives as they entered. 'A man was just in here, but disappeared when he heard you bashing on the front door.'

'Then he can't have got far,' Joseph replied. He punched the number for Ian's mobile, only to discover he had no signal. 'Why the hell isn't my phone working? This isn't a dead zone.'

One of the TST officers, a big guy built like a rugby player, appeared with a black router-like box with a series of aerials sticking out of it.

'It's because of this jammer. That's what took the cameras down, and all our phones as well. The thing is powered by batteries, but I just turned it off, so you should get reception again any moment now.'

Joseph pushed past him into the corridor to see a female TST officer.

'No sign of anyone anywhere else in the flat,' she said.

The DI nodded, as a worrying thought spun inside his brain. Why hadn't Ian spotted the intruder entering through the back door?

Joseph headed out through it onto the top of steps, looking over the rear fence at the Volvo Ian had parked in the lane. The driver's door was open, and his heart clenched when he spotted Ian sprawled on the ground next to the vehicle, not moving.

Joseph whirled around. 'Officer down!' he shouted inside.

The male TST officer thundered down the stairs and out the front, as Joseph headed down the steps and into the garden.

'Where are you going?' Megan asked, appearing in the doorway.

'Whoever it is, they can't have got far. Somewhere round here there has to be the entrance to that old sewer, and I intend to bloody find it.' Joseph checked his phone signal and, seeing it was back, quickly sent the map image to Megan's phone. 'Use this to stand guard over the other end of the old sewer in Christ Church Meadow and call for backup.' He turned to the female TST officer. 'You stay here and keep guard over Joanna.'

Both women gave him a nod.

He turned on his phone's torch as he spun away, his eyes scanning for any hint that might show that their suspect had come this way. Then he spotted the clear impressions of shoe prints in the frost on the grass, one set heading up to the rear flat steps from the garden, and another trailing away.

Less than a minute had passed since they'd first entered the flat. He still had a chance to catch the bastard.

Joseph directed his phone's torch into every corner of the small garden, but there was nothing more than a rusting barbecue and some battered plastic garden chairs. There certainly wasn't a manhole cover in sight, and he couldn't see any more shoe prints.

A sinking feeling was already filling the DI's stomach as he pulled up Dylan's map again, trying to match it to the layout of buildings around him. According to the blue line, Joseph was standing right on top of the sewer, but he was damned if he could spot the entrance to the fecking thing.

He checked the map once more. The end of the blue line showed where the old sewer emptied into the stream, and it wasn't too far.

He began moving towards it, trying to follow the path of the blue line on the map.

As Joseph reached the rear of the garden, he hauled himself over a fence into the lane Ian had been watching. He saw the TST officer had reached the DC and was checking his pulse. As much as Joseph's instinct was to rush over and help, he needed to keep on the intruder's trail.

Just opposite him was a grove of trees, leaves lit by an amber streetlight and casting deep shadows. But it was the railings just beyond that, which bordered one of Oxford's many streams, that seized his attention.

Joseph raced towards them. A few moments later, he was staring down into the rapidly flowing water, swollen from all of the rain over the last few days. Quickly, he checked the map again. According to it, he had to be right on top of the sewer's exit. Unable to see anything yet, the DI leaned over the railing as far as he could, aiming his phone's torch down and back towards the wall beneath him.

Then he spotted it, the top of an arched tunnel less than a metre above the surface of the fast-moving stream, but still just about high enough to pass a small boat through with someone lying flat down inside it.

His every instinct was screaming at him there was a chance that Joanna's would-be abductor was still in the tunnel. They could, of course, have headed to the other end where hopefully Megan was standing guard by now, but odds were they would try to escape through the shorter section and exit the sewer here. Then the intruder could easily head back to the Isis to make their escape. This might be his one and only chance to catch them before the trail went cold again.

Before he could challenge his impulse of utter stupidity, Joseph lowered himself over the railing towards the sewer's exit. As his feet plunged into the icy water, the current grabbed hold of him. He knew from memory the stream wasn't usually that deep here, but he was still concerned the swollen water might be strong enough to carry him away before he could enter the tunnel. Then he thought of Hannah and Millie's bodies in the autopsy room. That was all the motivation he needed to take the next desperate step.

Joseph let go and dropped straight into the stream.

Frigid water clamped around his chest like a fist as the water surged up to his neck before his feet struck the bottom. The current slammed into his body like a hammer blow, pushing him sideways. He had just enough time as he was carried past to reach out and grab onto the edge of the tunnel. Fighting to hang on, his phone was torn from his hand and carried away by the torrent, the small pool of light it had been casting in the sewer entrance disappearing. Before him, the tunnel was now nothing but a dark mouth of shadows. But somewhere in there, the murderer could still be getting ready to make their escape.

With Herculean effort, Joseph heaved himself over the lip of the tunnel entrance and into the old sewer. As Joseph gathered himself, breathing hard, part of his caveman brain baulked at the idea of heading into the primordial darkness ahead of him. But he swallowed his fear and did it anyway.

He walked into utter gloom with his arms out to touch the top of the arched ceiling, slimy algae sliding under his fingertips as he went.

Moving further away from the exit, the sound of the fast-running stream grew fainter behind him as night clamped in around him, the stench of putrid mud filling his nose.

So much adrenaline was powering through his system that, despite the freezing water, his body was humming, ready for whatever was going to happen next. But he also knew that, down here in this hellhole, he was totally alone and without any backup. That seemed to be something he had a certain knack for. Some might even say it was a calling.

Joseph edged forward, occasionally stumbling on something unseen on the floor of the old sewer beneath the waterline. The darkness and the quiet were so complete that it seemed like his breath thundered in the confined space.

Right at the edge of his hearing, the sound of gentle, rippling water reached his ears. Before Joseph could react, something hard smashed into his chest like a wrecking ball and he was shoved aside as an object slid past him. He tried to reach out and grab whatever it was, and felt wood scrape beneath his fingers.

A boat, it had to be.

But even as Joseph desperately tried to grab onto it, something came crashing down onto his head. Then the darkness rushed into his mind. He lost consciousness and toppled backwards into the icy water.

CHAPTER TWENTY-ONE

LIGHT PRESSED in on Joseph's eyelids before they fluttered open to reveal he was lying on a bed in a dimly lit room.

'Oh, thank God, you're awake at last,' Megan's voice said from close by.

As Joseph's eyes focused, he took in the white walls, and a lone bedside light casting a soft glow across what had to be a hospital room. The hands on the clock above the door showed it was five o'clock. That had to be the early version of five, going by the darkness visible through the slats of the blind in a window. In a chair next to the bed, Megan pulled off the blanket she'd covered herself with and looked at him with a palpable sense of relief.

Joseph sat up in bed, a teeth-grinding headache making itself known.

'Feck, what the hell happened?' Joseph asked, helping himself to a glass that had been filled with water and sipping it to relieve the desperate dryness of his throat.

'To start with, you're lucky to be alive. We're assuming Joanna's intruder hit you over the head and left you to drown. Thankfully, Martin Seven, one of the TST officers, began a search of the immediate area when you didn't respond to their calls. Luckily for you, he spotted you floating on your back as you drifted back out of the old sewer and into the stream.'

'Jesus, that was a close call.'

Megan nodded. 'If Martin hadn't dived in and pulled you out, I'd probably be visiting you in the morgue right now. I think you may owe him a drink, as you would have almost certainly drowned otherwise.'

'At the very least,' Joseph said. His fingers probed a large bandage that covered the wound on the top of his head where he'd been struck, and he flinched as a spike of pain went through his skull.

Megan grimaced. 'Yes, ten stitches, I'm afraid. They've already given you a CT scan; thankfully, that all looked fine. The doctors said to let nature take its course and that you would wake up eventually.'

Joseph's memories of what had happened rushed back. Something, almost certainly a boat, had loomed out of the darkness and then he'd been struck over the head.

'The bastard hit me with something—an oar, I think.'

'That would make sense. Amy has already been in to see you and said that the trauma looked like it was caused by a blow with the edge of some sort of flat object.'

Joseph nodded, immediately regretting it as it made his head pound, but then the image of Ian out cold, lying on the road by his car, filled his mind.

'Jesus, what happened to Ian? Please tell me he's alright.'

Megan immediately held up her hands. 'Relax, Joseph. He's doing fine now and only has a slight concussion. He's in a room a couple down from you, and apparently he's already demanding his body weight in grapes—oh, and a kebab.'

That last detail made Joseph smile. 'Then we need to make sure he gets one.'

The DC leant forward in her chair. 'Now, for the million-dollar question everyone is dying to know. Did you see who attacked you?'

'Didn't get a chance. It was absolutely pitch black in that sewer. I would've been lucky to see my hand in front of my face, let alone whoever clobbered me over the head. But what about Ian or Joanna? Did either of them get a clear look at our attacker?'

'I'm afraid not. Ian got out of the car when he thought he heard something. That's when someone snuck up behind him and knocked him out.'

Joseph groaned. 'That's exactly why there should always be two officers in a car during a stakeout.'

Megan nodded. 'Yes, DCI Faulkner is already on the warpath about that one. According to the grapevine, he made a point of getting the DSU out of his bed to shout at him, saying if he'd had proper resources, none of this would have happened.'

'So what about Joanna? Did she get a look at the intruder?'

'No, she was fast asleep when a man grabbed her by the throat and was trying to force something over her mouth that smelled of chemicals. The assumption is that it was chloroform.'

Joseph nodded, almost swearing as another spike of pain hit him. But he needed to ask the most important question of all.

'Just please tell me you caught the bastard?'

The corners of Megan's mouth turned down. 'I'm so sorry to be the one to have to break it to you, but there's no sign of the intruder after they escaped down that stream in their boat.'

A stone ball filled the DI's gut. 'Right... This is all my fault, Megan. I almost had the toerag in my grasp, but I let them slip away.'

'No, this isn't on you. Even Chris said that. Although, he is furious that you headed into a potentially dangerous situation without any backup. Mind you, if he's furious, I'm incandescent. What the hell were you thinking, Joseph?'

'What can I say? Apart from it seemed like a good idea at the time.'

'Next time, for God's sake, take a moment to think or you'll have me to answer to.'

Joseph snapped her a salute. 'Right you are, sir.'

She gave him an exasperated look, followed by a small smile. 'You're impossible, Joseph.'

'I'm told that's one of my better qualities.'

Megan laughed as she shook her head at him.

'Okay, you'd better get me up to speed with what's been happening,' he said. 'I imagine DCI Faulkner is throwing everything, including the kitchen sink, at trying to catch our intruder?'

'You better believe it. The DCI has pulled everyone in. He even demanded Walker give him unlimited manpower for the investigation.'

'That's great news, and in that case, can you find my clothes for me and we can head into the station?'

Megan stared at him. 'Are you stark raving bonkers? You can't go anywhere. You just suffered a concussion and need to rest.'

Joseph waved a dismissive hand at her. 'To hell with that. A couple of Ibuprofen and I'll be as right as rain. All I need for you to do is distract whoever is on the desk long enough for me to make my escape.'

'You, Joseph, are as stubborn as a bloody mule.'

'You better believe it,' he said, grinning at her as he swung his legs off the bed.

When Megan and Joseph turned up at the station around 6 am, it was already a hive of activity. It looked like there wasn't a single desk that didn't have a half-finished cup of coffee, as everyone attempted to sharpen their brains with a caffeine hit.

As soon as they entered the room, all conversations fell away.

Joseph immediately raised his palms. 'It's worse than it looks, but I'm fine, thanks for asking.'

There were a lot of relieved expressions as Chris came over. 'Is that a doctor's definition of *fine*, or DI Stone's self-diagnostic version?'

Megan raised her eyebrows at him. 'What do you think, Boss?'

Chris shook his head at Joseph. 'What would happen if I ordered you to return to the hospital?'

'I think you might find me suddenly very hard of hearing,' Joseph replied.

The DCI smiled, and Megan rolled her eyes.

'You are a right royal pain in the arse, DI Stone, but then again, I wouldn't have you any other way,' Chris said.

'Glad to hear it, because I'm unlikely to change anytime soon. Now, what's been happening here?'

'We've sent a lot of uniforms out to begin an intensive search along the river, concentrating our efforts on every single boat moored up along it. Police launches are travelling up and down the Isis to see if they can find anything. We're also hitting local radio and social media hard, asking people to keep a lookout for any suspicious activity, especially along the river. Also, despite the early hour, we've already had divers checking along that sewer to see if they could find anything, and we struck gold there. They discovered two recently excavated tunnels, leading to the nearby gardens of Millie Dexter and Joanna Keene's flats. The bastard seems to have burrowed up under a neighbour's compost heap near Millie's flat, and beneath a shed near Joanna's, removing the boards so they could sneak in and out without being seen.'

'So you're saying that our murderer spent a long time planning this?' Megan asked.

'It certainly seems that way. Oh, and the TST guys have confirmed that the jammer retrieved from Joanna's flat prevented the victims from being able to ring for help. Whoever is responsible obviously didn't mean to leave it behind, but they were in a rush when you started knocking on the front door.'

'Okay, so what about our two chief suspects?' Joseph asked. 'Where were they during all of this?'

'Brian was definitely at home. All access points in and out of his student accommodation were closely monitored. According to our surveillance team, he entered his flat at ten last night, and didn't leave it until about ten minutes ago, when he apparently set off for an early morning training session with the boat team. We're as certain as we can be that he was home all night, as there is no other way out of the apartment block.'

'That sounds like it rules him out as a prime suspect. What about Charles Norton?'

Chris clenched his jaw. 'There, it's not so clear cut. He entered his family home, which backs onto the canal in north Oxford, at 9 pm last night, but there's no footpath. That was why we'd written it off as a way out of the house. That was, until this morning, when he turned up at the boat club thirty minutes ago without having been seen leaving the house. It turns out that occasionally the coach likes to take a single-person scull boat to work.'

'Jesus, why didn't anyone ask me?' Joseph said. 'I could have told you that at least half the houses along that stretch have a small boat to use on the canal.'

'Yes, an oversight on my part, and I won't be doing that

again. From now on, I intend to work far more closely with you, Joseph, and make full use of your considerable experience and expertise.'

The DI gave the younger man a straight look, but couldn't see any hint he was taking the piss. He actually seemed to mean what he was saying. It looked to be that this newfound mutual respect was starting to run both ways.

Megan was glancing between them, obviously not quite sure how to process this new relationship between Joseph and their senior officer.

'That's good to hear, Boss,' the DI replied. 'As for Norton, if he slipped our surveillance net, he certainly could have been the one at Joanna's last night. Also, whoever hit me over the head was definitely using a boat of some kind.'

'It's certainly easy to imagine the coach, who by all accounts is a top-class rower in his own right, using the old sewer to carry out the abductions,' Megan added.

'Sounds to me like we need to haul him in ASAP, if you haven't already?' Joseph asked.

'We're about to. I'm getting ready to head over to the boat club training session and bring Norton in for questioning. Would you like to tag along?'

Joseph nodded. 'Absolutely, if only to see the look on his pompous face when we do it. Men like Norton sicken me.'

'Then let's just hope he cracks under interrogation and tells us all his sordid little secrets.'

'As long as he really is our man,' Joseph replied.

Chris nodded. 'I do realise that even with everything pointing towards Norton, he still might not be the murderer. But if he isn't, to use a rather apt saying, we'll be up shit creek without a paddle. Anyway, I would like you to join me when I interview him, Joseph. You have a knack for getting suspects to crack under questioning.'

The DI was slightly taken aback by the DCI's vote of confidence in his skills. 'Of course. Do I take it I'm to be bad cop, then?'

'I think it may be more a case of me taking on the role of bad cop, and you as the even more annoyed cop who just had someone try to knock his brains out,' Chris said.

'In that case, let's drag this bastard in, and make him sing whilst I hold him and you punch him,' Joseph replied.

Megan's eyes widened.

He caught her look and quickly shook his head. 'Not literally, Megan, just a figure of speech.'

'Right, you had me worried there,' she replied.

The DCI nodded, as he and Joseph headed out of the door together.

'A figure of speech, hey?' Joseph said, as soon as they were out of earshot of Megan.

'Whatever it takes, DI Stone, we're going to make him talk,' the DCI said, raising his eyebrows at him while they walked away.

CHAPTER TWENTY-TWO

JOSEPH WAS STILL BEMUSED the DCI had insisted on driving. The journey to the boat club on foot from St Aldates station was at most a ten-minute walk. But Chris, for reasons best known to himself, had insisted on taking a vehicle. Whatever the reason, the DI resented the decision, because Chris wasn't taking any prisoners.

In the unmarked Volvo V90, Chris was driving them towards the Isis in the growing light of a dreary dawn, far too quickly for Joseph's liking. The car's pace was brisk enough for the few pedestrians and cyclists out at that early hour of the morning to have to jump or swerve aside. Many shook their heads as they passed them, and probably tutted too. That pretty much amounted to the British equivalent of an angry mob. Joseph more than sympathised with them. They tore down the tree-lined avenue, his palms growing increasingly sweaty.

'You do know PC Burford is already there keeping Norton under surveillance?' he said. 'We really could have afforded to take our time and walk there, Chris.'

'Yes, but I'm not going to waste an opportunity to escape from behind my desk and drive,' the DCI replied, looking at

Joseph. More significantly, he seemed totally unaware of the Isis now rushing towards them as they ran out of road.

'Boss!' Joseph said, with a definite bit of squeaky bum creeping into his tone.

Chris glanced ahead and, seeing the river, casually pressed the electronic handbrake button, and spun the wheel over. He sent the Volvo into a sideways skid like they were bloody auditioning for the opening credits of a seventies cop show.

Joseph had to hang onto the roof strap as the car's traction control eventually caught up. The wheels dug in, spraying gravel but saving them from an imminent watery demise. Then they were racing along the bank of the river towards a footbridge ahead of them. Unlike Joseph, Chris was having the time of his life, at least based on the eejit grin that almost reached his ears. He brought the Volvo to a totally unnecessary, hard-braking, head-lurching stop just before the bridge.

Joseph swore if he'd been wearing a St Christopher medallion at that point, he would have kissed it.

'Are you a rally driver when you're off duty?' Joseph asked, casting a hard stare in the DCI's direction, as he climbed out of the vehicle.

'Funny you should mention it. I actually have an old Triumph TR4 that I restored. I like to take her out on track days.'

'I never would have guessed,' Joseph said, wishing he'd taken an extra paracetamol to deal with his headache that was pounding again.

'I can always invite you to join me on a track day if you fancy it?'

Joseph quickly shook his head. 'With all due respect, that's really not my thing. I think I would rather have all my teeth extracted without an anaesthetic.'

The DCI chuckled as they walked towards the bridge and the boat clubs on the other side.

PC Paul Burford, who was wearing plain clothes as part of the surveillance operation around the coach, headed over the bridge to meet them.

'Where's our man, officer?' Chris asked him.

Paul hitched his thumb over his shoulder towards the Isis. 'Right now, he's out on the water in a boat, trailing the women's Blue team as they train. Apparently, it's flat-out training from now until the big race on Saturday. '

Chris nodded. 'How much longer until Norton and the women's team come back in?'

'About ten minutes, sir,' Paul replied.

'Then we'd better arrange a little reception committee for him,' Joseph said.

The three of them headed over the curved bridge, where two swans were gliding along the stream bordering the edge of Christ Church Meadow. Large puddles were everywhere on the grass and some even had delusions of becoming lakes.

Chris was looking out over the meadow, too. 'There's even more rain forecast. They're saying now that with the ground so saturated, we could easily be looking at another flood, maybe even the highest on record.'

'That's all we need,' Joseph replied. 'The last time we had a really big one was about ten years ago. That was when Botley Road was under water. The fire brigade had to pump the water out into adjacent fields to stop the houses on either side from flooding. It was a surreal sight.'

'I wouldn't know. I was still working as a DC at the Bridewell station in Bristol back then,' Chris said.

'So what made you move to Oxford?' Joseph asked.

'Fancied a change. Let's just say that I wasn't exactly a fan of the DSU there, nor her, me.' He shrugged.

'Ah, right you are,' Joseph said, giving the DCI an appraising sideways glance. It seemed Chris had a better understanding of Joseph's situation at St Aldates than he'd first given him credit for. Certainly, that the man confided in him spoke volumes.

A short while later, they were approaching a hive of activity in front of the Oxford University Boat Club as the men's team carried a boat down towards the river. Every single one of them was giving the DI a questioning glance. But that was nothing compared to the group of women in Oxford boat crew tracksuits, who were openly staring at Joseph, their heads already bent together in whispered conversations.

'Something tells me that none of them will be that surprised when we haul their coach away for questioning,' Chris said.

Joseph nodded, then noticed someone training on the open-air gym balcony above them. Whoever was training was just out of the DI's line of sight, although he could see Brian spotting for them. They lifted a very heavy weight on a barbell, then with the barest groan, returned it to the rack, bench pressing far more than the DI would ever be capable of. That was why Joseph was so taken aback when he saw that the person who sat up and wiped sweat from their forehead was none other than the small-statured cox.

'Isn't that lad who talked Brian Reed down off the ledge and stopped him punching Ian in the pub the other night?' Chris asked.

'Yes, that's Craig Franks, the cox to the women's Blue team,' the DI replied.

As the other man began to put the weights away, Craig spotted Joseph and gave him a wave.

'It looks like you've turned up mob-handed to finally take our coach away for questioning,' he called out.

The DCI's gaze narrowed on him. 'How would you know about that?'

'It's common knowledge that you've been keeping an eye on Joanna. Something about a stalker. So it doesn't take a lot to put two and two together when your plain-clothes officer turns up first thing, asking where Charles is.' He gestured towards Paul, who grimaced. 'Anyway, I expect Joanna finally came forward and made an official statement to you guys. It's about bloody time someone did.'

'I'm afraid we can't say anything about that,' Chris replied, before turning to Paul. 'So much for the surveillance operation being kept confidential,' he muttered under his breath.

'Sorry, sir,' Paul replied, looking distinctly uncomfortable.

Joseph raised his chin towards the cox. 'I'm surprised to see you training so hard, Craig. I always thought the coxes had a relatively easy time of it, since they don't need to be at the peak of physical fitness.'

'That might usually be the case, but I like to keep my hand in. Anyway, if you're after Charles, that's him coming in now with the women's team.' Craig gestured along the river. 'I'm letting the reserve cox keep her hand in, although I'll be heading straight out with them again in another thirty minutes.'

The three officers turned to see Norton had a megaphone pressed to his mouth and was sitting in the prow of a small twin-hulled launch trailing the women's Eights boat, shouting instructions to the rowing team.

Even though Joanna had her back to them, Joseph recognised her head as she rowed with absolute precision and power.

'Put your fucking backs into it, ladies, you're not out on a Sunday bloody stroll now,' Norton shouted at them.

'Charming,' Chris said, as they began to make their way towards the slipway.

'Yes, the man is a fecking bully when it comes to his teams,' Joseph replied. 'How do you want to play this, Boss?'

'Softly at first. At least until we are so far into questioning Norton that it dawns on him he might actually need a solicitor.'

'Then softly it is.'

The women's boat was surging towards them now in the growing light, the cry of their female cox calling out like some sort of water bird crying its dawn chorus. As they neared, the DI could tell Joanna and every single one of the team were giving it their all as the cox called out the strokes. Not that any of that seemed to be good enough for Norton, who kept looking at his stopwatch and shaking his head.

The women's rowing team sped past the boathouse, and the moment they had done so, they all dropped their heads, paddles raised from the water. There was no doubt each of them had given it everything they had and were utterly exhausted.

'With a performance like that, it's a wonder that I allowed any of you on the Blue team,' Charles bellowed at them.

Then Norton spotted the DI waiting on the slipway, and his entire demeanour changed. He lowered the megaphone and sat back in his seat, shoulders slumped, with something of a frightened rabbit look.

'If someone could be convicted just by how guilty they looked, then it would have been an open and shut case, and we would be getting ready to shove him in a cell and throw away the key,' Joseph said.

'If only it was that easy, but sadly we need something called proof,' Chris replied, as they headed out to meet the coach's small twin-hulled launch as it came in to land.

The reserve women's team was already disembarking from the racing boat. Joanna shot the two detectives a questioning look. In the way of an answer, the DI just raised his eyebrows at her. She nodded, and a moment later she had a scrum of women around her, all watching Norton step off the launch and wade up the slipway in his blue wellies.

Norton peered at Joseph. 'Is there anything I can help you with, DI Stone?'

'We need you to come to the station to answer some questions as part of our ongoing investigation.'

'Is this to do with Millie?' he asked, his face pale.

'Among other things,' Joseph replied.

'Okay. Just let me grab my things and I'll let the assistant coaches know that I'll be stepping out for a short while.'

Chris nodded and as the coach headed away, he bent his head towards Paul. 'Keep close to him in case he gets any ideas about making a run for it.'

The PC nodded and trailed Norton as he headed over to a group of men who had been watching him talk to the detectives.

Chris turned to Joseph. 'Like a lamb to the slaughter.'

'Here's hoping so, Boss,' the DI replied, watching the coach grab a sports bag from one of the men and turn back, looking as nervous as hell.

CHAPTER TWENTY-THREE

CHRIS AND JOSEPH deliberately made the coach wait twenty minutes. They'd watched him on the camera feed, getting more and more agitated as he paced inside the interview room. Once they both thought the man had stewed long enough to hopefully loosen his tongue a fraction, they

decided the time had come to rattle his cage.

As they headed in, Norton was draining his second glass of water. He looked up, giving them a haunted look.

Megan would be watching them on the camera feed from the room next door. Joseph was hoping by the end of the interview, she might pick up a few tips.

'So, what's this all about?' Norton said as the detectives sat down opposite him. 'I hate to rush you, but this is a critical couple of days before the race on Saturday. I really need to get back to the training session as soon as possible.'

'Hopefully, we won't delay you too much longer,' Chris said, with a passable attempt at a reassuring smile.

This was the tactic the two detectives had agreed on beforehand. The intention was to gradually lure Norton in, so when they hit him with the hard stuff, he wouldn't see it coming.

Chris was going to lead, before letting Joseph loose with his *very pissed-off cop* role, to see if they could squeeze the truth out of the man.

'Let's get this show on the road,' the DI said, as he leant over and flicked the switch on the audio recorder and its green light turned red.

Chris clasped his hands together and leant on the table. 'To start with, I would like you to tell us where you were last night?'

Norton gave the DCI a confused look. 'At home with my family.'

'I see, and what time did you arrive home yesterday?'

'Around 9 pm. It was a long day of training, but then again, it always is this close to race day.'

'I see. So what time did you leave for work this morning?'

'5:30 am sharp,' Norton replied.

'And how did you get there? Car, bike, or maybe you walked?' Chris asked, even though they already knew the answer.

This was again deliberate, an agreed upon test to see where Norton began lying. Catch him with a small lie, and it might quickly move on to snaring him with a bigger one they could then use to trip him up.

'Actually, I took a single scull boat into work. It's a great way to travel through Oxford, and puts me into the right frame of mind for the training sessions.'

So much for the man taking the bait with a small lie, Joseph thought.

'Do you use that way of getting to the boat club regularly?' Chris continued.

'It's actually a bit of a good luck tradition for me, in the last few days building up to the race.'

'But you didn't use it last night by any chance?' the DCI

asked, as casually as if he was asking whether he'd popped out to the shops.

Joseph knew this was Chris going after the meat in the sandwich. Playing his part, he gave the coach a cold, stony look as he warmed up to his role for his upcoming performance.

'Sorry, why would I do that?' Norton replied.

Joseph peered at him. 'Why don't you tell us?' he said with a low, dangerous tone.

Norton blinked rapidly. 'I don't know what you're driving at. As I said, I was home last night with my family. Just ask my wife, she'll tell you.'

'Don't worry, we will,' Joseph replied.

Norton's gaze darted between the two detectives. 'Has someone said something that I need to be aware of?'

Joseph leant forward over the table a fraction. 'Such as?'

The coach paused a moment and refilled his glass again before taking a long gulp. 'Is this something to do with someone on the boat team making allegations against me?'

So the slimy toerag already had at least an inkling of why they'd brought him in. Joseph cast a glance at the video camera in the corner of the room. The DI wondered what Megan was making of Norton's performance. The thing was, so far at least, the man wasn't exactly radiating the guilt of a murderer.

Chris gave Joseph the barest nod to indicate the DI should carry on tightening the screw.

'You sound like someone who has a guilty conscience?' Joseph said, as he sat back.

Again, the coach's eyes darted between them. 'Why, what's been said?'

Neither Chris nor Joseph said anything, both of them deliberately letting the silence linger.

Then Norton closed his eyes for a moment, obviously grappling with whether or not to say something.

'Just tell us,' Chris urged him gently.

The coach opened his eyes again. 'Look, I have to push the teams to deliver their very best. That is basically my job, even if some of them don't like me for it.'

So the man was going to play it innocent, like so many others who had sat in this interview room before him.

The DCI timed his moment perfectly and gave Norton a puzzled look. 'Are you absolutely sure about your methods to achieve that?'

Norton drew his lip over his teeth. 'What are you driving at?'

'Then, let's put that another way,' Chris said with the tone of a disappointed headmaster, 'were you involved in a personal relationship with Hannah Emmerson, Millie Dexter, or Joanna Keene?'

Norton stared at them, his mouth flapping like a landed fish.

Joseph drummed his fingers on the table. 'Come on now, why be so shy, Charles?'

Now to push things forward in what definitely would be construed as leading a witness. If a solicitor was there, he would be all over them like a rash. But thankfully they weren't.

The DI fixed the coach with a penetrating stare. 'You're a healthy guy. I'm sure you've got a good sexual appetite as well. And here you are, a fox put in charge of a hen house. After all, what's a little bit on the side if it doesn't do anyone any harm?'

'I... I...' Norton replied, stammering, before the rest of the sentence got stuck in his throat.

'Just confirm for us that you had relationships with the three women mentioned,' Chris asked.

The coach began fiddling with his ring, staring down at the table as he sensed a precipice rushing up towards him.

Joseph slapped his hand on the table. 'Bloody answer the question, man!'

The coach jerked in his chair, and glanced over at the red light on the recorder, then returned his gaze to the detectives and slowly nodded.

'Yes, I had relationships with them,' he replied in the small voice of a broken man.

'Sexual ones?' Chris pressed.

'Yes,' Norton replied, red blotches appearing on his neck.

'And you didn't think that was significant enough to step forward and inform us about after the murder of two of those women?'

'I... I was trying to protect my family.'

'You should have maybe thought about that before you unzipped your trousers,' Joseph said, realising it was only a matter of time before Norton asked for a solicitor. They needed to make hay whilst there was still sunshine, and quickly direct this interview to what they really needed to know.

Norton had now sunk into himself as though someone had let the air out of him.

'So, were there others, apart from the three women we mentioned?' Chris asked.

'Yes, a few more over the years,' Norton replied, without even attempting to lie, and not making eye contact.

In the DI's experience, that was a good thing, as once a suspect started to talk, their mouths had a tendency to run away with them. It often seemed to be a relief for them as they attempted to unburden themselves of the things they'd been keeping buried.

Chris's eyes narrowed on the coach. 'So, does your wife have any idea about these affairs?'

Norton shot them both a pleading look. 'No, she doesn't, and please don't tell her.'

'I'm afraid this is bound to come out one way or another, so I would suggest you speak with her sooner rather than later.'

'I will,' Norton replied, looking as wretched as any man could as his sins came home to roost.

'So where did these sexual liaisons take place?'

'Local hotels usually.'

'And how did you manage to keep these affairs hidden all this time from your family?'

'By using my scull and slipping away in the middle of the night. You see, my wife and I sleep in separate bedrooms, which makes it easier not to get caught.'

Joseph immediately exchanged a subtle look with Chris. Norton had basically just told them he could have had the opportunity to slip away from his house the previous night to abduct Joanna. If he had, his wife would have been none the wiser.

'So, who ended these affairs?' Chris asked, almost casually, although Joseph knew immediately what he was up to, setting the man up for the bigger lie to hang himself with.

And just like that, their man took the bait.

'It was always me. They got too attached, but I only wanted a casual fling, nothing more. But you know what young women are like, drawn to men in positions of power like moths to a flame.'

Joseph caught the brief smile flickering across the bastard's face. He gripped his hands under the table, fighting the desire to slap the eejit.

Once again, Chris gave Joseph the barest nod to give him the go-ahead, not to lay into the man physically, but certainly giving him permission to hit him verbally as the DI went in for the kill.

'And I don't suppose you would know anything about Millie giving up her position on the team and at the university, because she couldn't handle your predatory sexual behaviour towards her?' Joseph asked.

Norton lifted his gaze to the DI's, his eyes wide as he went to answer, but Joseph wasn't going to give the gobshite the chance to defend himself.

'And you can't explain why Joanna Keene said that she was the one who broke off the affair with you, but then you tried to blackmail her?' Joseph continued, his voice growing louder. 'Did you do the same thing with Hannah Emmerson? Kept on at her, not taking no for an answer?'

A flicker of realisation passed through Norton's eyes. 'Hang on, if you are saying that I had something to do with their murders, then you've got this all wrong.'

Joseph drummed his finger on the table. 'I never said that. But I'm interested in why you would automatically jump to that conclusion?'

The red spots on Norton's neck had now merged into one large scarlet ring. 'I just thought...' He shrugged, realising that he was damned if he spoke and damned if he didn't.

'Okay, let's return to where you were last night,' Chris said, the very voice of reasonableness. 'Is there anything that you would like to confess now? Because it will go so much easier for you if you do, Charles.'

'I keep telling you that I was at home.'

'So no secret night excursions, then?' Joseph asked.

'I don't know what you mean.'

'It's an easy enough bloody question. Did you slip away from your home last night to deal with one of the women on the boat team who was prepared to give evidence against you?'

'You mean Joanna?' Then his gaze flicked again to the red light of the recorder, and Joseph knew immediately that they were about to lose their moment. Sure enough, Norton frowned and then he shook his head.

'I think I need to get a solicitor in here with me,' he said in an uncertain tone.

Joseph peered at Norton. 'That sounds to me like you're guilty and have something to hide. So let's just make this easier on all of us and you tell us the bloody truth! That you were the one fecking responsible for the murder of those poor women!'

Norton stared at him. 'I know what this looks like, but I swear it wasn't me. You've got to believe me, Detectives.'

Chris sucked his cheeks in. 'It's not exactly looking great for you, Charles. Especially when you've just shot down your own alibis for the murders of Hannah Emmerson and Millie Dexter, when you claimed you were at home with your wife.'

Joseph nodded. 'Yes, a wife who sleeps in another bedroom. And didn't you just tell us that you sometimes slip away at night using your scull boat? So let me paint you a little picture, and you tell me how right I am. The women that you had affairs with all eventually came to their senses and tried to break things off with you, not the other way around. But you didn't like that one little bit, especially when you knew if they said anything, you would lose everything. So at first, you tried playing mind games with them, breaking into their flats and deliberately moving things around. But when that didn't work, and you believed they might actually blow the whistle on your cosy little harem, you took the next step.'

'What next step?' Norton asked, staring at the DI with an appalled expression.

'You murdered them, you arsewipe.' Joseph stood up and leant over the table, resting his fists on it like a gorilla. 'That's the truth, isn't it? You couldn't stand a woman saying no to you and were determined to have their silence, whatever the cost!'

Norton looked at Joseph with his mouth agape. 'I never broke into any of their flats, and I would never murder anyone. I don't know who you've been talking to, but that's simply not what happened.'

'Why, who do you think we've been talking to?' Chris asked

in a relaxed tone, as though the DI wasn't standing over the coach like he was about to rip his head off.

'Joanna, obviously, and others on the boat team...' His eyes widened. 'I bet you've been talking to that little shit-stirrer, Craig Franks. He's always had it in for me, probably because he's jealous.'

'Sorry, what do you mean?' Chris asked.

'I mean, that bloody hobbit fancies himself a lady's man, but they all see him as a mate and nothing more. If ever a man had an inferiority complex, it's Craig. And I've seen the way he's tried to turn everyone against me. I bet he's the one who's been trying to stab me in the back.'

'I think you've done a pretty good job of that all by yourself,' Joseph replied.

But Norton's words had also set a cog spinning in the back of the DI's brain. After all, it was Craig who'd first told Joseph and Megan they should talk to the women's team about how the coach behaved towards them. He was probably just looking out for them, just like any decent person would do, but even so...

Norton crossed his arms. 'Okay, I'm not saying another word until I have a solicitor here.'

'If that's the way you want to play it,' Joseph replied, glancing at Chris, who nodded for him to give the go ahead. 'Charles Norton, I am arresting you on suspicion of the murders of Hannah Emerson, and Millie Dexter, as well as the attempted abduction of Joanna Keene. You do not have to say anything, but it may harm your defence if you do not mention, when questioned, something which you later rely on in court. Anything you do say may be given in evidence.'

Norton shook his head. 'This must be some sort of joke.'

'Does it look like we're laughing?' Chris replied. 'Okay, interview with Charles Norton is paused at 8:30 am.' He leant across and stopped the recorder. 'We will reconvene when your solicitor has arrived, Mr Norton. If you can't afford one, a duty solicitor can be provided.'

'Of course I can bloody afford one,' the coach replied, real anger flashing in his eyes for the first time.

'Then I hope you can afford a great one, especially when your wife hears about what you've been up to,' Joseph said, as he and Chris stood and headed out of the interview room.

'So what do you think, Boss?' the DI asked after the door closed behind them.

'I think we haven't got any hard evidence other than he may have been lying about his whereabouts when Hannah and Millie were murdered. He certainly seemed none the wiser about the attempted abduction of Joanna last night. I'm afraid that right now, we haven't got much to hold him on.'

'I know that, but obviously we need to organise a search of his home to see if he has anything there that could be used as evidence, specifically the missing rowing medals.'

Chris nodded. 'So the question is, do you really think we have our man, Joseph?'

The DI rubbed the back of his neck. 'The only thing I know for sure right now is that man is a philanderer who blackmailed the women he targeted into keeping quiet. That's certainly enough for a conviction if Joanna holds her nerve and is prepared to go to court. But to convict him of murder is a long stretch from where we're standing right now.'

'I know, and that's what I'm worried about. If we don't unearth something during the search, by showing our hand too early, we won't be able to secure a conviction.'

'If he *is* our man,' Joseph replied.

'Why, are you thinking that we should take another look at Brian Reed?'

'Maybe, but there's another line of inquiry I'd like to chase up, with your permission?'

'Go for it. And, Joseph, I just wanted to say good work in there. You do rather well with the bad cop role.'

'Megan will just be relieved that I never actually laid hands on the man.'

'I think we can leave that to his wife. Anyway, I'd better get the wheels spinning and let Walker know the progress we've made.'

The moment Joseph stepped into the observation booth, Megan looked away from the monitor where she'd been watching the coach. The man was currently pacing the room like a caged animal on the other side of the glass.

'So, what do you think?' Joseph asked, as he sat on a desk.

'I think we should look into Craig Franks's background as a matter of urgency. Something that Norton said got me wondering about him.'

'You're not the only one. I want as much information as you can dig up on the cox. Call it a hunch, but if I've learned anything over the years, it's not to ignore them. Let's start with checking whether Craig owns any sort of boat, and widen the search from there.'

'I'm all over this like a rash,' Megan said as she got up.

The detectives headed out of the room, just as on the monitor, Norton slumped into a chair. He held his head in his hands.

CHAPTER TWENTY-FOUR

It was the end of a very long day, especially as Joseph had started it in a hospital bed. Unfortunately, the last few hours of work with Megan, attempting to shine a searchlight on Craig Franks's background, so far had yielded little in the way of success.

After staring at the screen for hours, Joseph's eyeballs felt like sandpaper. He looked up at Sue as she entered the incident room, and noticed how dejected she looked, which wasn't a good sign. She'd been one of the detectives on-site as the team had combed Norton's house for any evidence that could help link him to the murders.

'What's with the long face?' the DI asked as she sat down, already suspecting he knew the answer.

'We didn't find a crumb of anything of real substance in Norton's house, although the technical forensic team have taken his laptop and mobile away to pore over them, and see if they can unearth anything there,' Sue replied.

Megan sat back in her chair. 'So, no smoking gun in the form of any stolen rowing medals from the women's flats?'

'Sadly not, and certainly nothing that will stop the DCI from having to release Norton tomorrow morning.'

'Damn it,' Joseph said. 'The solicitor has also got Norton on the whole no-comment strategy now, and the bugger is playing his part to a tee.'

Sue shook her head. 'Why am I not surprised? Anyway, I heard via the grapevine that you're also looking into the cox, Craig Franks. How's that going?'

'Badly,' Megan said. 'We've not found so much as a speeding ticket for Craig,' 'The man seems to have a squeaky clean past from the little we've been able to find on him.'

'Sounds a bit too good to be true,' Sue observed.

Joseph took a sip of his cold tea and shuddered at the horror of it. 'It does, but there's absolutely nothing on the police database about him. But then again, I suppose there wasn't about Charles Norton either.'

'That's the problem about criminals who fly under the radar —it's hard to pin anything on them until they surface.'

'Tell me about it. I thought we might be on to something, tracing a boat under his name, but no joy there—just like the coach and Brian Reed.'

'What about asking where he was on the days that Hannah and Millie went missing?'

Joseph clicked his tongue. 'And right there is a huge problem with this hunch of mine. At the time of Hannah's disappearance, Craig wasn't even living in Oxford. He was only eighteen back then and still in sixth form at Bampton Private School in Richmond upon Thames. And before you ask, according to the Oxford University entry team—because yes, I've already checked—Craig had nothing but glowing testimonials from Bampton. By all accounts, the lad was a star student, especially when it came to the rowing team. It actually turns out that Joanna Keene went there as well and started at Oxford a year before he did.'

'Now that is an interesting coincidence. But if you can't find anything out online, it sounds like you might want to pull him in for questioning, or at least have a friendly chat with him, if only to rule him out?'

Joseph sat back in his chair. 'That's why I popped over to the boat club earlier to do exactly that. But nothing doing, as Craig was up to his neck with last-minute training with the women's Blue team for the big race tomorrow with Cambridge.'

Sue shrugged. 'Then there's not exactly a lot you can do, short of arresting him on a hunch and holding him for twenty-four hours. The great and the good of Oxford will want your head on a silver platter if you do that.'

Joseph nodded. 'Don't I know it. That would make me about as popular as a herpes outbreak at a nudist colony. That's why it's not really an option right now, especially as there's nothing else to implicate Craig, other than that the coach isn't his biggest fan.'

'That sounds like a positive to me,' Megan said, looking up from her screen.

'I know it does, but until we get to talk to Craig in person, we really haven't got anything to go on, other than he may be a person of interest in our investigation. But don't you worry, the moment the boat race is over and done with, I'll grab hold of the lad for a chat. Besides, with Chris agreeing to have a protection team in place to keep a close eye on Joanna, and without an imminent threat to her life, I suppose we can afford to wait another day.'

Megan pulled a face. 'That didn't exactly work out well last time, did it?'

'I know, but this time they don't have a secret underground

sewer they can use. Besides, they'd be crazy to try a second time. Once, they might have got away with it, but twice?'

PC Greg Robson wandered into the incident room, looking just as long-faced as Sue had a few moments before.

Megan shot him a questioning look. 'Someone else not having a good day of it?'

'You can say that again,' Greg replied. 'I swear, there isn't a stone that we haven't turned over trying to locate where the murderer was holding his victims. We've even done a boat-to-boat search, but absolutely nothing there, either. The DCI has finally ordered the search to be wound down as we're just chasing our own tails.'

'Then it sounds like we are in danger of running into yet another blind alley with this investigation,' Sue said.

Megan sighed. 'I really thought we were on the edge of a breakthrough when we arrested Norton.'

'You never know, he might still crack under questioning,' Joseph replied.

Sue nodded as she glanced at the clock that was on its way towards 7 pm. 'As it's long past the end of our shifts, who fancies a cheeky one at the Scholar's Retreat to drown our sorrows?'

Joseph shook his head. 'I'll cry off from the pub if you don't mind, especially as I'm technically meant to be recovering from nearly having my skull caved in last night. I just need to get home to my boat and rest.'

'I'm not surprised after the day you've had,' Megan said. 'I can run you back, if you like?'

'Only if you let me buy you some Thai takeaway from the Dancing Frog, as a thank you.'

'I don't mind if I do. I've barely eaten all day.'

'That makes two of us,' Joseph said as he stood, grabbing his coat. 'See you tomorrow, guys, and let's just hope that it brings better news.'

Sue and Greg nodded as the two detectives headed towards the door.

The rain was lashing down on the roof of *Tús Nua* as Joseph and Megan sat at the table with Dylan, finishing the last of the Thai takeaway. The professor's dogs, having tried their luck begging for scraps, and with some disgust after getting nothing for their efforts, had set up camp as close as possible to the radiator.

Joseph had invited his neighbour over because, as usual, he'd completely over-ordered, and they needed his help with putting a dent in the mountain of food. However, that wasn't his only reason.

Often, when no one else could, Dylan had an unnerving knack of unearthing things other people missed. That was why Joseph had wanted to pick his brain about this case from the start. Megan had been taken aback by just how much information Joseph had been prepared to share with someone who wasn't a police officer, even if he was an honorary one in the DI's head.

'So let me get this straight, you've run out of leads,' Dylan said as he finished the last of the Massaman curry.

'Yes, with the one possible exception of Craig Franks, but that's an outside bet at best,' Joseph replied.

Dylan nodded. 'So, what have you been able to find out about the cox?'

'Just that he was a star student along with Joanna Keene at Bampton. Other than that, there's not a lot more to discover.'

'Oh, Bampton. I know the headteacher there, Sophie Devlin, really well. They specialise in turning out some of the best rowers in the country, so no wonder that a lot of their students end up here in Oxford or at Cambridge. The talent scouts are all over them. Is there some reason that you want to investigate Craig?'

'Only that we thought there might be something to what Charles Norton said about Craig being a *"little shit-stirrer,"* although he could just be throwing mud to try and distract us.'

'Yes, but it does feel like Craig has often been there to point us in the right direction,' Megan added.

'That sounds like someone just trying to be a good citizen,' Dylan said. 'But one thing that makes little sense to me. You say he's the cox of the women's Blue team—aren't they usually quite small to avoid adding weight to the boats? From what you've told me, that doesn't exactly sound like the sort of man who would be physically capable of carrying an unconscious woman from her flat.'

'I would have said the same until I saw Craig doing bench presses and managing some very impressive weights,' Joseph replied. 'The man may not be a giant by any measure, but I suspect he might be capable of lifting a knocked-out woman.'

Dylan scratched his grey beard. 'Then it sounds like he can't be ruled out of the equation by his physique alone. Out of interest, what course is he doing at Oxford?'

'Engineering Science at Lincoln College,' Megan said. 'That's one thing that could link him to the abductions.'

'Why's that?' the professor asked.

'Because we recovered a very sophisticated wide frequency jammer that the intruder left behind in Joanna's flat,' Megan said. 'According to TST, it was a lot more advanced than the usual thing that criminals buy on the black market, and that are banned in this country. That alone suggests that it was chosen by someone who knew exactly what they were doing.'

Dylan took a sip of his red wine. 'That sounds like a slightly more promising lead.'

'Maybe, but one swallow, a summer doesn't make,' Joseph replied.

Megan powered up the iPad she'd been using to browse the internet to see if she could dig up anything more on Craig, but once again came up empty. On the screen, she now showed Dylan a smiling photo of Craig from the Oxford boat team's page.

'As you can see, he doesn't look like the murdering sort,' Megan said.

Dylan exchanged a frown with Joseph.

'What's that look about?' the DC asked.

'Because they rarely do,' Joseph replied. 'A person never *looks* like a psychotic killer in real life. Just think of Helen back at the Pitt River Museum. She looked like a regular girl next door, apart from the fact that she was into ritualistic slaughter. That's why it's always best to keep an open mind about these things. Having said that, I increasingly think that we're clutching at straws here when it comes to Craig.'

'In which case, it seems that we have circled back towards Norton again,' Megan said.

Joseph nodded. 'Who we know for sure he is guilty of something, just not necessarily of murder.'

'Whoever the real killer is, the question is, will they kill again?' Dylan asked.

'That's certainly what's going to keep us up at night if we don't catch them soon,' Joseph said. 'Because of that, we need to look at everyone, however unlikely. That's why, if Chris is okay with it, I'd like to be there at the finish line for the boat race in London tomorrow to grab Craig afterwards.'

A thoughtful look filled the professor's face. 'Actually, if you're really serious about looking into Craig's background, you could do a lot worse than talk to his old headteacher. Bampton School is more or less on the way from here if you're planning on heading to the boat race in London. I could call her and set up a meeting if you like?'

Joseph glanced across at Megan polishing off the last of the green curry. 'What do you think?' he asked.

'I think it certainly can't hurt. If anyone knows the dirt on somebody, it will be an old teacher of theirs.'

The DI shrugged. 'In that case, why not?'

Dylan raised his glass of red wine to the two detectives. 'Then, good luck tomorrow, my friends. Oh, and here's to Oxford winning.'

Megan and Joseph both raised their glasses and clinked them against his.

'Right, I don't know about anyone else, but I absolutely need my bed,' Joseph said.

Megan nodded, stifling a yawn. 'Yes, I have to admit to being a bit shattered.'

'You're telling me,' Joseph said, his fingers probing his bandaged head. There was still a dull ache, although it was beginning to subside.

Megan spotted what he was doing. 'I could always take you back to the hospital, if you like?'

Joseph just gave her the *look*. 'Do you actually know me, DC Anderson?'

She laughed. 'Just a suggestion. Anyway, I'd better head off and get my beauty sleep. See you first thing in the morning. Dylan, it's been a pleasure, as always.'

'Likewise,' the professor replied.

Megan slipped on a coat, and having patted both Max and White Fang, who gave her sleepy looks from their positions in front of the radiator, she headed outside into the growing rainstorm.

'I think that's me done too,' Dylan said as he finished the last of his wine. As he stirred himself from his seat, his gaze travelled to the bandaged wound on Joseph's head. 'Just do me a favour next time, and try not to sail so close to the wind.'

Joseph gave him a smile. 'I'll do my best, my friend.' He patted the professor's shoulder and stood, both dogs getting to their feet as well.

When Joseph was alone at last, he didn't even bother to undress. Instead, he just flopped onto his bed and didn't so much go to sleep, but pass out the moment his head hit the pillow.

CHAPTER TWENTY-FIVE

JOSEPH AND MEGAN were driving through the ever-increasing downpour towards Richmond upon Thames. It had rapidly become an epic journey, thanks to all the flooded roads. The rain had become so heavy that day had almost been reduced to night, forcing Megan to turn the headlights on. More than once, the car had lost grip as they had hit a larger puddle and briefly aquaplaned before its traction control had kicked in. Joseph was grateful he wasn't the one doing the driving. He would have been a nervous wreck doing that in these conditions.

For the DI, it was also an uncomfortable reminder of the stormy night the deer had run out onto the road and caused the crash that had killed his baby son, Eoin. No wonder Joseph had a cold sweat running down his back by the time they neared their destination.

They travelled the last mile along a main road with a tall brick wall on their side and towering, mature trees on the other.

Joseph's gaze went to the satnav screen. According to it, this was the boundary of Bampton School's extensive grounds. The one detail he couldn't help noticing was the razor wire running along the top of the wall.

He pointed it out to Megan. 'Are we sure this school doesn't double as a prison?'

The DC gave him a wry smile. 'I think we'll find the students here enjoy slightly better living standards than that.'

'*One hundred yards ahead, turn left,*' the satnav announced.

Megan slowed the Peugeot and they turned off the main road towards a large entrance. The blue sign in front of it read, *Bampton School,* and beneath that, *Striving Towards Success.*

'Remind me, what are the fees they charge for this place?' Joseph asked.

'Around sixty thousand for boarders,' Megan replied.

The DI whistled. 'Bloody hell, you'd think they could have come up with a better slogan than that if the parents are shelling out that sort of cash.'

Megan laughed as they stopped in front of the gates next to an intercom box. She leaned out and pressed the green *Call* button and a moment later they heard a ringing sound.

'Hi, how can I help you?' a man's voice said.

'We're here to see the head teacher, Mrs Devlin. It's DI Stone and DC Anderson. We have a meeting arranged with her.'

There was a short pause at the other end. 'Ah yes, she's expecting you. I'll buzz you in.'

The gates swung open.

'Yep, definitely a Parkhurst Prison vibe to the place,' Joseph said with a lopsided smile as they drove through the highly ornate gate.

A moment later they were heading along the obligatory tree-lined driveway through the slanting rain. They passed rugby and football pitches, along with at least a dozen outdoor tennis courts. It was obvious that this particular educational establishment took their sports very seriously indeed.

After what seemed like at least another mile, a large, sprawling series of buildings came into view.

'That looks more like a secondary comp to me, rather than a posh school,' Megan said.

'It's not exactly your standard converted Victorian manor I'd envisaged for this place, either,' Joseph replied.

They pulled up in a large and very full car park, filled with Range Rovers, Mercedes, BMWs, Jaguars, and Porsches, the usual transport of the well-heeled. There were even a few Rolls Royces thrown in, just to make sure you weren't left in any doubt.

Joseph's brow knitted as they got out into the driving rain, and he pulled his zip right up to his collar.

'If those are staff cars, I think they may be paying them too much,' he said.

Megan shook her head and pointed towards a large banner attached to one building.

'Bampton Welcomes You to Our Annual Regatta.'

'I was reading about this on the school website,' the DC said. 'They hold a rowing race just before the Oxford and Cambridge Boat Race kicks off. I'm pretty sure all these cars belong to the parents.'

'That figures. Our police Peugeot definitely doesn't look like it belongs.'

'We could always pretend it's our nanny's car as the Bentley is in for a service,' Megan said, casting him a grin.

As they headed towards a large glass atrium with an entrance sign next to it, they heard rhythmic shouts in the distance. That drew their attention to the river lined with coppiced willows on the far side of the school. Joseph knew from the satnav that this was the Thames that ran like a thread through their case, linking the murders and the attempted abduction together. The question was, why?

A sizable crowd of drenched onlookers huddled next to the river, many in Barbour jackets, while others tried to protect themselves with oversized golf umbrellas. The more sensible ones had taken shelter from the lashing rain in a large marquee.

All were watching a couple of rowing teams slug it out on the river. The shouts the detectives had heard were coming from the coxes calling out instructions to their four-person racing sculls as they powered down the middle of the river. Neither team was giving the other a millimetre as they raced towards the red and white flag marking the finish line.

'Not exactly great weather for a race on the river,' Joseph said.

Megan glanced at her watch. 'It will be the same for the Oxford and Cambridge women's team, when they start their race in an hour. You'd think they'd cancel it in these conditions.'

'Only as an absolute last resort, thanks to all the training that's gone into it. Mind you, there was that time the Cambridge boat sank in rough water, so the organisers don't always make the right call.'

The DC nodded as they headed towards the entrance, putting on their police lanyards at the same time as a gaggle of students came racing out. All of them were wearing two-toned blue sashes, the team colours of Oxford and Cambridge. They ran past the two detectives, towards the rain-lashed spectators on the embankment. That was all except one boy, who, noticing them, doubled back to hold the door open.

'Thank you,' Megan said as they walked past him.

The boy gave her a beaming smile in return before heading off to rejoin his classmates.

'Yes, definitely not your typical comprehensive with those manners,' Joseph said, looking around as they entered the large, impressive atrium area with a high glass ceiling.

On the far side was a set of blue doors, and a sizable display case filled with trophies and plaques. Above that, the school motto, *Striving Towards Success*, was written in a large flowing script on the wall. It was no doubt a reminder for the students, teachers, and probably the parents who entered this hallowed educational establishment.

The detectives headed over to a wooden counter with a glass screen. Behind it, was a small office where a man and two women were working. Joseph counted at least six camera feeds on a bank of screens, including one covering the main gates. Yes, they definitely took their security seriously here.

'DI Stone and DC Anderson, I presume?' the woman said as they approached.

Megan and Joseph both nodded and showed their police lanyards.

Once the woman had examined their IDs, she smiled at them. 'If you would both like to just stand in front of the camera, I'll get some passes sorted out for you, and then I'll buzz you through and take you to Mrs Devlin's office.'

A few moments later, Joseph had a very unflattering photo of himself in a plastic wallet hanging from its own blue lanyard.

'You'd think our police IDs would be enough for them,' Joseph whispered to his colleague.

'Apparently not,' Megan replied.

Once they'd cleared the Parkhurst-like security door, and followed the receptionist down a wooden panelled corridor, he glanced at his colleague's photo.

'Bloody hell, you actually look alright in yours,' he said, gesturing at it.

'That's because I'm part of the social media generation who were born knowing how to take a selfie.'

'Maybe you should give me lessons. Ellie seems determined to set me up for a date. It's only a matter of time before she gets round to putting my face on Tinder, or whatever. But based on the typical mugshot I manage to take, that would be enough to scare anyone off.'

Megan laughed. 'We can't have that. If you like, I can shoot a decent one of you. Besides, there's nothing that Photoshop can't sort out with your face.'

Joseph narrowed his eyes at her. 'Thanks for that, really.'

'Oh, anytime,' the DC said, grinning at him.

The DI also caught the receptionist, who'd overheard their little exchange, smiling to herself when she opened the door and ushered them into a plush room.

Comfortable leather seats were waiting for them, arranged around a low table with glossy magazines on it along with a smart-looking school prospectus. The walls were filled with a series of black and white action photos of students in various sports, everything from rowing to polo, all obviously taken by a professional photographer.

'Mrs Devlin will be here to see you shortly,' the receptionist said. 'She is just overseeing the last-minute preparations of the live coverage of the Oxford and Cambridge Boat Race that's going to be shown in our auditorium. Everyone is very excited, because two of our old students are on the Oxford Blue women's team. Joanna Keene who's a rower, and Craig Franks who's their cox.'

'Yes, we know both of them,' Joseph replied.

'Oh, really? They were such wonderful students. Craig in particular, was such a charming lad who could never do enough for you when he was here at Bampton. That aside, they are both excellent role models for our current pupils.'

'I'm sure they are,' Megan said.

The receptionist smiled. 'Absolutely. Anyway, can I get you a coffee or tea while you're waiting for Mrs Devlin?'

'Yes, a coffee would be grand,' the DI said.

'Of course. Would you prefer an espresso, an Americano, latte, a flat white, or a cappuccino?'

'An Americano would certainly hit the mark.'

'And a flat white for me,' Megan added.

The receptionist smiled at them. 'I won't be a moment,' she said, before heading out of the room.

'You know we're not in a comprehensive when they have a range of coffees on offer, and I guarantee you it won't be instant,' Joseph said.

'At least the school is spending part of those exorbitant fees on something worthwhile,' Megan replied.

The detectives made themselves comfortable, and, a short time later, were enjoying two exceptionally good coffees.

'I could get used to this,' Megan said, also tucking into a delicious chocolate chip cookie from the selection the receptionist had left for them.

'Maybe you should put in a request with our superintendent for a barista for St Aldates.'

The corners of Megan's mouth curled upwards. 'Yes, I'm sure DSU Walker will think that's an excellent use of police funds.'

The door opened and a dark-haired woman in her late forties, wearing a smart dark trouser suit, walked in. Joseph took in the kind face and warm smile headed towards them, the woman's hand already outstretched.

'DI Stone, DC Anderson, I'm so sorry for keeping you waiting. I'm afraid things have been rather hectic here today with our annual regatta.'

'Yes, we saw for ourselves on the way in,' Joseph said, as he and Megan took turns shaking her hand. 'We certainly appreciate you taking the time out of your busy day to talk to us.'

'Not at all. Always happy to help a friend of Professor Shaw. Such a remarkable man.'

'Aye, that he is,' Joseph replied before the head teacher ushered them through into her private office.

Inside, there were even more photos of the Bampton students, this time focused on their academic studies. Joseph's attention was drawn to a collection of photos on the head teacher's desk. They appeared to be mainly of Mrs Devlin and a man, along with two teenage girls, presumably her family.

After they'd sat down, the head teacher gave the detectives a thoughtful look. 'So, I have to say, Dylan left me quite intrigued when he told me you wanted to find out more about Craig Franks, but wouldn't say why exactly. He's not in any trouble, is he?'

Joseph raised his hands in a placatory manner. 'No, but let's just say that we're keen to get an idea about his character as part of an ongoing investigation. This is nothing more than a formality, Mrs Devlin.'

'I see. And please, call me Sophie.' She glanced across at a photo on the wall.

When Joseph followed her gaze, he saw it was a photo of a younger Craig, his arm draped around the shoulders of two female students of roughly the same age, each of them holding an oar. One of them was Joanna.

'Is that Craig and Joanna?' Megan asked, also looking over at the photo.

'It is. Craig in particular was such a sunny student,' Sophie replied. 'All the staff adored him whilst he was here. He, and Joanna, won scholarships to be here. Along with Grace, the other girl in the picture, they were our star students. They were always highly competitive, pushing each other to deliver their very best. That was true whether it was academic work or rowing, which they were all passionate about. They had everything to look forward to, but then...' She looked out the window at the boats coming towards the embankment, being cheered on by a huddle of spectators. When the head teacher turned back, Joseph was surprised to see her eyes glistening.

'What is it?' he asked gently, already wondering what history they might be about to unearth.

Sophie closed her eyes for a moment. 'What happened will haunt the staff at Bampton forever...' Her nostrils flared. 'You see, Grace was found drowned in the Thames.'

Joseph traded a wide-eyed look with Megan, who already had her notebook out.

'What happened exactly?' he asked.

'It's worse than you can imagine. Grace was doing so well, excelling at everything, even beating Craig and Joanna's team, who'd been tipped to win the rowing race finals for Regatta Day. The final has always been rather a big deal among the students, staff, and parents. Anyway, Grace's team squarely beat theirs, but of course, they were the first to congratulate her.'

'I see, but when did Grace drown exactly?' Joseph asked.

'It was a few weeks after the final. Grace should have been riding high on her success, especially when a talent scout offered her a position on the Oxford women's rowing team after her chosen college had already accepted her. It seemed then that the world was literally throwing itself at her feet. But Grace didn't seem to be herself, and had become really withdrawn after the race. She and Craig seemed distant too, which didn't help matters. The rumour around the school was that he'd finally plucked up the courage to ask her out, but she'd rejected him. Then, one morning, Grace went missing from her dorm. A few days later she was found drowned in some reed beds further downstream.'

Joseph sat up straighter as cogs started spinning in his brain.

'I'm so sorry, that's just awful,' Megan said, shooting him a sideways glance.

'But I haven't even got to the worst part,' the head teacher continued. 'As we waited to hear the coroner's report, everyone convinced themselves that Grace had become so depressed that she'd taken her own life. Craig was beside himself at losing someone he considered to be his best friend, and blamed himself for not being there for her with whatever she was going through. Then the truth came out...'

'Go on,' Joseph said, as a bad feeling of where this was heading took hold.

'When the police finally released details of the full post-mortem, it turned out that not only had Grace been strangled to death, but that there were indicators that she'd been beaten, too, with some sort of blunt object. You can't begin to imagine the fear that created among our female students. The detectives who investigated interviewed everyone here. However, by the end of their investigation, they thought an intruder had broken into Grace's bedroom, which was on the first floor. It turned out that a rowing medal that she kept in a display case had also been taken. The detectives thought it likely that the killer took it as some sort of trophy.'

Joseph and Megan traded looks.

'You see, there had been a series of aggravated burglaries of the larger houses in Richmond, and another private school down the road had also been targeted,' Sophie continued. 'Obviously, when we'd first heard that, we increased our security precautions here at Bampton.'

'Yes, we noticed,' Joseph replied, thinking of the barbed wire and cameras.

'But despite everything we put in place, none of it turned out to be enough. No one in their wildest dreams would have believed that anyone would attempt to break into the boarding house and abduct an innocent girl, before murdering her in such a brutal manner.'

The cogs in Joseph's brain were well and truly spinning

now, as everything fell into place in his mind. Megan was staring at him as well. It sounded like at last they had their prime suspect, but the DI needed to make sure.

'And all this happened when exactly?' Joseph asked, as he tried to form a mental timeline that could link Craig to the other killings.

'Five years ago,' Sophie replied.

'I see... And can you tell me a bit more about what Craig did after Grace's death?'

Sophie narrowed her eyes at him, but nodded. 'At first, Craig was inconsolable, but everyone rallied round him, especially Joanna. Then, he slowly started to pick himself up and became determined to get into Oxford as a rower, as a way of honouring Grace's memory. Although Craig hadn't been picked by a talent scout like Grace had, the year after her death, he secured a provisional offer from a college there to study electrical engineering. Then he took himself to Oxford to try out for a rower's seat. However, the coach there said that even though Craig was physically strong, he simply didn't have the physique to row at the level required to be on the men's team. I think that was especially hard for Craig as Joanna was immediately accepted for women's reserve Osiris team.'

Just like that, Joseph realised they had their motive, and a reason why Craig might have a vendetta against Norton. But now to fill in the missing gap about Hannah.

'So, did he stay in Oxford when he tried out?' the DI asked.

'Yes, for a summer. He lived on an old narrowboat that belonged to his uncle whilst he was there.'

Joseph sat up straighter. 'Do you know the name of the boat by any chance?'

'Let me think... He told me before he left school... Oh yes, *Dawn Treader*. I wasn't going to forget that in a hurry, because it was obviously named after that boat from the C. S. Lewis' Narnia book.'

Megan had already scribbled the name down when another part of the jigsaw slotted into place.

'So how did he eventually secure the cox position on the Oxford team?' Joseph continued.

'That was a dream that Craig never gave up on. Even though he hadn't been able to get a seat on the men's Blue team, he was tenacious. He even used his own one-man scull to shadow the Oxford men and women's teams when they were out on the river training. Eventually, after a gap year, he finally achieved his dream of joining the boat team, albeit, not as a rower, but as a cox on the women's team. But I'm afraid that Craig is one of those people for whom tragedy seems to follow him around. You see, that position only became available because the women's cox on the Blue team disappeared.' Then the head teacher's expression widened. 'I saw on the news that her body recently turned up. Is that why you're here?'

Joseph needed to wrap this interview up sooner rather than later, to avoid getting caught up in the quagmire Sophie's line of thinking would inevitably lead to. The same one he'd already jumped to, and he was certain Megan had as well.

'I'm afraid we can't talk about that,' Joseph said. 'Is there anything else you can tell me about Craig Franks?'

'Just that he was very popular and we're very proud of what he went on to achieve. I suppose you could say he's the shining embodiment of the values we try to instil in all our students, to have resilience and to never give up.'

The irony of what she'd wasn't lost on Joseph, and he just nodded. 'Then, I think that's all we need, don't you DC Anderson?'

Megan nodded. 'More than enough, DI Stone.'

Sophie looked between the two detectives, a troubled

expression spreading across her face. 'Are you sure that Craig isn't in any sort of trouble?'

'Just dotting all our i's and crossing our t's,' Joseph replied.

'I see...' the head teacher started to say.

A knock interrupted them.

'Come in,' Sophie said.

A woman in a tracksuit came breezing in. 'The Oxford and Cambridge women's Boat Race coverage is about to begin, Mrs Devlin. Stuart thought you might want to say a few words to the parents and students beforehand.'

When Sophie looked at the detectives, Joseph nodded. 'We're all done here. I must thank you again for answering all our questions. It's been incredibly helpful.'

'I'm glad I could be of help,' Sophie replied, standing. 'I'll see you out.'

'There's really no need, especially as you have somewhere you need to be in a hurry.'

She nodded. 'Yes, I'd better get my skates on.' With a smile, albeit a much more concerned one than the one she'd given them when they first met, Sophie shook their hands and then headed off with the woman in the tracksuit.

The moment the two detectives were outside, and walking back to their car, Megan turned to the DI.

'It all fits, Joseph. The timeline, the MO of stealing rowing medals, everything.'

'Yes, and my guess is that Craig got a taste for it when he murdered Grace after she rejected him. Then he went on to do the same with Hannah to free up her seat on the Oxford team as their cox.'

'So what about Millie, and his attempt to abduct Joanna?'

'Maybe a long standing jealousy that she was immediately accepted onto the team? But that's something we need to ask Craig himself when we formally arrest him. We should ring

Joanna's protection team. Have them grab Craig now, in case he tries anything.'

Megan glanced at her watch and grimaced. 'I'm afraid the women's teams, including Craig, will already be out on the water by now.'

'There's not exactly a lot he can do whilst the race is on, but alert the protection team to arrest him the moment they finish the race.'

'Actually, it's only a fifteen-minute drive away from here, and we could be there to help do that in person.'

'Then let's get there as fast as we can. We can form a little reception committee to meet Craig the moment they land,' Joseph said, climbing into the car.

CHAPTER TWENTY-SIX

RACING along the wrong side of the road past the column of stationary London traffic, blue lights strobing, Megan glanced over at Joseph in the passenger seat.

'You doing okay there?' she asked.

'Eyes on the bloody road,' Joseph said through gritted teeth, as they raced towards an oncoming van.

Megan almost rolled her eyes at him, before returning her attention to what Joseph was convinced was going to be an imminent crash. However, the van driver wasn't one for a game of chicken with an unmarked police vehicle. Spotting the kamikaze Peugeot closing in on him like a proverbial bat out of hell, he swerved to one side and in his haste to avoid a head-on crash, mounted the pavement to get out of their way.

'See, I had everything under control,' Megan said, speeding past the now-stationary van, its male driver looking as pale as Joseph felt.

The DI didn't bother to grace that statement with a response, but instead looked at the satnav screen, wondering just how much more of this torture he was going to have to put up with. Thankfully, according to the display, they were only about ten minutes from their destination.

'Why don't you find the live coverage of the Boat Race on the radio for us to listen to?' Megan said, casting him another glance. 'If nothing else, it will take your mind off my driving.'

'Sorry,' he said. 'Don't take it personally. I'm always stressed out in a car that's travelling at anything over a snail's pace.'

'Says the Lycra warrior who I've seen out plenty of times on his bicycle, rocketing along and weaving in and out of the traffic.'

'Yes, but I didn't kill my son with a bike so the same psychological rules don't apply,' the DI replied, his tone flat.

Megan grimaced, but didn't say anything else. That was probably a good thing. Even though Joseph knew many aspects of the car crash all those years ago had been beyond his control, the irrational part of his brain would always hold himself accountable for what had happened to his son.

The DI scanned through the stored stations on the car's DBS radio and pressed the button for the BBC Sports channel.

'It's do or die for the Dark Blues women's team right now, as Cambridge is pulling away from them,' the male announcer said. *'They now have a four-second lead approaching Barnes Bridge.'*

Joseph's attention returned to the race course map along the Thames, which he'd opened on his phone. 'Shite, that means there's only about three minutes left until they reach the finish line. We're not going to make it in time, Megan.'

'Relax. The boat crew will still have to turn round and head back to the boathouse at the Putney Embankment. Even with the Thames current in their favour, that will still take them a good fifteen minutes. Besides, we don't actually need to be there, since we have a team already on the ground ready to arrest Craig the moment he steps ashore.'

'Then let's just hope they listen to my briefing about doing it somewhere well away from all the cameras and reporters covering the race. The last thing we need is a public arrest jeopardising Craig's prosecution. I can already hear his solicitor banging on about how the bag of shite isn't able to have a fair trial because any jury will have been influenced by his arrest being splashed across the news.'

'I'm sure that even if we don't get there in time, the team will be as discreet as possible when they arrest him.'

Before Joseph could reply, the announcer, who had been burbling along in the background about the race, suddenly got very excited.

'*Good grief, I don't know how the Dark Blues have done it, but they have closed the gap and pulled level with the Light Blues. Both teams are driving hard for the finish line with nothing to separate them but sheer determination. It's now anyone's race...*'

'Is it wrong to be rooting for our home team when we're in the middle of an arrest operation?' Megan asked.

'I'm sure if the situation were reversed, and it was Cambridge detectives chasing down a suspect on their home crew, they would do exactly the same thing.'

'Then, come on, Oxford!' Megan shouted.

She grinned at Joseph as they sped straight over a mini-roundabout, making a driver, who'd also been approaching at speed from the opposite direction, slam on his brakes.

'Just as well we're heading somewhere in a hurry, otherwise, I would book him for dangerous driving,' Megan said, with absolutely zero irony.

Continuing down the road, they listened to the announcer's excitement reach a fever pitch. '*Cambridge finds itself in dangerous territory here as Oxford is on the brink of breaking clear by an entire length. There's just two hundred metres to go...*'

'You can do it, Dark Blues!' Megan said, swerving the car into the bus lane and hurtling down it.

'I would prefer to arrive in one piece, if it's all the same to you,' Joseph said, his jaw clenched.

'Has anyone ever told you that you worry far too much? Have a bit of faith in my driving skills.'

Joseph didn't bother answering, but instead tried to keep his attention on the satnav display, rather than daring to look out the windscreen at what was increasingly resembling a console racing game. The map showed they were speeding along the north circular road towards their destination at the Putney boathouse.

'Oxford is extending their lead and Cambridge has nothing left to respond with, as their competitors shoot towards the finish line at Chiswick Bridge,' the announcer said.

Joseph tried to imagine he was there on the embankment of the Thames, watching this play out live. Both Oxford and Cambridge women crews, having trained flat out for months and months, would be giving this everything they had. All that preparation, and it all came down to this one race, where two teams at the top of their game were pitted against each other. And there, on one of the boats, was Craig Franks, a man who had been so determined to pursue his dream that he'd killed multiple times to clear the way towards today's increasingly probable victory. What would be going through the man's mind as his team raced towards the finish line? Was he a big enough psychopath to really believe every murder he'd committed had been worth it?

Then the announcer interrupted the detective's runaway train of thought.

'And the Oxford women's team has crossed the finish line first, with two clear boat lengths over Cambridge. That was a sterling performance from an outstanding Dark Blue crew.'

Megan whooped and tapped the steering wheel. 'Way to go, ladies!'

'*The Oxford team have dropped their heads, but they are smiling too, especially the cox, Craig Franks,*' the announcer continued. '*He's punching the air as he turns their boat round, getting ready to head back upstream to the Putney boathouse for a well-earned celebration.*'

'A dream come true for Craig, even if he got blood on his hands to make it happen,' Joseph said.

'I'm certainly looking forward to wiping that smug look off his face when—' Megan peered ahead. 'Oh, bloody hell.'

As they slowed, Joseph risked reconnecting to reality by glancing through the windscreen. Ahead of them was nothing but stationary traffic, and this time on both sides of the road, with absolutely nowhere for them to squeeze through.

'Yep, that's the South Circular I know and loathe,' the DI said. 'Just lean on the siren and try to get them to let us through.'

Megan nodded, but despite all her efforts, a short while later their progress had been reduced to a crawl as cars bumped up onto the pavement, trying to clear a path for them.

Joseph was already calculating in their ETA, which was ticking up by the minute. 'This is not good.'

'Look, apart from being there to see this thing through, where's the rush? Our team will have the situation under control long before we arrive,' Megan replied.

Joseph scowled at her. 'Says the woman who had a driving death wish only a moment ago.'

Megan shrugged. 'So I can adapt to the situation, sue me.'

For the next ten minutes, they listened to the announcer talk about statistics and how this performance from Oxford women's crew would rank as one of the all-time outstanding performances.

Joseph knew that when Craig eventually heard this, he would lap up all the adulation.

As the detectives continued to crawl along in their car, slowly making their way through the almost stationary traffic, inevitably the sports commentator finally announced, '*The women's team has returned victorious to Putney Embankment and has disembarked. Now, as tradition dictates, the team has got hold of the cox, Craig Franks, and...*' There was a pause. '*Yes, and, to much applause, they have thrown him into the Thames!*'

Joseph turned off the radio. 'So that's it then. Let's just hope our team is on their toes.'

The words were barely out of his mouth when, miraculously, the road ahead of them suddenly emptied of traffic. However, rather than return to treating the streets of London like her own personal racetrack, Megan kept the car's speed down to an almost legal speed.

'What are you waiting for?' Joseph said. 'Put your bloody foot down.'

'But I thought you said—'

The DI waved for her to be quiet. 'I know what I said, but like you just pointed out, we want to be there to see that smug look wiped off Craig's face.'

'Make up your mind,' Megan said, shaking her head. She floored the accelerator and the Peugeot shot ahead, making Joseph immediately regret his request.

Even with the siren blaring, it was a good five minutes later that Joseph and Megan finally arrived at the boathouse. But now, at least they were on foot, squeezing their way through the hordes of spectators who thronged the Putney Embankment, vying to get a look at the winning Oxford team.

As they got their first glimpse of the rowers, Joseph noticed the dejected-looking Cambridge crew. They had drawn into a huddle and were being comforted by their other team members, family and friends. To have trained so hard and lost was obviously hard to come to terms with.

The mood in the Oxford camp couldn't have been in greater contrast. They were all smiles, hugs, and patting each other on the back, while sharing an enormous bottle of champagne between them.

Joseph was surprised to see Norton among them, beaming at his rowing students. Chris had talked about putting a restraining order on the coach to keep his distance from the teams, but had obviously allowed him this last opportunity to see them, no doubt under the watchful eye of the police already on the ground.

Enjoy it while you can, because it's the last time you're ever going to be doing this, you little shite, Joseph thought to himself.

The detective's gaze had already moved on to try and spot his much bigger priority, namely Craig. But his heart quickly sank when he found no sign of the cox anywhere. Perhaps they'd already arrested him?

'Can you see Joanna down there among the other rowers?' Megan asked.

Joseph realised she was right. Joanna was nowhere to be seen, either.

'We'd better get down there and find out what the hell is going on,' the DI said, spotting DC Dave Roberts in plain clothes.

With a final push, they squeezed past the Oxford supporters, all wearing dark blue scarves, and reached the cordoned-off slipway. They both flashed their police lanyards to the security guard, who immediately let them through.

Straightaway, Dave headed over to them. His grim face told

the DI everything he needed to know before the man even opened his mouth.

'I've got bad news. Craig Franks slipped away with Joanna Keene whilst the team were celebrating.'

Joseph stared at the PC. 'How the hell did you let that happen?'

'As per your orders, we were keeping a safe distance until we could arrest him somewhere away from all those reporters. One moment he was talking to the Cambridge team and the next we lost sight of him. A moment later we realised Joanna had vanished, too.'

Joseph's blood ran ice cold. 'Oh shite. Have you thrown up a cordon yet?'

'It literally happened two minutes ago and we're about to.'

'Then what are you waiting for, a personal bloody order from the King? For feck's sake, get on with it already, man.'

The officer gave him an ashen look and nodded, grabbing his phone from his pocket and heading away.

'They can't have got far, there's still a chance we can find them in time,' Megan said.

'I just pray so,' Joseph replied.

It was then he realised Norton was staring directly at them, his eyes slitted.

'Someone doesn't exactly look thrilled to see us,' Megan said.

'There's also a chance he might have an idea where Craig and Joanna went, so come on.'

'You couldn't bloody even give me this moment, detective?' Norton said the moment they'd reached him. 'Isn't it enough that you've already destroyed my career? My marriage?'

'That will be down to you, but there's one way that you can do the right thing and help us,' Joseph replied.

The coach peered at him. 'Go on?'

'Have you seen either Craig Franks or Joanna Keene since they arrived back here?'

Norton crossed his arms. 'And why do you need to know that exactly?'

'Because Joanna's life may be in danger unless we can find her quickly!'

The coach's eyes widened. 'You're saying that Craig's the murderer?'

'I'm not saying anything, but have you bloody seen them?'

Norton nodded and pointed to a far set of steps leading up from the river to the other side of the boathouse. 'I saw Craig head up those just a few minutes ago.'

'And what about Joanna?' Megan asked.

'She was celebrating with the others when she took a call and then went very pale. The next thing I knew, she was slipping away and heading in the same direction that Craig had gone.'

'And you didn't think to let any of her protection squad officers know?'

'For your bloody information, that's exactly what I was about to do, Detective,' Norton said, squaring up to Joseph.

But the DI was already ignoring the pumped-up gobshite. He and the DC pushed past the man, and raced for the far steps.

Joseph yanked his phone out as they ran, looking through the call history until he got to Joanna's number.

He punched it in and listened to it ringing on his mobile. After a few agonising seconds, his heart lifted when Joanna answered.

'Hi, what can I do for you?' she said.

'It's DI Stone. Okay, you need to listen to me very carefully, Joanna. Are you with Craig, right now? Just say uh-huh, if that's the case.'

'Uh-huh...' Joanna replied.

Joseph balled his hands into fists as he heard the sudden tension in her voice.

'Who's that?' Craig's voice said in the background.

'Just the coach, asking if we want to go for a celebratory drink at a pub in Covent Garden,' Joanna replied.

'Okay, but we still need to have that chat first, right?' Craig said.

'Whatever you do, you mustn't do that,' Joseph quickly said. 'Is it possible for you to get away from him? If yes, just say, uh-huh again.'

Joseph's heart lifted when she said, 'Uh-huh.'

Megan, who'd been listening in, shot him a relieved look.

'Okay, I want you to head back to the slipway where I and another officer will be waiting for you.'

'Uh-huh, sure, I'll be right there,' she replied, the sound becoming muffled. 'No problem, Craig,' Joanna said. 'But I just need to head back and fetch something I left behind.'

'Don't worry. I'm sure someone will grab it for you.'

'No, it's okay, really. I won't be a moment, and then we can have a proper talk.'

Joseph immediately cupped his hand over the mobile. 'I have a feeling that this situation is about to go south quickly, Megan. We need to find them before it's too late.'

She nodded and the two of them headed up the steps, Joseph desperately hoping to catch the cox before it was too late.

Joseph continued to listen to the conversation, already dreading where this was headed, but Craig's response was muffled.

'Ouch, you're hurting my wrist,' Joanna said next. 'Why are you doing this?'

The line suddenly went dead as a high pitch scream came from the other side of the boathouse.

Joseph was already dialling the number for Dave as he and Megan ran through a passageway towards where the scream had come from.

The DC picked up, and Joseph talked as they ran. 'Listen, Joanna Keene is being abducted by Craig Franks south of the boathouse. Get all units there as fast as possible.'

'On it, sir,' Dave replied.

The detective killed the call just as a second scream, this time much closer, was suddenly cut off. That was followed in a matter of seconds by the sound of an engine revving into life.

Megan cast Joseph an apprehensive look before they burst through a gate and emerged onto an adjacent road. The detectives were just in time to see a white transit van speeding away down a side road. It turned and disappeared from view.

Joseph spun round to face Megan. 'Did you get its number?'

She immediately shook her head. 'It was too far away.'

'Shite!' Joseph shouted, as Dave and two other protection officers came running towards them.

The DI immediately stabbed the dial button for Joanna, but heard an answering ring a short distance away. He glanced down to see a mobile on the road, its cracked display glowing as it vibrated on the tarmac.

Joseph put both hands on his head. 'Double shite,' he roared as he turned to the approaching officers.

'Contact DCI Faulkner and lock down every bloody road out of here, and do whatever it takes to get a police chopper in the air, now!'

CHAPTER TWENTY-SEVEN

A FEW HOURS LATER, the rain was hammering against the windows of St Aldates Police Station, where Joseph and Chris were currently standing in the superintendent's glass-walled office. Several heads had turned to watch the spectacle of the two detectives being laid into by the DSU.

'What do you fucking mean you don't have a clue where Craig Franks took Joanna?' Derrick bellowed at Chris.

'I'm afraid there was absolutely no way we could track down a white Ford Transit van heading out of London without knowing its number plate. If we'd tried to stop every white Ford Transit van, we would have quickly brought London to a standstill.'

'That might be true, but Franks should never have been able to escape in the first place,' Derrick replied. 'This whole fucking mess has the powerful stench of someone screwing up.'

As Joseph knew he would, the DSU's gaze sought him out, but before he could respond, Chris leapt to his defence.

'DI Stone and DC Anderson, along with the team on the ground, did everything they could. As the SIO in charge of the operation, I take full responsibility for what happened in Putney.'

Joseph appreciated the man trying to act as a lightning conductor to deflect the superintendent's wrath away from him, but he wouldn't let his senior officer take the blame, either.

Joseph stood taller and met Derrick's icy gaze head-on. 'I'm afraid if it's anyone's fault, it's mine. I was the senior attending officer who asked the team to hold back until they could make an arrest out of the public's eye. If they'd acted immediately, Craig Franks would now be in custody and Joanna Keene would be safe.'

'Bloody hell! I might have known that it was your incompetence that led to this shit show. I've already had the head office demanding that heads roll. Tell me why I shouldn't offer them yours, Stone?'

Joseph had to fight the compulsion to eyeball the man and tell the little bollox to his face that if they were going to start talking about incompetence, maybe they should start with the superintendent's decision to suppress evidence on the Hannah Emmerson case.

Instead, the DI just stared over Derrick's shoulder at the wall. 'We've all made mistakes on this, and Hannah's case.'

Just like a switch had been thrown, the fire in Derrick's eyes flickered out. He obviously realised that if he threw Joseph under the bus, then the DI would hang onto his ankle and drag the superintendent down with him.

The DSU's gaze tightened on Joseph. 'I will try to talk head office down, but the question remains—what are we going to bloody do about this fucking mess?' he said much more calmly, despite the swears.

It's remarkable what fear can do to a man, Joseph thought.

'Somewhere out there, if she isn't already dead, Joanna's life will be hanging by a thread,' Derrick continued. 'Her fate is on us, gentlemen,'

'Right now, Franks doesn't know that we're looking for him, which should work in our favour,' Chris replied. 'I've already issued a general alert across the country for his arrest. We've also checked the database, but, perhaps unsurprisingly, there's no record of any Ford Transit van belonging to Craig. No one has seen him at the student accommodation block in Oxford where he lives, either. We got the site manager to discreetly let us into his room, so any friends of his couldn't tip him off that the police are looking for him. Unfortunately, we found nothing useful there.'

'If he's been this careful so far, he's certainly not going to leave any evidence lying around,' Joseph said. A thought struck him. 'It might be worth checking if there's a Transit van registered to his uncle, like the narrowboat was. Talking of which, any joy tracking down *Dawn Treader*?'

'When we did our sweep along the canal last week, it was spotted moored near Iffley Lock,' Chris said. 'It was checked, but it was locked and the officers couldn't see anything suspicious through its cabin windows.'

'But that was then, and this is now,' Joseph said. 'Definitely worth sending some police launches up and down the river to look for it, in case Franks is using it as a floating hideaway. It may even be where he's holding Joanna.'

Chris nodded. 'When we find it, it will be worth having Amy and the forensic team go over it with a fine-tooth comb.'

Derrick frowned. 'But he may not be holding her there at all,' the superintendent said, for once sounding like a police officer rather than someone determined to give everyone else on the case ball-ache. 'There would be a greater risk of a member of the public noticing something if he was holding a woman against her will for any length of time on a boat.'

Joseph nodded. 'I agree. My money is still on Franks keeping her somewhere well away from any witnesses.'

'But you think he would be stupid enough to come back here to Oxford?' Derrick asked, now a completely different man than the one he had been at the start of this conversation.

'There's a good chance,' Joseph replied. 'Wherever Franks holds his victims, he's managed to evade our best efforts to find it so far. Also, I'm sure he had to be aware that Joanna had a protection team monitoring her, and don't forget he broke into her flat and nearly abducted her when we had a surveillance team in place. That tells me we're dealing with an arrogant son of a bitch. Yes, he could have whisked Joanna away to another hiding place, but there is a common thread running through all these murders.'

'Which is?' Chris asked.

'The river itself. If Franks isn't holding his victims on his uncle's boat, then my guess is that it's somewhere very close to the Isis or Thames, so why not return to Oxford, especially if he doesn't realise that we're onto him yet.'

'That makes sense,' Chris said. 'I think our best course of action is to search right along the river on both banks, extending as far out from Oxford as we have to.'

'That is going to take significant manpower, especially when we have another flood warning in place,' Derrick said. 'We're going to be fully stretched, dealing with the fallout from that.'

'Whatever needs to be done to save Joanna, please do it,' Joseph replied. 'Even if we have to pull in officers from right across the country,'

'But the cost—'

'Sod the cost,' Joseph said, narrowing his eyes at the superintendent.

Chris looked between them, and it was evident by the look

on his face he had no idea how Joseph could talk to the DSU like that and expect to get away with it.

Derrick sighed and nodded. 'Yes, none of us want the blood of another victim on our hands. I'll call in a helicopter search as well. Happy now, Joseph?'

'Ecstatic.'

'Then both of you get out of my sight and do whatever it takes to catch this bastard before it's too late.'

The incident room was crammed with what seemed like every available officer from St Aldates and Cowley stations, as the manhunt for Franks and Joanna ramped up. Derrick had certainly put his money where his mouth was. Dozens of officers had been pulled from flood duty and were now out scouring the embankment of the Isis. Joseph's instinct had also been proved right. It turned out Craig's uncle, who was a builder, did indeed own a white Transit van, and its number plate had now been factored into the search.

Chris put his phone down and groaned.

'Problem?' Joseph asked as he looked up from studying a detailed Ordnance Survey map of the Thames Valley, looking for anything that might jump out.

'I've just heard back from the police launches, and so far there's been absolutely no sign of *Dawn Treader*. It's like it's vanished off the face of the planet.'

'Something that big has to be out there somewhere, and it can't have got far since it was spotted at Iffley Lock only a week ago. After all, a narrowboat isn't exactly a speedboat, and I should know.'

Megan looked up from her screen, where she'd also been

searching for potential candidate sites that could have been missed. 'What if Craig is hiding it in plain sight?'

'What do you mean?' Chris asked.

'Isn't the search team relying on identifying the boats by their names? Like a car with false plates, what if Franks has done the same and disguised the name somehow?'

Chris and Joseph both stared at her.

'Bloody hell, talk about missing something so fecking obvious,' Joseph said, shaking his head. 'He wouldn't have the time to change its green paint job, but its name, absolutely. Chris, you may want to get the launches to do another sweep, this time looking for a boat matching the description of *Dawn Treader*, rather than relying just on the name painted on its side.'

Chris nodded and had already picked up the phone to start dialling before Joseph had even finished talking. The boss was soon issuing fresh orders to the officer coordinating the river launch search team.

Ian walked in, his head bandaged and a box of doughnuts in his hands, like a wise king arriving with a chest of gold.

'Will you look at this place? I'm gone five minutes, and it seems everything has gone to shit without me.'

Sue was already on her feet and headed over, scowling at him. 'What the hell are you doing here, Ian? The doctor said you were meant to rest at home.'

In the way of an answer, Ian simply gestured with his chin towards Joseph. 'If it's okay for my Irish friend to be here, then it certainly is for me as well. That's especially true when I heard that you've sent out an SOS for all hands on deck.'

Chris cupped his hand over his phone. 'It's great to see you back, Ian, but desk duty only for the time being, do you hear me?'

'Fair enough, Boss, and that's why I've brought supplies,' Ian said, holding up the box of doughnuts.

Joseph was pleased to see that Megan, who was learning fast, was one of the first to dig in before they all vanished. Within seconds, the vultures had circled away, leaving the box empty. That was when Chris's phone went off again. However, this time when he picked it up, his eyes quickly widened.

'Great work, and we'll take it from here.'

Everyone in the incident room gave the SIO an expectant look as he put down the phone and stood up.

'Okay, listen up everyone. We may have just had a break-through. The white van registered to Franks's uncle has just been spotted parked at the end of a green lane track near Yarnton.'

'Hang on, I was looking there a moment ago, at a site that we hadn't checked before, and thought it might be worth something,' Joseph said. He returned his attention to the Thames Valley map on his screen. He quickly scrolled through it until he was looking directly at the village of Yarnton again. Then his gaze narrowed as he spotted what he'd noticed before. 'That's it. I bet the bastard is holding Joanna there. It's the disused sewage plant that green lane leads to.'

As Chris, Megan, and the others crowded around the screen, he pointed to a series of rectangular buildings next to a lane.

Megan nodded. 'And that green lane continues straight down to the Oxford canal. How did we miss it before now?'

'Because we weren't searching that far north of the city,' Chris replied.

'Okay, we obviously need to chase this lead up as a matter of priority,' Joseph said. 'Can the police helicopter monitor the scene until we get there?'

'Unfortunately not,' Chris replied. 'It needs to return to base for fuel. We need to get feet on the ground as fast as possible, so let's get over there straight away.'

But Ian was already holding up his hands. 'That might not be quite as straightforward as you think, Boss. I drove past Yarnton on my way here. I barely got through. The rising flood-waters have almost completely cut off the village.'

Chris blew his cheeks out. 'Damn it, and I bet it's not deep enough for the police launches to reach it.'

Ian nodded.

'Then what about taking one of the Land Rovers?' Megan asked. 'I'm sure they could cope with a bit of water, and I'm also more than happy to drive.'

But Chris was already grabbing his coat. 'No, I'll cover that duty. Megan and Joseph, you're with me. Let's go and nail that bastard before it's too late.'

CHAPTER TWENTY-EIGHT

CHRIS DROVE Joseph and Megan through the growing darkness, day slipping away to night. Their vehicle ploughed through the water, its wipers barely making a dent in the biblical amount of rain currently falling from the sky. Around them, Joseph watched the sheets of rain swirl over the Oxfordshire countryside, beginning to resemble one large lake punctuated with trees.

The dual carriageway had been cordoned off by highway patrol, but they'd waved the police Land Rover through. The problem was the road was all but invisible under the floodwater. It was giving Chris a serious challenge trying to navigate along it, but one he seemed to be relishing.

Thankfully, Megan's choice of vehicles for this journey had been spot on. The Land Rover's ground clearance helped to keep it above the water level. Its ability to cope with the extreme conditions was also helped by the adapted air intake snorkel system that ran up the side of the windscreen to exit at roof level, which meant it wouldn't get blocked by floodwater. That little adaptation had meant the Land Rover had been more than up to this formidable task, and, so far at least, with dry feet for the detectives inside the vehicle.

They were making slow but steady progress, the headlights catching the peaks of the bow wave their vehicle was creating, rolling out towards the sides of the invisible carriageway.

'Nice night for it,' Joseph said.

'You're telling me,' Chris replied, with the grin of a man having the time of his life.

But Joseph was painfully aware of the time ticking past. It should have taken less than five minutes to reach Yarnton, but in these conditions, their progress had been reduced to a snail's pace. It took them another good fifteen minutes before they reached the village.

Finally, they began passing the houses set well back from the road, sandbags already piled up in front of their doors. Joseph spotted a Thames Water van, the water already halfway up to its wheel arches. Two men wearing fluorescent vests were desperately trying to erect some temporary flood barriers. Beyond them, a fire engine was pumping out a pool of water edging towards people's homes. This was going to be a long night for the emergency services and also a very worrying one for homeowners.

'I think this flood is going to set a new record,' Megan said, looking around them.

Chris nodded. 'Apparently, Botley Road is already underwater and cutting the city off from the western side. The sooner the government spends some serious money on flood defences, the better.'

'Talking of floods, what about *Tús Nua*, Joseph?' Megan asked. 'Will she be safe in this?'

'Dylan already rang to say both our boats are safely moored and not going anywhere,' Joseph replied. 'Apparently, the lock-keepers have already opened all the gates along the Thames to drain as much water as possible to prevent the city from flooding.'

'I think it's going to be a close-run thing,' Chris replied.

With a bang, the Land Rover lurched hard down onto its suspension, the front tyres dropping into some unseen pothole, sending a huge spray of water over the windscreen.

'Shit, we need to be careful of those,' Chris said. 'Even this Land Rover will grind to a halt if her engine gets submerged.'

'Yes, slow and steady is the only way we're going to make it all the way to the abandoned sewage plant,' Joseph replied.

'Won't that be in danger of being underwater by now as well?' Megan asked.

Joseph scanned the contours on the Ordnance Survey map he'd downloaded from his computer. 'It should be okay. According to this, the old sewage plant is slightly elevated, so it should be just above the floodplain.'

'It's the *just* part of that statement that worries me. If it keeps tipping down like this, we may need to trade this Land Rover in for a boat.'

'Don't you listen to the woman, old girl, you've absolutely got this,' Chris said, tapping the steering wheel with his fingers.

It was hard for Joseph not to notice, especially considering they were currently chasing down a murderer and his next potential victim, just how much the DCI had mellowed since he'd first met him. Getting away from his desk was obviously good for the man, and maybe he needed to do that more often. The DI also liked to think that maybe his influence—bad or otherwise—was helping to round off some of the man's sharp corners, much like river water smoothed even the most jagged stones given enough time.

Following the satnav's directions, they turned off at an almost invisible roundabout. The only parts of it that could be seen were the bushes rising above the floodwater like the bristles of a giant's shaving brush.

As the road began gently climbing, the water level began to drop around the vehicle. With a final spray of water from the Land Rover's wheels, which put Joseph in mind of a dog shaking itself after a dip, they were finally clear of the flood.

Chris didn't waste any time in putting his foot down. Soon they were racing away through the outskirts of the village, their strobing lights tinting the surrounding houses blue.

'There is one upside of this flood,' Megan said. 'If most cars can't make it through, I doubt that a Ford Transit van could have either. Hopefully, that means Craig will still be trapped at the sewer plant with Joanna.'

'If either of them are still there,' Joseph replied, not voicing the fact that Joanna could already be dead. 'He could have just dumped the vehicle, or left it parked there when he's not using it.'

'I wouldn't be so sure about that,' Chris said. 'The police helicopter used a thermal camera when they found the van and the engine block was still warm. That was only fifteen minutes ago. So I've got a good feeling about this.'

'Let's hope your instinct is on the money then, Boss,' the DI replied.

The problem was that deep down, Joseph couldn't help but feel that Franks was like a cat with nine lives, always evading them, despite their best efforts. Would it be any different this time?

'Talking of the helicopter, exactly how long until it returns from refuelling?' Megan asked.

'They were going to make a fast turnaround, so should be back here in another twenty minutes,' Chris replied. 'Unfortunately for us, that means we're going to be on our own until then.' He glanced at the satnav. 'That said, the sooner we get there and apprehend Franks, the happier I'll be.'

He gunned the engine when the road levelled out, the vehicle bouncing over the potholes as the coiled spring suspension fought to keep the Land Rover level.

'The boss is obviously from the same school of driving that you and Ian went to,' Joseph said to Megan, hanging onto the grab handles as they were thrown around inside.

'Nothing wrong with a bit of speed,' Megan said.

'Absolutely not,' Chris replied, smiling at her.

Joseph just shook his head at them. 'Two peas in a bloody pod.' He peered at the destination marker on the map on his phone. 'There should be the entrance to the green lane where the sewer plant is coming up on the right any moment, Chris.'

'Got it,' he replied, as it came into view, along with a white Ford Transit parked up on the road.

The DCI killed the blue lights, and a short time later they pulled up behind the van, blocking the exit.

The detectives got out into the stinging rain, which made it hard to make out anything.

'I'll check the vehicle,' Megan called out, heading over to the Transit van.

She peered through the windscreen, but seeing nothing there, headed around the back and pulled on the door to find it locked.

'Allow me,' Joseph said, stepping forwards. 'Chris, you may want to avert your eye for this bit.'

'If you think you're going to pick the lock, you can think again, Joseph,' the DCI said as he headed around the back of the Land Rover. A moment later, he reappeared with a pair of mole grips from a toolkit kept in the back of the police vehicle. Without even hesitating, he headed up to the Transit's back doors, took hold of the lock, and rotated it a couple of times. The barrel made a crunching sound, and then Chris was pulling the door open.

He met their impressed gazes. 'An old trick I learnt from a lad I arrested for breaking into a whole series of builders' vans. Anyway, we had due cause to check this van out, don't you think, officers?'

Joseph and Megan duly nodded. The DCI winked at them and then disappeared into the back of the van, slipping his latex gloves on. A moment later he reappeared with a bottle, along with some rags and some large plastic ties, all of which he slipped into evidence bags.

He unscrewed the bottle and smelled it, quickly pulling it away from his nose. 'As I suspected, chloroform. I would say that's a pretty good indicator that Franks probably drugged and bound Joanna, before transporting her here from the boat race.'

'This is starting to look more promising,' Megan replied.

'It certainly is.' Chris replied, looking down the green lane. 'How far is it to the sewer plant from here, Joseph?'

The DI glanced at his phone's screen, beaded with countless jewels of water. 'About half a kilometre according to the Ordnance Survey map. If Franks is still there, I think we might want to keep the element of surprise on our side. We should head in on foot, rather than risk him hearing the Land Rover approaching. Besides, that green lane already looks pretty boggy to me.'

Chris gave the lane an appraising look. 'Yes, I don't fancy even the Land Rover's chances in that muck.'

'Hang on, won't Franks have been alerted already by the police helicopter overhead earlier?' Megan asked.

'Hopefully, he'll just put that down to something to do with the flood at Yarnton, especially as the crew deliberately kept their distance.'

'Then let's pray this hasn't been a wild goose chase,' Joseph said.

Soon the three of them, all wearing wellies and holding torches currently turned off, were making their way down the unpaved passage as the rain continued its barrage. The weather had already penetrated the defences of Joseph's cagoule and soaked him to the skin.

Although the lane might not have been flooded, it was still a sticky quagmire and their progress wasn't swift. Muddy step by muddy step, they closed in on the marker for the disused sewage plant on the map.

They had finally got to within a hundred metres of it when at last the DI spotted a series of squat brick buildings with concrete roofs, barely visible over the top of the hedge running along the side of the lane.

Without the detectives needing to say a word to each other, they all took their batons out as they crept towards a padlocked entrance gate.

Joseph spotted a pair of muddy bootprints leading from the trail directly towards it. 'Those look fresh to me,' he whispered, pointing them out to the others.

Chris cast him a sideways glance. 'Starting to have a better feeling about our odds, Joseph?'

'By the minute.'

As quietly as they could, they all climbed over the gate. Megan was the last, but the gate rocked on its hinges as she lowered herself off it and clanked against the padlocked chain. Joseph strained to hear any reaction. They all collectively held their breaths. Thankfully, there wasn't even a murmur beyond the steady drumming of the rain.

With a nod to each other, they all crept forward again through the storm's growing darkness.

Ahead of them lay the abandoned sewage plant. It was

partly overgrown with bushes, and a circular filtration bed was covered with moss. Some of the walls of the largest building were covered with graffiti, a sure sign that the local yobs had discovered this place at some point.

What drew Joseph's attention, and gave him hope they might have really found Frank's hideaway, was a rectangular mound of earth with a hatch built into the top of it.

'That looks like an old water storage reservoir for the sewage plant,' Chris said. 'Are you all thinking what I'm thinking?'

'Absolutely,' Megan replied.

'I agree, but we should still split up to cover this site in case Franks has spotted us and is hiding in here somewhere,' Joseph said. 'The last thing we want is to risk him getting away.'

Chris nodded. 'Apart from the storage tank, there's really only one other place that Franks could hide. Whilst Megan and I check the tank, Joseph, could you check out that building?'

'Leave it to me, Boss.'

A few moments later, Joseph was edging towards the open doorway, his baton at the ready, his breathing shallow. The hum of adrenaline pumped through his veins as he stepped towards the dark, foreboding shadows that lay inside.

Joseph cautiously peered in, but the interior was just a jumbled mess of indistinct shapes. With no other option, he pressed the button on his compact LED flashlight. The beam of cold white light blazed out, piercing the darkness and illuminating the interior.

He stepped forward into the room, his heartbeat thundering in his ears. Rainwater slanted through a series of large glassless windows along one wall, forming large puddles of water beneath each of them. The torch's beam picked out fragments of glittering glass and broken tiles scattered over the floor, most likely the work of those local yobs.

As Joseph ventured further into the room, he spotted a bank

of metal cabinets lining the left-hand wall. Most had been gutted, with their wires trailing from the gaps where the equipment had been ripped out. A series of dials ran along the rear wall, many of them cracked and broken, a testament to the destruction probably caused by vandals.

But it was the three light blue metal cylinders with large pipes and valves that really caught the DI's attention. They curved down into large square holes in the ground, most likely part of some sort of pumping mechanism.

As Joseph moved forward, the sound of his boots crunching on broken glass filled the room, impossibly loud in this confined space. But once again, beyond the sound of the rain, he couldn't hear anything.

It was then he noticed multiple sets of footprints criss-crossing through the debris-covered floor, leading to and from the doorway he'd just entered. But of more immediate interest were the footprints congregating around the furthest pipe descending through a hole in the floor. As he aimed his torch beam towards it, he saw a large section of the pipe had been cut off, presumably with an angle grinder, and was pushed to one side of the open hole in the floor.

Interesting...

Joseph headed over, keeping his torch beam focused on it.

As the DI closed in, he noticed a blue shape beneath the hole. Leaning over it, he peered down and then his heart leapt. There, floating in a wide sewer pipe visible through the hole in the floor, was a rowboat, and more importantly, a figure was lying in the bottom of the boat. Joseph's mind reeled. He wasn't looking at Joanna, but Craig, his eyes closed, a gag around his mouth.

Even as his brain struggled to process this new piece of information, he was already calling out, 'Joanna, are you okay?'

Too late, Joseph heard someone running up behind him. The DI turned and just had time to lock eyes with Joanna.

'Stop!' the DI shouted.

He raised his arm to protect himself, as the woman swung a bar down towards him. Joseph's forearm deflected most of the blow, but the bar still hurtled onwards, striking his forehead hard. Like a switch had been thrown, the DI's world went dark and he lost consciousness.

CHAPTER TWENTY-NINE

JOSEPH CAME ROUND, his head feeling like a rhinoceros had charged him, and then trampled on his skull for good measure. He opened his eyes to see Megan's worried face staring down at him.

'Oh, thank God, you're back in the land of the living,' she said.

As Joseph took a quick physical inventory, the main headline was there was a stabbing pain coming from the top of his head.

With a considerable effort, he gathered his thoughts. 'Joanna Keene hit me round the fecking head!'

'You mean Franks, surely?' Megan asked, staring at him.

'No, Keene had Craig tied up in a boat on the other end of that pipe...' The DI tried to sit up, but a wave of nausea swirled through him.

'Bloody hell,' Megan said. 'Steady there. That's the second nasty head wound you've received in as many days.'

'Aye. But in that old sewer the last person to smack me round the head can't have been Keene, because she was still with you in the house.'

'Then she had an accomplice?'

Joseph's eyes widened. 'Feck!' Ignoring her advice, the DI pushed himself up into a sitting position. He peered down into the hole in the pumping station floor to see exactly what he'd been dreading. The boat, Joanna, and Craig had all vanished.

'Damn it, how long have I been out?' Joseph asked.

'Just a couple of minutes. We were checking the inside of the water tank—which is definitely where Joanna has been holding her victims. We had just found the end of a sawn-off oar handle that we figure was used to beat the female victims when we heard you cry out. We rushed straight here, and as soon as we saw you were knocked out next to this hole in the floor, we quickly put two and two together, although obviously we still thought Craig was responsible. Chris was straight onto the station and someone there was able to dig up some information, confirming that this pipe runs directly to the Oxford Canal about a kilometre away. The boss set off in pursuit along the green lane that runs parallel to the pipe, whilst I stayed with you.'

Joseph nodded, and immediately wished he hadn't, with the mother of all headaches roaring inside his skull. 'Is backup on its way?'

'Yes, a police launch is heading along the Oxford Canal from the Thames, and the helicopter is ten minutes out. A police Land Rover from the Cowley Police Station is also trying to get here, although it's slow going because of the flood.'

'Okay, but at least Keene can't get that far in a rowing boat,' the DI replied. 'But right now, Chris will need backup with that psychopath, so let's get moving.' Joseph grabbed hold of the pump and, gritting his teeth, hauled himself to his feet.

'Where the hell do you think you're going?' Megan asked.

'To do what needs to be done. I'm not going to let our SIO face that monster alone.'

'Bloody hell, has anyone told you that you'd beat a mule in a bloody stubbornness competition?' Megan said, following Joseph through the doorway.

'All the time, and it's a badge of honour that I wear with considerable pride.'

Megan shook her head as they headed outside, straight into the snarling rain.

Joseph noticed the puddles had already grown considerably larger in the short time he'd been knocked out. That meant the flood was still rising. It had to be only a matter of time before this whole area was underwater too.

They reached the gate and clambered over it, the whole manoeuvre making his head spin like a Ferris wheel. He jammed his jaws together and ignored the feeling of vertigo. Fishing his mobile out, he punched the contact number for Chris's phone. It went straight to voicemail.

'Shite, the boss isn't answering. That can't be a good sign.'

Megan nodded, and they hurried down the green lane together, splashing through the water that had risen over it.

Ahead of them, they could see the lane led to a small stone bridge, rising like the hump of a whale's back above the floodwater.

Joseph gestured towards it. 'That's where this lane crosses over the Oxford Canal.'

'Let's hope Chris is okay, and he's just lost signal,' Megan replied, without any conviction in her voice.

They redoubled their efforts, their feet sending spray flying as they half ran, half waded towards the bridge ahead of them.

Joseph felt the last of his strength ebbing. He knew he couldn't keep this up. But that stubborn part of his soul that he was so proud of would not let him give up before he'd seen this thing through to the bitter end.

At last, they reached the bridge and raced to the middle to look down at the canal roaring past at an astonishing speed.

'Shine your torch along the embankment to see if we can locate the exit from that pipe,' he said.

As Megan's beam travelled along the edge of the canal, they both spotted the dark mouth of a tunnel. The bars covering it had been cut.

'That must be where Joanna escaped with Craig,' Joseph said.

'So where the hell are they now?' Megan asked, peering along the rushing canal into the distance.

'They could be miles away when the river is travelling at this speed—' A cry cut off the rest of Joseph's words.

'For God's sake, help me!' Chris called out from somewhere beneath them.

Megan immediately directed the torch beam to just beyond the tunnel exit and there, a bit further downstream, they spotted the DCI desperately hanging onto a branch that had partly sheared off the trunk and bent down into the water.

'I'm losing my grip here—for Christ's sake, hurry,' Chris shouted as he blinked into the torch beam.

Joseph found a deep reserve somewhere in his body and the two detectives set off at a run. Less than thirty seconds later, they were wading through the floodwater that had burst the embankments of the canal. The current pulled hard at their legs. They splashed their way to where Chris was clinging on, his knuckles white, arms trembling with the strain, a man right on the edge of letting go.

Without hesitation, Joseph stepped onto the unstable branch, now attached to the main trunk only by a strip of bark. He held on to the branch above him tightly and moved carefully towards the DCI, whose grip was already faltering. The raging stormwater swirled around them as Megan urgently spoke into her phone.

'Nearly there, Chris,' Joseph said, closing the distance.

His boss's gaze locked onto his, his teeth chattering. 'It is seriously fucking cold in here, Joseph.'

'Then let's see what we can do about getting you out of there, and tucked up back at the station with a nice cosy hot water bottle,' the DI replied, with his best attempt at a calm voice. 'But you're going to have to trust me, Chris. I'm going to reach down in a moment and grab hold of you. When I say let go, do it, and I'll haul you out of there and back to the embankment.'

'I'm not sure I can, Joseph. My hands keep spasming and have locked on.'

'You have to try—'

The DI's words were lost in the sound of a loud splintering noise behind him. The thin strip of bark that held the branch to the trunk had finally begun to tear away. A vibration shuddered through the branch, and Chris's eyes widened as his hands were shaken free.

Time seemed to slow down for Joseph. In a quick movement, he reached down and grabbed his SIO with one hand, while maintaining his grip with the other on the branch above him. He began towing Chris back towards the embankment. But then, as he knew it would, the branch shuddered again violently, finally breaking free of its tether.

The bitter taste of bile rose to the back of Joseph's throat.

In the split second he had left, he desperately hauled Chris out of the water towards Megan's waiting arms. She grabbed them both just as he felt the toe of his boot hit the edge of the embankment. With a last desperate effort, Joseph pushed off the branch and stepped onto solid ground. Megan pulled them both to safety as the branch was swept away down the canal.

Breathing heavily, Joseph supported Chris with Megan's help, and they made their way back to the safety of the bridge.

'Fecking hell, that was close,' Joseph said.

'You're telling me,' Megan replied, as Chris's whole body began to shake.

'Chris has hypothermia setting in!' Joseph shouted.

'I've already contacted the police helicopter, and it's going to land in the field next to us,' Megan replied, taking Chris's hands in hers. 'It's going to fly you straight to hospital, Boss.'

The DCI's eyes locked onto hers. 'We had it wrong. It's Joanna who abducted Craig,' he said through chattering teeth. 'I almost had her, and that little bitch smacked me over the head with an oar. She dragged Craig onto his uncle's narrowboat, which she'd hidden under the trees, and took off downstream with him.'

Joseph's mind raced. 'Okay, leave that to us, Chris. The police launch is just a few minutes out. Wherever that psychopath thinks she's going, she won't get far. Even running with the current, a narrowboat isn't exactly fast.'

Megan's gaze tightened on Joseph's head. 'That doesn't look good. You've been in the wars, and should go to the hospital, too. Leave this to me.'

When the DI put his hand to it, he felt the warmth of blood on his fingers, but he shook his head.

'No, I'm seeing this through. Besides, Keene has some serious payback coming.'

Chris managed a faint smile. 'I wouldn't try arguing with the man, Megan. The two of you get that bitch for me, and that's an order.'

As they heard a helicopter coming into land, Joseph managed a smile. 'Leave that to us, Boss.'

CHAPTER THIRTY

Joseph and Megan clung tightly to the police launch as it raced down the canal in the direction Chris had indicated the narrowboat had gone.

Considering the awful conditions, in near total darkness, the officer steering the RIB was doing an astonishing job of navigating the numerous branches being carried along by the floodwater. Another officer at the prow was using a spotlight to illuminate their way so they could avoid any debris that might damage the hull if they struck it at speed.

'I don't understand what Keene's game plan here is,' Megan shouted over the roar of powerful twin Mercury outboard engines. 'She knows we're onto her, so what does she hope to gain by fleeing? It's not like she's going to get far in that boat. Also, why take Craig?'

'Because she wants to use him as a hostage,' Joseph replied. 'But she's deluding herself if she thinks we're just going to let her waltz away with him.'

'Surely she must know the game is up?'

'Almost certainly, but I think this is just her last desperate throw of the dice. That's especially true when she knows the alternative is spending the rest of her life behind bars on multiple murder charges.'

Megan frowned at Joseph. 'So, in other words, she's got nothing left to lose?'

'Exactly. Desperate people do desperate things, and when we're talking about cornering a psychopath, that's when they can be the most dangerous.'

The DC nodded as the RIB boat swung around a gradual bend in the canal. When it straightened out again, they passed a flooded road running parallel to the waterway. Several cars had been left abandoned there in the rising floodwater. It was halfway up the patio doors of a lone house as they sped past it.

'This is as bad as I've ever seen it,' Joseph said. 'I hate to imagine what state Oxford is in by now.'

'Not good, but that's someone else's problem right now,' Megan replied.

'Aye, that it is.'

A loud thud came from the hull, and the boat rocked violently before the officer swiftly steered the police launch to the right.

The detectives both looked down to see a partly submerged log, scraping along the side before falling away behind them.

'Sorry, sir, it's hard to spot everything under these conditions,' the officer who'd been steering said. 'We really should consider breaking off the pursuit.'

'Not when there's a life in danger, we won't,' Joseph replied. 'I don't want any argument, so we keep going. Understood?'

'Of course, sir,' the officer replied.

Megan looked at Joseph. 'We could hand this over to the air search team. That would be a lot safer for everyone involved.'

But Joseph shook his head. 'We have a small window of time here. As long as Joanna thinks that keeping Craig alive is her best bet, she'll do exactly that. Besides, it will take too long for the police helicopter to get back here after dropping Chris off at the hospital. And if we lose Keene now, there will be nothing stopping her from killing Craig. I let Millie and Hannah down, and I can't let the same thing happen to him.'

Megan reached over and squeezed the DI's shoulder. 'You do realise that this isn't all down to you? If there's any blame, we should share responsibility equally across the team.'

'That's not how I see it,' Joseph replied.

'Then maybe you should start trying to.'

Joseph fell silent. Deep down, he knew Megan was right, but part of him refused to see it that way. If Craig died, Joseph would have his blood on his hands—just like he did with both of Keene's other victims.

The police officer at the front of the boat suddenly turned around to look at them. 'There's a narrowboat dead ahead of us.'

Relief surged through Joseph. 'Okay, let's see if we can get this situation resolved peacefully. Pull up just behind it and we'll try to talk Keene down off the metaphorical ledge.'

The other officer nodded and gradually pulled back on the throttle as they slowed to match the speed of the other craft.

He handed the DI a megaphone. 'You'll probably want this, sir.'

'Thanks,' Joseph said, as the officer at the helm directed the spotlight towards the back of the narrowboat. Glancing back, Joanna spotted the launch and gunned the boat's engine.

Joseph flicked the megaphone's switch on and raised it to his mouth. 'It's over, Keene. You've got nowhere left to run to. Give it up.'

'And why would I do that, DI Stone?' Joanna shouted back. 'I can't exactly plea bargain my way out of murder. Better to go out swinging, I say.'

'What exactly do you mean by that?' Joseph said, a feeling of apprehension taking hold.

'That I'm going to push for the finish line, whatever the cost,' she replied.

'I don't like the sound of that,' Megan whispered. 'What about Craig?'

Joseph lowered the megaphone and nodded. 'We definitely need to prioritise his rescue above everything else. So let's just pray Joanna hasn't already tipped him overboard and is still using him as a hostage.' He raised the megaphone back to his mouth. 'Okay, how about this? You release Craig, and we'll let you be on your way.'

They heard Joanna laughing as the RIB boat slowed to match the speed of the narrowboat, just twenty metres off its stern.

'And lose what little leverage I have?' she replied. 'Just how gullible do you think I am, Stone?'

'That's the last thing I think you are,' Joseph replied. 'You've shown remarkable resourcefulness in getting this far, but we both know this is only going to end one way.'

'Do we? Are you sure about that?'

'Look, you know you can't outrun us, and we can follow you until you're forced to land. The moment you do, you'll be arrested. So there's no point in prolonging the inevitable.'

'But you're still thinking two-dimensionally about my current situation, Stone,' Keene replied in a mocking tone. 'I'm used to winning, doing whatever it takes, including murdering, to achieve my objectives. To do that requires a mind that is prepared to not play by the rules. Let me demonstrate...'

Still picked out by the spotlight, they watched Joanna tie off the rudder and disappear into the cabin.

'What the hell is she doing now?' Megan asked.

'I don't know, but let's grab this opportunity to board the boat,' Joseph replied. He nodded to the PC piloting their craft.

The officer accelerated the launch until they were drawing

alongside the narrowboat. At that exact moment, Joanna re-emerged from the cabin carrying a length of heavy chain and pushing Craig before her, his mouth still gagged and his hands tied together.

Immediately, Joseph gestured for the officer to pull away until the boats were traveling abreast of each other down the fast flowing canal, a metre between them.

'So predictable, Stone,' Joanna called out. 'If anyone isn't capable of thinking outside the box, it's you.'

'Aye, I was always the slow one back at school,' Joseph replied with a shrug. 'But you really don't need Craig. Just humour me and let him cross onto our boat. Saving his life is our only priority right now. Catching you can wait for another day.'

Keene's gaze tightened on him. 'Yes, of course your prime concern would be yet another person who has had life handed to them on a silver platter, just like Hannah and Millie's were. All of those stupid arseholes looked down their noses at me. Isn't that right, Craig?' She ran her fingers through his blond hair. He tried to pull away from her, but she yanked him closer.

Joanna turned back towards the police launch, her eyes slitted. 'He was meant to be my plaything, but you spoiled our party before I had a chance to get all nice and cosy with him. So what use is he to me now, Stone? Especially now that I've finished using him to do things for me, including trying to draw you away in the sewer?'

'That was Craig who hit me over the head?'

'Only because he panicked. But that was all part of my little pantomime. You were meant to think he was the one responsible for the murders, before I heroically fought him off back at the sewer plant and killed him. But you spoiled all of that when you spotted Craig knocked out in the boat.'

'But why would he have done any of this to help you?' Megan called out.

'The same old story. He's always fancied me. Haven't you my lovely? Although, you didn't take it well when I rejected you at Bampton.' She nudged Craig in the back and he moaned. 'So easy to get someone to do anything for you when they worship the ground you walk on, even if they don't understand exactly why they are doing it.' She started to wrap the length of chain around Craig's wrists. 'And like I said, in a situation like this, it's all about thinking outside the box.'

Before Joseph could reply, Keene stepped up behind Craig and shoved him hard in the back. With a muffled scream, he fell into the raging, frothing water. The moment he hit, Craig began frantically kicking his legs, desperately trying to keep his head above the surface. But despite his best efforts, he was pulled under by the raging current.

'Fecking bitch!' Joseph shouted.

'Absolutely, and that should keep you busy until I'm long gone,' Joanna said, grinning at them.

'Get back to Craig and do whatever you can to save him,' he shouted to Megan and the two officers on the police launch. With a snarl, Joseph leapt for the narrowboat's side and clung on.

The DC nodded and began pulling her jacket and boots off as the police launch circled back towards where Craig had vanished beneath the surface.

'What the hell do you think you're doing, Megan?' Joseph shouted after them.

'What I have to do to save a life,' she called back. Then, without hesitating, she leapt into the canal at the spot where Craig had disappeared.

'Wow, she certainly has courage, I'll give her that,' Joanna said as she picked up a lever used for the locks from the floor. 'I'm impressed, Stone. You're definitely thinking outside the box now. Shame you won't live long enough to arrest me.'

'We'll have to see about that, you gobshite,' Joseph said, pulling himself up towards the roof of the narrowboat.

'You think?' Joanna said. 'Time to scrape an unwanted barnacle off my boat.' She grinned at the detective as she leaned hard on the tiller, steering the craft towards a bank of trees.

The branches scraped over Joseph's body like curved claws. Then one branch, thicker than the rest, sliced into the back of his hand, leaving a deep, open gash and breaking his grip. He was left dangling by his other hand from the roof railing, his feet ploughing through the surface of the floodwater as he lost sight of Keene.

A wave of primordial anger rose through him. *I'll give you bloody thinking outside the fecking box,* the detective thought.

It was often when Joseph was in the tightest of corners that he did the craziest things, so why should it be different this time? If he couldn't currently see Joanna, that also meant the murderer couldn't see him.

Before the DI could give himself a chance to think his plan through, he let go of the railing and dropped further down the side of the boat. As his lower body made contact with the water, a large splash erupted. With split-second timing, he reached out and desperately grasped the edge of the boat's hull with just the tips of his fingers as it slid past. Now with only his head and arms above the floodwater, Keene thankfully took the bait. No doubt thinking she'd scraped the detective off the boat, the woman began to steer the boat away from the trees and back towards the middle of the canal.

Joseph heard her chuckling to herself. Now, to put the second part of his downright stupid plan into operation.

The DI began to shuffle his hands along the lip of the narrowboat's hull towards the cockpit.

Just then, an open lock gate came into view. Joseph thought he knew this section of the canal well, but the floodwaters had made the terrain almost unrecognisable. Nevertheless, his instinct was they were approaching Duke's Lock, just beyond Wolvercote. If he was right, there would also be a left-hand channel just before it, which would be a shortcut from the Oxford Canal leading directly to the Thames.

When the channel came into view, Keene turned the narrowboat sharply towards the shortcut through to the river and gunned the engine. So that was her plan: try to escape through it to the Thames. Joseph would place good money she had another boat waiting to guarantee she would be long gone before anyone realised what had happened.

That might be her plan, but it was one Joseph was determined to spoil, especially as the fecker had probably just claimed her third victim right in front of the detective's eyes.

With fresh determination, Joseph continued to shuffle his hands along the lip of the hull, the current savagely pulling at his body. He hung on with grim determination, inching himself along the boat until he pulled level with the cockpit. The top of Keene's head was just visible, but thankfully, the woman's full attention was focused on the difficult manoeuvre in progress as she negotiated the right hand bend in the fast flowing current.

Joseph knew it was now or never.

They entered another open lock, and the roar of the water bellowed around them as it bounced between the brick canyon walls. Joseph took a deep breath, and then with every ounce of strength he had left, he pulled himself upward in one fluid movement.

Hearing him, Joanna turned, her eyes widening as she saw the detective clambering over the side of the boat. Without hesitating, she swung the lock lever, striking Joseph in the side before he had a chance to defend himself.

A searing pain burned through the DI as several of his ribs cracked. He snarled and lunged at Joanna, wrapping his arms around her. She fought back, a wild, cornered creature, driving the lock lever into the detective's stomach.

Agony erupted in Joseph's gut as he clung tightly to Keene in a desperate bear hug. Through the pain, he saw the brick wall of the lock rushing towards them. With a deafening crash, the boat smashed into the wall, twisting sideways.

Even as raw, burning agony pumped through his stomach, Joseph determinedly hung on to the lever. The stern of the boat swung around and smashed into the opposite bank in a tremendous crash of splintering wood. Within seconds, it was jammed fast between the two lock walls with the floodwater surging over it. The craft tilted, breaking Joseph's grip on the weapon, and Joanna was thrown backwards.

The rower staggered, regained her balance, and swung the lever in an arc towards Joseph's head. The DI ducked and threw a desperate punch straight up towards the woman's face. With a sickening crunch, his fist connected with his opponent's nose, hard enough to topple Joanna backwards into the raging water. With a surprised cry, the rower hit the surface hard. Her head bobbed up briefly as she was swept away, her gaze locking onto Joseph before she was pulled into the swirling terrible depths.

Joseph's focus snapped back as the boat lurched beneath him, the weight of thundering water breaking the vessel apart. Within moments, he was sinking into the rushing current with what remained of the narrowboat.

With nothing left to fight, the floodwater came up to claim him. With a roar, it surged over his head and suddenly he was beneath the surface, the impossible strength of the current pummelling into his body, and driving the air from his lungs.

A strange sense of peace took hold of Joseph as his life slipped away. He had done all he could, and at least Joanna wouldn't live to kill again. He just hoped Ellie would be proud of him when she learned what had happened.

The water was clawing its way into his nose and throat, and into his lungs. As his consciousness faded, Joseph thought he could hear a constant thudding getting louder. Then a bright light, like the moon, was blazing down through the surface just above him.

No, not the moon...

He felt hands reach down through the water and grasp onto him. The next moment he was being pulled out, and he saw Megan's face over him. Her mouth was moving, but he couldn't make out her words as his world faded to black.

CHAPTER THIRTY-ONE

ELLIE RUSHED into Joseph's hospital room, her face ashen. Sobbing, she threw her arms around him. 'Bloody hell!' she said, as tears rolled down her face and she clung to her father.

'I know, lass, but *ow*. Could you not squeeze so hard, your old man is a bit worse for wear.'

She grimaced as she pulled away, smearing her tears with the back of her hand. 'Sorry...' She took in the bandages wrapped around his chest and stomach, not to mention the fresh ones on his head.

'Are you going to be okay?'

'Yes, although on top of everything else, I could have done without Keene driving that lock lever into my spleen.'

Ellie put her hands over her mouth.

'Honestly, I'm going to be okay. According to the doctor, my liver will take over its function while my spleen heals, although I will need to stay in here for a while to be monitored, so it will be lots of decent painkillers for a while.'

Taking a shaky breath, she nodded.

'You just wait and see. I'll be as right as rain before you know it.'

'But what about your ribs and the fresh head injury?'

Joseph smiled and pointed to his head. 'It will take a lot more than a murderer braining me to get through this thick noggin. As for the ribs, they just need time.'

His daughter took his hands in hers. 'So, you're really going to be okay?'

'I don't think I'll ever be okay because I'll always be me, so no change there, I'm afraid.' He grinned at her.

'Dad!' Ellie gave him an exasperated look, but then laughed.

'That's better,' Joseph said, gazing at his daughter with a softness in his eyes.

There was a knock on his door and Joseph looked over to see Chris, wearing a dressing gown and leaning on the doorframe.

'Space for another visitor?' the DCI asked.

'Always,' Joseph said, gesturing towards a free seat next to the bed.

Chris fixed him with a long look. 'It seems I owe you my life.'

'You would have done the same for me if the roles had been reversed.'

'Absolutely. But that aside, your dad is a regular hero, Ellie.'

'Tell me something I don't know already,' she replied.

Chris smiled, and returned his attention to Joseph. 'It's good to see you awake, especially after nearly getting yourself drowned on top of everything else Keene did to you.'

'Yes, I was lucky that Megan and the launch officers turned up when they did.'

Ellie's eyes widened and she clamped her hand onto her father's bandaged one, which had been torn open by the branch.

'Ow, again,' Joseph said.

'Sorry, but if I had lost you...' She wiped away fresh tears. 'Especially because of *her*...'

'Well, you didn't, which is the main thing to focus on.' His gaze softened on her. 'Would you be an absolute love and run along to the hospital Pret, and grab me a coffee? One for you, Chris?'

'A double espresso would be great,' the DCI replied.

'Of course,' Ellie said, leaning over and kissing her father on the forehead before heading out of the room.

Chris grimaced the moment she'd gone. 'Sorry, me and my big mouth.'

'Don't worry about it. Ellie might not like my job sometimes, but she also understands that's the nature of it. Having said that, I thought it was better that we spoke alone rather than putting her through it. Can you get me up to speed on the case? To start with, how's Craig doing?'

'Thankful to be alive. The launch officers said they'd never seen anything like it when Megan dived in to save him. Not a lot of people could have managed to make it to the bottom of the canal when the current was running that fast. Especially to rescue someone wrapped in chains, and not end up getting themselves drowned in the process.'

Joseph nodded. 'I can testify to Megan's exceptional swimming abilities, after seeing her take part in a river race recently. I certainly doubt there are many other people who could have pulled off a rescue in those awful conditions.'

'Craig definitely owes his life to Megan. Although, technically, I should lecture the DC about risking herself like that.'

'If that's true, then I should be next in line for that as well.'

Chris chuckled. 'Isn't that the truth? But we both know that would be a waste of my breath.'

Joseph snorted. 'You might have a point there. Anyway, please don't be too hard on Megan. I think she has the makings of an exceptional detective. She certainly has the guts for it.'

'I agree. I misjudged her when we first met. I actually thought she wasn't up to the job at all. However, she's more than proved herself to me, just like you have, Joseph. I'm sorry I didn't realise straight away what an exceptional officer you are, but I certainly do now.'

'Yes, I tend to grow on people once they get to know me, a bit like a slow-growing nail fungus.'

Chris chuckled. 'Now, that's quite the comparison. Anyway, I'm proud to have you on the team, even if I think you should be my boss, rather than the other way round.'

'Really?'

He nodded. 'The truth is—and should you ever repeat this, I'll completely deny it—I'm a bit intimidated by you, Joseph. You have far more experience, and a better-honed instinct. In the future, I intend to listen to you far more closely, instead of DSU Walker. He's definitely got a blind spot when it comes to you.'

Joseph shrugged. 'There's history between us that accounts for that, and it runs both ways.'

'I thought as much,' Chris replied, raising his eyebrows at the DI. 'Anyway, in future, I intend to utilise your talents to the full extent, and Megan's too. Maybe, when the other officers see me doing that, they might even stop calling me *Fucker* behind my back.'

The DI grimaced. 'Just office banter. You should hear what they call the superintendent.'

'Actually, I have. Although in his case, I think it's a bit more deserved.'

Joseph roared with laughter. 'You'll get no argument from me there, Boss. Office politics aside, any update on the search for Keene's body?

'Yes, it finally surfaced in the Thames and has been recovered. I suppose it's fitting in a way that Joanna's life ended in the river, since her whole obsession seems to have revolved around it.'

'The Irishman in me can certainly see the poetic justice to it.'

Chris nodded. 'I was wondering if you had any thoughts about why she did any of this?'

'I'm pretty sure that it was partly jealousy. She definitely had a bit of a chip on her shoulder as it turns out she'd won a scholarship to Bampton, unlike the other students who had rich parents. That made her highly competitive with them. She certainly hated to see others getting ahead of her. Like Grace did back at her old school, when she won the rowing race. Suddenly Grace had all of these offers coming in and Joanna couldn't handle that, so she murdered Grace. After that, she seemed to get a taste for it. Killing Hannah was a means to an end to secure a seat on the team for Craig as a cox, when he started at Oxford.'

'But why would she want to do that?'

'Probably so she could use him to do her bidding within the boat team. I'm just not sure why she killed Millie.'

'I may be able to cast some light on that. Megan came to see me whilst you were in surgery. She told me that when she and Ian were interviewing Craig, he told them that Joanna had tried it on with Millie, just like she once had with Grace back at Bampton, but they'd both turned her down. It looks like she just couldn't deal with it, especially when she saw how Millie was with Norton, a man she looked up to and was in love with. And how Grace was with Craig. I think that's why she initially set the coach up to take the fall for the murders, then switched to Craig in the end. Despite that, it's almost like she saw Norton as a role model. At least she didn't have a chance to beat Craig with that damned sawn-off oar handle of hers.'

'That's one less trauma that he has to deal with. I think Millie's beating was ultimately all about control. It seems she was jealous of Craig being into Millie, and she was determined to have the last laugh. But setting Craig up to take the fall was a genius move. Especially when she made it look like he had abducted her from the Boat Race, rather than the other way round.'

'That makes sense. So how did Keene manage to get into her victim's homes?'

'I think that's the easy part,' Joseph said. 'She would have used the same changing room in the boat club as the other women. That was where she probably managed to make copies of their keys.'

'Yes, that all fits. Then I suppose the only question that remains is, would Keene have done it again if she'd got away with it?'

'We'll never know for sure, but my hunch is yes,' Joseph said. 'In her own way, she had an even bigger ego than Norton, and referred to her victims as her *playthings*. I think she would have kept heading down that path until she was eventually caught. She had the makings of a true serial killer about her, and she wasn't about to stop anytime soon.'

'At least that career was cut short, sooner rather than later,' Chris said.

'But not soon enough,' Joseph replied, thinking of Millie and Hannah, and of Grace too, women who were the same age as Ellie. 'And that will haunt me forever.'

'These sorts of cases always do,' Chris said. 'I always find myself running over old cases, second guessing myself about why I didn't do something that could have saved a life.'

'We all do that,' Joseph replied.

The DCI sighed and nodded. 'I suppose that's just part of the job. Anyway, when we get out of here, I'd like to take you and Megan out for a drink to say thanks for saving my life. What do you say?'

Joseph arched his eyebrows at him. 'If you're buying, who am I to look a gift horse in the mouth?'

Chris snorted as another knock on the door came and they looked over to see Dylan and Megan standing there.

'Will you see who the wind has blown in now?' Joseph said, beaming at them both.

'And we come bearing gifts,' Megan said, holding up a box. 'I have those Pastel de Natas from that place you love on the high street.'

'Pastel de Natas?' Chris asked.

'Portuguese custard tarts,' Joseph replied.

'Oh, right.'

Dylan looked up and down the corridor in a theatrical take on checking the coast was clear, before producing a green and white bottle, with a crystal cut pattern on it, out of a carrier bag. 'And I've got an exceptional Shivering Mountains craft gin here with all our names on it.'

Joseph turned to Chris. 'It seems like we're going to have that drink together sooner than we thought.'

Two months later, Joseph was adjusting the collar of his shirt in the small family-run Italian restaurant Ellie had insisted he book for his *hot date*.

The detective had already fortified himself with a single malt Bushmills Whiskey, in an attempt to suppress the sense of pure animal terror currently rolling around in his gut. Joseph was seriously out of practice when it came to the dating game. He also still wasn't at all convinced that any of this was a good idea.

He'd already been toying with the idea of getting Megan to ring him once the date had begun. Maybe with something along the lines of an urgent investigation that needed his specific expertise. Maybe a hostage incident to add urgency. He even knew that Chris, with whom his friendship with had deepened since the Keene case had been closed, would back him up if he needed the lie confirmed. But the problem with that strategy was that his date would see straight through it. That would make life more than awkward whenever he came across her at work.

Mixing business with pleasure was currently looking like the worst idea he'd ever allowed himself to be cajoled into. Kate had been as thick as thieves with their daughter about this too, comparing notes on Joseph's future romantic life. Why he'd agreed to it, he still wasn't sure. But then again, Ellie was a force of nature and when she told him to jump, his role was to ask: *how high?*

At least she'd let him choose the restaurant, the owner of which he knew personally, and who was going to cook them something special that wasn't on the menu. Something involving clams, white wine, and garlic, which certainly sounded like a winning combination to Joseph.

As the restaurant door opened, his heart sped up.

Oh, Jesus, here we go... he thought. But then he saw it was just a young couple coming in, and the waiter was already heading over to welcome them.

Joseph emptied his glass, desperately trying to slow the spin of his nerves.

It was then a shadow fell across his table. He glanced up, expecting to see the waiter coming back to ask if he wanted a refill. Instead, he found himself looking at Amy. Her fair hair was hanging loose and framing those dazzling blue eyes of hers, which were currently looking at him as a smile formed on her lips.

'I didn't hear you come in,' Joseph said as he quickly stood.

'I just sneaked in behind that other couple who just came in.'

'Right...'

He hurried around the table to help her out of her coat. The air caught in Joseph's throat when he saw the stylish black dress she was wearing. Amy looked absolutely beautiful and dressed to kill.

'Are you okay?' she asked, peering at him.

'Sorry, I'm just not used to seeing you in civvies.'

'What, this old thing?' she said, pointing to her dress and actually doing a little twirl. 'You like it?'

'I love it...' He grimaced, wishing he could take the words back and not sound quite so desperate.

Amy cocked her head. 'Joseph, will you please relax. You look like a frightened rabbit, which makes me feel like some sort of fox who's about to pounce on you.'

'Sorry...' Joseph said as he pulled her chair out for her.

Amy shook her head, her smile widening as she sat down. 'Please stop apologising. So, what are you drinking?'

'Bushmills.'

'Then let me get you another, and see if we can't get you to relax. I'm under strict instructions from Ellie that you are to have a lovely evening, and I, for one, don't intend to cross her.'

His gaze widened. 'Oh dear God, she hasn't been at you, too, has she?'

'You better believe it. Ellic has been leaving nothing to chance for tonight.'

'That lass, what am I going to do with her?' Joseph said, at last finding his smile as the spin of his heart slowed.

Amy laughed, and the two of them ended up talking and talking until the owner finally had to throw them out. Whatever else they found that night, they both discovered a deep connection, and maybe even the glimmer of something more.

JOIN THE J.R. SINCLAIR VIP CLUB

Get instant access to exclusive photos of locations used from the series, and the latest news from J.R. Sinclair.

Just click here to start receiving your free content: https://www.subscribepage.com/n4zom8

PRE-ORDER SUMMER OF EMBERS

DI Joseph Stone will return in
Summer of Embers

Pre-order now: https://geni.us/EmbersofSummer

GO BEHIND THE SCENES

If you are intrigued to learn more about real life locations in Oxford and the surrounding area, from A Flood of Sorrow, author J.R. Sinclair has created an online gallery of images with brief notes for each image.

See everything from the Radcliffe Camera, to the Hawk Stone itself, in an ever expanding gallery of photos.

Get your access to the Location Photos here: https://www. jrsinclair.net/vip-club

Made in United States
Troutdale, OR
03/09/2025

29599694R00173